W9-BTD-202

DISCOVER

READ

EXPLORE

LEARN

**NEW HANOVER COUNTY
PUBLIC LIBRARY**

DYING TO LIVE

ALSO BY MICHAEL STANLEY

DYING
TO
LIVE

A DETECTIVE KUBU MYSTERY

MICHAEL STANLEY

MINOTAUR BOOKS
ST. MARTIN'S PRESS 🦂 NEW YORK

DYING TO LIVE. Copyright © 2017 by Michael Sears and Stanley Trollip. All rights reserved. Printed in the United States of America. For information, address St. Martin's Press, 175 Fifth Avenue, New York, NY 10010.

www.minotaurbooks.com

Designed by Kelly S. Too

The Library of Congress Cataloging-in-Publication Data is available upon request.

ISBN 978-1-250-07090-6 (hardcover)
ISBN 978-1-4668-8156-3 (ebook)

Our books may be purchased in bulk for promotional, educational, or business use. Please contact your local bookseller or the Macmillan Corporate and Premium Sales Department at 1-800-221-7945, extension 5442, or by email at MacmillanSpecialMarkets@macmillan.com.

First Edition: October 2017

10 9 8 7 6 5 4 3 2 1

To our partners,
Pat Cretchley and Mette Nielsen,
with thanks

NOTE

The peoples of Southern Africa have integrated many words of their own languages into colloquial English. For authenticity and color, we have used these occasionally when appropriate. Most of the time, the meanings are clear from the context, but for interest, we have included a glossary at the end of the book.

For information about Botswana, the book, and its protagonist, please visit http://www.detectivekubu.com. You can sign up there for an occasional newsletter. We are also active on Facebook at www.facebook.com/MichaelStanleyBooks, and on Twitter as @detectivekubu.

CAST OF CHARACTERS

Approximate phonetic pronunciations are given in square brackets. Foreign and unfamiliar words are listed in a glossary at the back of the book.

Banda, Edison	Detective in the Botswana Criminal Investigation Department [Edison BUN-duh]
Bengu, Amantle	Kubu's mother [Uh-MUN-tleh BEN-goo]
Bengu, David "Kubu"	Assistant superintendent in the Botswana Criminal Investigation Department [David "KOO-boo" BEN-goo]
Bengu, Joy	Kubu's wife [Joy BEN-goo]
Bengu, Nono	Joy and Kubu's adopted daughter [NO-no BEN-goo (*no* pronounced as the no in *nor*)]

Bengu, Tumi   Joy and Kubu's daughter [TOO-me BEN-goo]

Chan   Official in the Chinese embassy in Gaborone

Collins, Christopher Researcher from the University of Minnesota

Collins, Petra   Christopher Collins's wife

Dlamini, Zanele   Forensics expert [Zuh-NEH-leh Dluh-MEE-nee]

Gampone, Jonah   Owner of import/export business in Gaborone [Jonah Gam-PONY]

Hairong, Feng   Chinese man living in Botswana

Heiseb   Old Bushman [HAY-seb]

Ixau   Bushman constable in the Botswana Police Service, based in New Xade [i-XAU, where the X is like the sound used to make a horse go faster and AU rhymes with the word *how*]

Khama, Samantha   First female detective in the Botswana Criminal Investigation Department [Samantha KAH-muh]

Mabaku, Jacob   Director of the Botswana Criminal Investigation Department [Jacob Mah-BAH-koo]

MacGregor, Ian   Pathologist for the Botswana Police Service

Moeng, Festus   Private eye in Gaborone [FEST-is MO-eng]

Ramala, Botlele   Famous witch doctor [Bot-LEH-leh Ruh-MAH-luh]

Ross, Brian   CEO of an American pharmaceutical company

Segodi, Batwe   Detective sergeant in the Botswana Police Service, based in Ghanzi [BUT-weh Se-GO-dee]

Serome, Pleasant   Joy Bengu's sister [Pleasant Seh-ROE-meh]

Thabo, Sichle   Professor of anthropology at the University of Botswana [SICH-leh TA-bow (CH as in *church*)]

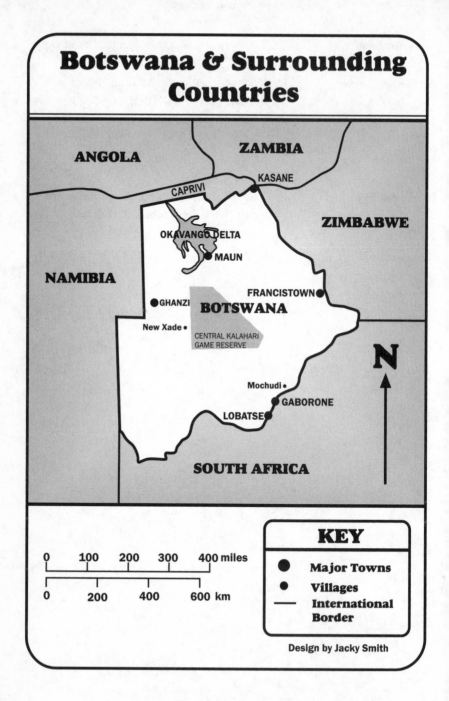

Botswana & Surrounding Countries

ANGOLA

ZAMBIA

KASANE

CAPRIVI

ZIMBABWE

OKAVANGO DELTA

MAUN

NAMIBIA

GHANZI

BOTSWANA

FRANCISTOWN

New Xade

CENTRAL KALAHARI
GAME RESERVE

N

Mochudi

GABORONE

LOBATSE

SOUTH AFRICA

KEY

● Major Towns

• Villages

— International
Border

0   100   200   300   400 miles

0   200   400   600 km

Design by Jacky Smith

 **PART 1**

CHAPTER 1

Detective Sergeant Segodi looked down at the dead Bushman and frowned. He didn't have much time for the diminutive people of the Kalahari. Somehow they always caused trouble, whether they meant to or not, and this was a case in point.

The Bushman was very old. That much was obvious. His skin was a web of wrinkles, and there wasn't a smooth area even the size of a *thebe* coin on his face. The lips were cracked and parched. But the most striking thing was the short crinkly hair covering the wizened head. It was pure white. Segodi couldn't remember ever seeing a Bushman with pure-white hair before; it was a sign of age so advanced that few Bushmen, with their challenging lifestyle, ever attained it.

The detective cursed.

What was the man doing out here alone? he wondered. He should have been with his family group in nearby New Xade. Or, if he'd walked into the desert to die in peace, why had he chosen to do so in sight of the road into the Central Kalahari Game Reserve rather than somewhere private in the middle of nowhere?

Instead, foreign tourists driving to the game reserve had spotted the body being checked out by a scavenger and reported it to the police station at New Xade, thirty miles up the road. Constable Ixau—who was the New Xade police force—had investigated and called the Criminal Investigation Department in Ghanzi. Which was why Segodi was sweltering in the Kalahari sun, with a mask over his nose and mouth, instead of being in the relative comfort of his office.

Now there would be paperwork and aggravation, to say nothing of having to share the Land Rover with the corpse for a hundred miles before it was disposed of in the public cemetery.

The area around the body was scuffed and trampled, which could have been caused by the shocked tourists. When he scanned the surroundings, he spotted something important—there were two sets of footprints coming out of the desert and ending at the body. This had been no lonely leave-taking; someone had walked with the Bushman to this spot before he died.

"What do you make of that?" Segodi asked the constable.

Constable Ixau followed the sergeant's eyes. "Someone was walking with him in the desert."

Segodi frowned, wondering why he wasted his breath. Ixau was clearly more than half Bushman. Surely he knew something about tracking in the desert. The detective examined the footprints more carefully. The sand was the soft, gray powder of the Kalahari, and it was difficult to make out much about the tracks.

Ixau joined him. "They came from there," he said, pointing to the left.

Looking down the road, the sergeant saw a second set of tracks—again of two people—some distance away. He walked over to check, and indeed, these were heading into the desert, away from the road.

"Fetch me the camera," he ordered the constable. "And bring the gloves." He was starting to have a bad feeling.

When he'd photographed the body from various angles and

taken multiple shots of the two sets of tracks—the one leading into the desert and the other ending at the body—he put on the latex gloves and kneeled next to the body. There were no obvious injuries. Without much difficulty, he lifted the right arm for a closer look. Apparently the man had been dead for some time, and the rigor mortis was starting to recede. There were contusions on the wrist. Perhaps that was the result of how the body had fallen, he thought.

He checked the other hand, but it seemed fine. But there was something odd about the neck. The angle didn't seem quite right. And there was a scratch and other abrasions on the side of the face.

Segodi sighed. There was more trouble here than just paperwork. Someone had walked out of the desert with the Bushman, perhaps there had been a fight, and now the Bushman was dead.

What had happened to the other person? he wondered. Only a Bushman could survive out here on foot in the middle of nowhere.

Segodi glanced at the road. There were tire marks at the side, but that was probably the tourists' vehicle. Nevertheless, he took a number of pictures.

Segodi told the constable to be careful with the body when they lifted it onto the body bag. He was going to send it for an autopsy. That would have to be in Gaborone, seven hours away from Ghanzi by van.

The corpse was even lighter than they'd imagined, and they carried the body bag to the Land Rover without difficulty. Segodi told the constable to mark the area where the body had been with stones while he noted the GPS coordinates. When that was done, Ixau drew the sergeant's attention back to the tracks. "I think these are the victim's," he said, pointing at the ones on the right. "He was a small man. You can see they are not as deep as the others, and not as big."

Segodi turned to the footprints again. He examined them closely and realized that the constable was right. He grunted agreement.

An idea struck him. Was it possible one of the tourists had

followed the Bushman's tracks? He'd need to check if he could contact them. It seemed unlikely, but that would explain the double tracks very neatly. He was of two minds whether to follow them. They might go a long way, and the corpse was already stinking up his vehicle.

"Shouldn't we see where they go?" Ixau asked.

Segodi gave him an angry look. Now he had no choice.

"Come on, then," he replied. "We'll start where they head into the desert."

"Wait a minute," Ixau said. "Someone was running along the road here." He pointed at scuff marks on the verge of the road.

To Segodi the marks could have been anything, but he was beginning to respect the Bushman's observations. "How do you know he was running?"

"The gaps between them are too long," Ixau replied.

"The Bushman?"

Ixau shook his head. "The gaps between them are too long," he repeated.

Segodi frowned, puzzled. "Someone ran from there?" he asked, pointing back to where the body had been. "Maybe after killing the Bushman?"

Ixau thought about it, then shook his head. "I think running *towards* the body."

It made no sense to Segodi, and he shrugged it off. "Let's follow the tracks."

Moving parallel to the pair of footprints so as not to disturb them, they walked for about a mile through the desert. The tracks wandered to and fro, crossed themselves, and then headed off again, as though the walkers had been looking for something.

In some places, the ground was the calcrete limestone common in this part of the Kalahari, and the tracks disappeared altogether. When that happened, Ixau headed straight on, and soon the tracks reappeared. The two people had made no effort to hide the signs of their progress.

Eventually they came to a depression surrounded by small sand drifts and calcrete scree. Apparently the men had spent some time here, and it seemed that they'd taken samples, because there were several small pits dug in the stony ground. Prospecting? Segodi wondered. Someone looking for the hidden gems of the Kalahari? He snorted. Not that old nonsense again. Or was it something else?

He squatted and felt around in one of the holes, still wearing the latex gloves, but found nothing except a few root fibers, sand, and calcrete pebbles. He let them run through his fingers and stood up.

"You make anything of this?" he asked the constable. Ixau shook his head.

After that, the tracks headed directly back toward the road, without the detours and crossings that had marked their progress into the desert. After a short time the two policemen were back at the vehicle.

"Okay, let's head back," Segodi said, wiping the sweat pouring off his face. "As soon as we get to New Xade, radio Ghanzi and tell them to drive a van towards New Xade. I'll meet them on the way. We need to get that body to Gaborone as soon as possible."

CHAPTER 2

It was a slow Friday. Assistant Superintendent David "Kubu" Bengu was looking forward to the weekend with his family, especially as his mother would be joining them.

It'll be a treat for the kids, he thought. In fact, for all of us.

He leaned back in his chair and crossed his legs on his desk. He was feeling content—there were no serious cases awaiting his attention, and he'd caught up with the dreaded paperwork.

Then he heard the sound he didn't want to hear: his telephone ringing. He grabbed it.

"Assistant Superintendent Bengu," he said gruffly.

"Kubu, it's Ian. Have you got a moment?"

Kubu sat up. Ian MacGregor was the forensic pathologist for the Botswana police and was very good at his job. He was also a friend and shared Kubu's taste for interesting cases. Kubu would always have a moment for him.

"Of course, Ian. What's up?"

"It's very odd." Uncharacteristically, the pathologist hesitated. "It's that Bushman they sent over from Ghanzi."

Kubu sighed. He'd had his fill of cases involving the Bushmen. "It's not my case, Ian. Ghanzi CID has the jurisdiction for that one."

Ian hesitated again. "I know that. But this is very strange indeed. It's hard to explain."

Kubu relented. "Try."

"Well, when I did the autopsy, it's true about his neck being broken, but . . ." The pathologist trailed off. "I think you'd better come over and see for yourself."

Kubu was intrigued. He'd known Ian for many years, more or less from when the pathologist had arrived in Gaborone from his native Scotland. He was many things, but certainly not indecisive. Kubu scanned his pleasantly clean desk. He had the time.

"I'll see you in half an hour," he said.

KUBU FOUND IAN in his tiny office off the mortuary, sucking on his usual pipe full of unlit tobacco and contemplating a desert scene he'd painted himself. He'd pulled down his surgical mask and left it hanging round his neck.

After a perfunctory greeting, Kubu asked him what was so puzzling.

"I'll show you," Ian replied. "Get togged up." He pointed to a lab coat that had some hope of getting around Kubu's bulk, handed him a mask, and passed him a box of latex gloves. He pulled on a pair himself, adjusted his mask, and led the way to the room where the autopsy had taken place. Kubu was glad that lunch was still a way off; he was not fond of dead bodies under the best of circumstances, and cut up ones that had been lying in the desert for a few days certainly weren't the best of circumstances.

They walked over to a corpse lying on a slab.

"Cause of death is a broken neck, snapped between C2 and C3—the second and third cervical vertebrae. The spinal cord is damaged there, so he would've stopped breathing and died within a couple of minutes. Now take a look at this." He indicated the left side of the head. "It looks as though he was hit on the side of the face. There's bruising, and there are abrasions as a result of the blow. It seems the blow was hard enough to break the neck. But that's *very* unusual. There's not *that* much damage to the face—no cracked cheekbones, for example—so I don't think the blow was very severe. You'd expect the head to whip sideways, but not the neck to break."

"What if someone broke his neck deliberately? Held him and then sharply twisted his head? If the bones are as brittle as you say, that would've been easy."

"Well, there's only bruising on one side of the head, and there's no evidence of a struggle. He would've fought back, and there would've been evidence. Skin under the fingernails or the like. There's nothing."

"Could it have been an accident? He was hit on the face and broke his neck in the fall?"

Ian shook his head. "I can't see how he'd fall on his head. And look at this."

He lifted the right arm and showed Kubu the wrist, which was badly bruised.

Kubu looked carefully at the damage and nodded.

"He also has a distal radial fracture," Ian added. "That's a broken wrist."

"What could've caused that?"

Ian shrugged. "Given how weak his bones are, a rough grip from a strong man might've done it. If he fell, that bone's the one that breaks when you try to save yourself, but given the damage to his spinal cord, that's very unlikely."

"When did he die?"

"Judging by what Detective Sergeant Segodi said about the state of rigor mortis, probably the day before the tourists found the body. I can't do much better than that at this point." He paused.

Kubu waited. So far, nothing particularly strange had been revealed, but he was sure there was more to come.

"He's old, all right," Ian continued. "Bushmen always have faces like walnuts from all that sun, even the young ones. But look at the hair. Pure white. And his bones are showing signs of severe osteoporosis. That's leaching of the calcium. It happens in old people and makes the bones brittle. That may be why that blow snapped his neck, and the radius cracked under a rough grip."

Kubu nodded. So the man was old. That was no surprise either.

Now doubt entered Ian's voice. "And yet, look at this." He offered Kubu an unidentified organ in a glass jar filled with clear liquid. "Go on, take it. Look closely." Kubu did, then handed it back, none the wiser.

"That's the liver of a young man, Kubu. Maybe a forty-year-old who didn't drink. And then there's this." He handed Kubu a container with what was clearly a heart. "That ticker would've gone on pumping for years. All of the internal organs are like that. It's only the skin, the bones, and the hair that belong to a seventy- or eighty-year-old."

Kubu frowned. "How can he be forty inside and seventy outside? Could it be just genetics? He chose his parents well?"

"I've never read of anything like this," Ian replied. "And here's something else."

He passed Kubu a petri dish containing a blackened lump of what Kubu took for metal.

"That's a bullet, no doubt about it. I found it by chance when I got intrigued by the young organs." Ian paused and corrected himself. "The young-*looking* organs, I should say. It was lodged in one of the rectus abdominis muscles, just under an inch below the skin. Probably pretty spent when it hit him, or it would've killed him. I was surprised."

"Surprised? Was it recent?"

"Not recent at all. I was surprised because there was no scar. Nothing. I take photos as well as examining the body before I start the autopsy. I went back to the photos to check. No scarring at all."

"If he was a nomadic Bushman and someone shot him long ago,

he wouldn't see a doctor in the desert. If he didn't die, he'd recover. How long would the scar take to disappear?"

Ian shook his head. "Never. The scar would never disappear. Certainly not without an expert plastic surgeon and proper medication at the time of the injury."

Kubu was starting to understand why Ian was so puzzled. "Could he have swallowed the bullet or something?"

Again Ian shook his head. "It would be impossible for it to get there from inside the body. And it's badly corroded. It's been there for a very long time. I'm surprised the lead didn't cause him more problems."

It was Kubu's turn to shake his head. The Bushmen were strange people, and strange things happened with them, but a young man in an old frame, who seemed immune to bullets, was another thing altogether. It didn't make any sense.

Ian glanced at his friend and realized that Kubu had followed the same path he'd walked earlier that morning. He nodded slowly.

Kubu had had enough. "Well, let's get out of here and go back to your office."

"So," KUBU SUMMARIZED, after they'd washed their hands and disposed of the masks and gloves, "what we have is a very old man, apparently in good health except for his skin and his bones. He was killed by a blow to the head. And he was shot long ago, but that, presumably, has nothing to do with his death. Correct?"

Ian nodded, but said nothing.

Kubu brooded about it. "Is it possible we have the wrong end of the stick? Maybe he's a middle-aged man and had some illness that affected the bones. Maybe a nutrition problem? You said that Bushmen all have wrinkled skin."

"What about the white hair?"

Kubu shrugged. "Can't that happen after an extreme shock of some kind, like being bitten by a scorpion or poisonous snake?"

Ian frowned. "I suppose it's possible. But that doesn't explain the bullet."

Kubu was sure Ian had more to say. He leaned back in his chair and waited.

Ian fiddled with his pipe and took a long draw. "You know I'm interested in the Bushmen, Kubu. Always have been. One of my colleagues at the University of Botswana told me about a visiting anthropologist from the US giving a seminar on what he called the 'oral memory' of the Bushmen peoples. I wasn't all that taken with the topic but went along to see what he was talking about.

"What made me think of it now was his story about a certain Bushman he'd met. He said the Bushman was a great raconteur of stories about historical events that had happened to his people. He'd tell them in the first person—as though he'd been there himself. The stories changed a little with each retelling, but all the main points stayed consistent. The anthropologist was fascinated by this. He postulated that it was a way history could be retained by a people without a written record—that they learned the events as though they had actually been present. He thought perhaps that the storyteller visualized himself experiencing events that had actually been seen by his father or grandfather—maybe with the help of a trance or drugs."

"It sounds as though that would lead to exaggeration rather than accuracy. I don't remember any Bushman doing that."

"His suggestion was that only special men were selected for this oral memory task." Ian shrugged. "I said I wasn't convinced. And he got a lot of questions after the talk, some pretty pointed."

Kubu caught on. "You think our corpse in there could be one of the Bushmen he was talking about?"

"I don't know, but I got to thinking. If he was some sort of genetic freak—and you've seen the evidence yourself—then perhaps he's a lot older than he looks. Maybe he's around ninety or even older. If Collins's subject was also that old, perhaps he was telling those stories in the first person because he actually *was* present at the events." Ian looked uncomfortable. "I know it's far-fetched, but just look at the internal shape this man was in." He hesitated. "One of the stories he told the anthropologist was of a hunting party from what is now Namibia that attacked his group and shot many of them. Men, women, and children. Disgusting, but we know these things happened. He claimed to have been shot himself, but it wasn't a bad wound. I was thinking about that bullet I found in him."

"But the last parties hunting Bushmen were nearly a hundred years ago!"

Ian nodded. "Yes, Kubu, I know. I said it's far-fetched. But still."

Kubu thought for a few moments. Ian's speculation wouldn't go down well with an unimaginative, by-the-book type of detective like Segodi. And why would Segodi care anyway? There was no reason to think there was any connection between the Bushman's age and his death. No *reason*, but intuition told Kubu differently. He understood why Ian had called him.

The two friends sat quietly, each lost in thought, puzzling about the anomalies they'd just talked about. Then Kubu's stomach announced that it was time for lunch. He grunted and climbed to his feet. "I'd just stick to the bland facts with Detective Sergeant Segodi, Ian. Let's see what he comes up with. I'll let you know."

They shook hands, and Kubu took his leave. When he reached the door, he hesitated. He'd learned over the years to take Ian's hunches as seriously as his own. He turned around.

"Is there a way of accurately estimating a dead person's age? Like that Bushman?"

Ian didn't reply for several seconds. "I'll have to look into it. I'm not sure there is. How long someone has been dead, yes. The longer the better. But not how long since the person was born."

"Well, send the bullet to forensics. See what they make of it."

Ian nodded. "I'll do that."

Kubu waved and left the pathologist sucking thoughtfully on his pipe.

CHAPTER 3

Kubu ate his lunch in his office. His wife, Joy, had abandoned her efforts to get him to eat healthy salads—which had only led to clandestine visits to local fast-food restaurants—and now supplied a lunch that included Kubu's favorites in modest amounts. This gave him something to look forward to and at least didn't increase his weight.

There was cold *bobotie* with *sambals* and a little rice, a salad, pieces of fruit, and an energy bar. Kubu washed it down with a cup of proper coffee from a flask filled at home, and settled back in his chair, more or less satisfied for the time being. He would have liked a second helping of the excellent *bobotie,* but there was none to be had. He consoled himself with the thought that Joy would cook something special for Amantle's visit, and that they'd enjoy a glass or two of wine with it.

There was a perfunctory knock on the door, and almost before he could respond, Detective Samantha Khama was in his office.

"I won't have it, Kubu. I'm going to see the director right now, and I expect you to back me up." She looked at the debris of Kubu's meal. "Even if it is lunchtime," she added with a hint of sarcasm.

Kubu sighed. Samantha was a fine junior detective—until something upset her. Then there was no holding her back.

"Sit down, Samantha. What's happened? Would you like a coffee? Joy makes it for me from real beans."

Samantha settled into a seat, but declined the coffee. "Kubu, you know I've been pushing for the police to take crimes against women much more seriously, and particularly crimes against young girls. But you also know how male dominated the CID is, and how no one really cares anyway. I'm sure Detective Sergeant Seleke beats his wife, but the director turns a blind eye to it!" She paused, but rushed on before Kubu could respond. "There's rape and domestic abuse everywhere! And girls just vanish, often taken by witch doctors for their *muti* potions. What's worse is that half the people in this office are scared of the very witch doctors who're behind everything. Well, this is the last straw!" She tossed a report onto Kubu's desk.

He picked it up and read it, but was none the wiser about Samantha's agitation.

"It's a missing persons report," he said. "A certain Botlele Ramala is reported missing by his wife. What's the matter? I don't get it."

"Haven't you heard of *Kgosi* Ramala, Kubu? He's a witch doctor! He calls himself a chief among witch doctors and promises to prolong life and heaven knows what else. Guess what he uses to try to do that. *Muti*, of course. We've been watching him, but haven't been able to connect him to anything illegal so far."

"Well, even a witch doctor can go missing," Kubu said mildly. He shrugged. "Maybe he got into a disagreement with a competitor—another witch doctor."

"That Detective Sergeant Seleke just came to my office and said, 'Here you are, my girl. You're interested in disappearances.' I'm not *his girl*!" Samantha paused for breath. "I know he sneers at me behind my back and makes nasty remarks. And now he expects me to investigate a missing witch doctor who's probably off kidnapping some girl, or worse."

Kubu sighed and spread his hands on his desk. Seleke did go out of his way to bait Samantha, and taking her the missing witch doctor report probably was his idea of a joke.

He tried to defuse the situation. "Samantha, calm down. Everyone has instructions to let you see copies of missing persons reports. At your request. And that's been great, letting you get on top of the cases while they're warm enough to follow. This Ramala has been missing since yesterday. He didn't come home and didn't have any plans to be away. He may not be your favorite person, but we have to investigate it. He's also a member of the public, and we're obliged to protect him."

"You're not suggesting I actually follow this up?" she said indignantly.

"Definitely. Wait till Monday, and if he hasn't reappeared, look into it," Kubu said. "That will show Detective Sergeant Seleke that you take your job seriously and follow up every case. Then he can't go around saying . . ." Kubu caught himself and made a show of finishing his coffee. It certainly wouldn't do to tell Samantha what Seleke reportedly said behind her back.

"Saying what?"

"That you don't follow up cases against men," Kubu improvised.

Samantha thought about it. "I don't care if Ramala *is* missing. In fact, if he disappeared for good, I'd be delighted."

Kubu spotted a way to turn Seleke's tease to Samantha's advantage.

"Samantha, you're missing something. You've been watching this guy and suspect he could be in on something really bad. Here's your chance to investigate what he's been doing, interview his wife, his clients! You couldn't do that before. Now you can. You've got a legitimate reason to investigate everything about him: to try to find him. Detective Sergeant Seleke has done you a favor."

For several moments, Samantha considered that. Much as she disliked Seleke, Kubu had a good point. Whether Ramala's customers and colleagues would actually cooperate was less clear, but now she had a solid reason to ask them questions and expect to get answers, at least until the odious man reappeared.

Grabbing the report, she headed for the door. "Thanks, Kubu," she said with a rare smile, and was gone.

Kubu relaxed. He'd redirected Samantha's anger toward the case. Even if she realized how he'd done it, a blowup in Director Mabaku's office had been avoided.

Kubu poured himself the last cup of coffee from the flask, added sweetener instead of sugar—another compromise agreed with Joy—and stirred well. Then his mind drifted back to the mysterious Bushman.

He turned to Google for help and looked up "longevity." Wikipedia seemed to be the place to start. He found some surprising facts there. For a start, there were documented cases of people who lived to over 120. That in itself was amazing. Then there was the genetics issue. Kubu subscribed to the popular belief that choosing your parents correctly was the most important factor determining longevity. That seemed to be false. Only around 30 percent was explained by genetics, the rest by lifestyle choices, such as exercise, healthy eating, and leisure. There was nothing about differential aging of the organs of the body, though.

Was it possible that the Bushman actually had been present at the events the anthropologist had described? He tried "Bushman hunting party," but this produced hits about the Bushmen doing the hunting. But when he added "German," he was more successful. The last permit to hunt a Bushman was issued by the South African government in 1936. That was eighty years ago and not impossible to fit into a human's normal life span. But Ian had said it was Germans who attacked the Bushmen, so that would move the attack back to the time of the First World War, twenty years earlier, or even before that. On the other hand, many Germans had stayed in what had become South West Africa, so perhaps the attack had happened later.

As usual with browsing the Web, time passed quickly, and

Kubu's stomach started sending signals that dinner wasn't far off. He turned off his computer and wondered what Joy would be making. Soon he was counting the minutes until it was time to go home for the weekend.

CHAPTER 4

When Kubu arrived home, he was met, as usual, with a frenzied welcome from Ilia, their fox terrier, who jumped into the car and sat in the passenger seat, panting happily. Normally, the barking would result in an equally enthusiastic welcome from Tumi, their daughter, and Nono, the daughter they'd adopted after all her family succumbed to the widespread AIDS epidemic.

Joy should be back by now, he thought. Probably the traffic was worse than normal for a Friday afternoon. Perhaps there's a concert in Gabs this evening, or a big football match.

He parked the Land Rover in the shade, spent a few minutes patting Ilia, then went inside to change into something more comfortable. He'd barely reached the bedroom when Ilia started barking again. The others had arrived.

Kubu walked out to the veranda and was immediately rushed by Tumi, who gave him a huge hug. Nono followed in a more reserved fashion and hugged him too. When Joy had parked, Kubu went to help his mother, who was struggling to climb out of the car.

"Good afternoon, Mother," he said quietly, taking hold of her hand. "Welcome to our home. It's so nice to see you again."

"Thank you, my son," she replied. "I never get used to being here without Wilmon."

"That's not surprising, Mother. You were married for nearly forty years. How are you?"

"I am well, thank you. Sometimes I feel very old, but today I am strong. I think the children give me energy."

"And how is Mochudi? Are you still happy living alone there?"

"Yes, I am. That is where my friends are."

"The traffic was terrible!" Joy exclaimed as she lifted Amantle's bag from the trunk. "And it took us at least an extra fifteen minutes. A herd of cows got loose on the road. They were wandering all over the place. I'm surprised none were hit."

"And I'm pleased to see you too," Kubu teased.

Joy rolled her eyes and came over to Kubu. "I'm sorry, darling. I'm feeling frazzled. So nice to see you," she said, and gave him a peck on the cheek.

It must have been a really bad drive, he thought. She's normally so affectionate.

"Let's go in," he said. "I'll make drinks."

FOR DINNER, JOY had prepared a delicious chicken curry, not too hot because of the children, accompanied by yellow rice, a cucumber *raita*, chopped bananas, and mango chutney—Mrs. Ball's, of course. It was one of Kubu's favorite meals.

"Eat up, Nono," Joy said, noticing that she'd hardly touched her food.

"I'm not hungry," Nono replied.

"You need to eat. You've had a long day."

"But I'm not hungry." She paused. "I'm very tired. Can I go to bed, please?"

"It's too early to go to sleep. You'll wake up in the middle of the night."

"I want to go to bed." Nono was beginning to whine, so Joy said she could leave the table.

"Remember that you and Tumi are camping out in our bedroom tonight. Grandmother is using your bedroom for the weekend. And don't forget to brush your teeth."

Nono stood up and carefully pushed the chair back into position. "Good night, Grandmother. Good night, Mommy and Daddy."

They all bade her a good night's sleep.

"She must be sick," Kubu said. "She always eats everything. Maybe it's the flu that's been going around."

"I hope that's all it is," Joy said quietly.

Kubu knew immediately what she was referring to. Nono had been born HIV positive but had controlled the disease through daily antiretrovirals.

"Finish up your dinner, Tumi," he said. "Then why don't you go and read one of your books? Then I'll come and read you a story, but you must decide which one."

"Isn't there any pudding?" she asked.

Joy shook her head. "Not tonight, darling. But tomorrow I have a big treat for you. One of your favorites."

"Ice cream?" Tumi shouted.

Joy shook her head.

"Milk tart?"

Joy shook her head again.

"That's all I like, Mommy. I want ice cream."

"I have something special. A big surprise. But you'll only get it if you go and read now."

Kubu thought Tumi was about to cry, but he was wrong. She smiled, said good night, and trotted off.

"What's the surprise?" Kubu was curious.

"Malva pudding," Joy answered. "She likes it a lot."

"Is it safe for Tumi to be with Nono?" Amantle interrupted.

"My mother," Joy replied, "we've told you before that Nono

doesn't have AIDS. She's what we call HIV positive. She takes pills every day to suppress it."

"And what happens if she forgets to take the pills?"

"She can't forget, because I give them to her. If she didn't take the pills, she *could* get sick. But I don't think that's the problem. She's very good about taking them."

"You should take her to my traditional healer."

Joy bristled. "They know nothing, my mother. They are part of the problem, persuading people to stop taking the antiretrovirals. That's why so many people die. The witch doctors don't understand the disease."

"They have served our people for hundreds of years. I do not understand why you reject them."

"My mother, HIV hasn't been around for hundreds of years—only about thirty. The witch doctors know nothing about it. And all they do is give bad advice. They should take a lot of the blame for what is happening."

"Something funny came up at work today concerning a witch doctor," Kubu interjected, hoping to nip the budding disagreement before it got out of hand. "A witch doctor has gone missing. And what's funny is that Samantha is in charge of finding him." He laughed. "You should've seen her face when I told her it was her responsibility. You know how much she hates witch doctors."

"Who is Samantha?" Amantle asked.

"You must remember her, Mother. She's the detective who was responsible for finding the witch doctor who murdered that young girl from Mochudi for *muti*."

"I remember her. But I don't understand why she isn't married and having children. The girls these days do not know what is best for them."

"And there's a second interesting bit of news," Kubu said, and proceeded to repeat what Ian MacGregor had told him about the strange Bushman. "It doesn't make sense," he said. "Being shot and having no scar; being old and having young organs. Ian didn't have a clue about what was going on."

"Some witch doctors live a long time—a few hundred years, I am told," Amantle said. "They take *muti* made from the leaves of a baobab tree. You know those trees live forever. Perhaps the Bushman was taking the same *muti*." She shook her head. "You cannot trust those Bushmen, you know. He probably did not pay, and so the witch doctor made him pay with his life."

Kubu decided not to comment. He'd given up long ago trying to change his mother's old-fashioned ideas.

"You say he was murdered?" Joy asked.

Kubu nodded. "It looks like it."

"Another murder?" Amantle frowned. "What is happening to our country? Not long ago, we were peaceful with each other. Now there are many murders. Look what happened to Wilmon." She turned to Joy. "And even worse things happen to women. God is angry with our people. You must be very careful when you go out."

"I'm always careful, my mother."

"Would you like some *rooibos* tea before you go to bed?" Kubu asked.

"Thank you, my son. That will help me to sleep. I am not sleeping well these days. I still think of Wilmon."

And so do I, thought Kubu, as he went to put the kettle on.

CHAPTER 5

On Monday, Detective Sergeant Segodi set out to solve the case of the dead Bushman, at least to his own satisfaction.

He started with the report from the pathologist in Gaborone, carefully working his way through the details, grateful for Ian MacGregor's straightforward style. It seemed the dead man was in very good health for someone of his age, except for the extreme brittleness of his bones. The peculiarities of the organs held no interest for Segodi, and neither did the bullet, which obviously had nothing to do with the Bushman's death. On the other hand, he read the piece concerning the blow to the face and the broken neck twice; the death could have been an accident or an altercation that went wrong. Segodi was relieved. Something like that could be dealt with.

It was time to pay a visit to New Xade to get more information.

He went to his police Land Rover in the parking lot and checked that it had been properly cleaned since it had been used as a hearse. It had an overpowering smell of disinfectant, made worse because it had been closed up for the weekend and covered only by shade cloth against the sun. He grunted, climbed into the vehicle, opened all the windows, and put the air conditioner on full blast. Then he drove to the service station to refuel. While he waited, he bought a couple of packets of cigarettes as gifts. He didn't smoke, but he had no objection to the Bushmen tarring their lungs if they wanted to. Then he set out to repeat the long drive he'd made the previous week.

Soon he was following the road to Hanahai. Initially, it was corrugated and potholed, then it became narrower but smoother when he turned east toward the Central Kalahari Game Reserve. It was uninspiring country. Scattered acacias, small shrubs, and patches of spiky grass were the highlights. The rest was grayish sand mixed with shards of the lighter gray calcrete. For some reason the donkeys, with no fences to inhibit them, preferred the middle of the road to the verges. At one point, he spotted an ostrich heading off into the distance, muscular legs pumping.

It took him nearly two hours to cover the seventy-five miles to New Xade, and he pulled into the small town with relief. The town was a discouraging mishmash of different styles—small concrete block houses in need of maintenance, mixed in with thatched huts, some neat, some dilapidated, built on a framework of branches. People sat along the road watching their goats, or squatted outside their houses. Recently, some problems with drunkenness and theft in the town had motivated locating Constable Ixau there as a community police resource. Segodi thought it was a waste of effort; in his opinion, the Bushmen would be best left to their own devices.

The day was hot, so he found a group of trees in the center of the town and tucked his car into the weak shade. He climbed out, stretched, and went in search of Constable Ixau. Segodi found him in the single office that constituted the police station, taking down a complaint from a Bushman woman, who seemed extremely angry. The exchange took place in Naro, the local language, replete with a variety of click sounds. Segodi had no idea what it was about.

At last, the woman seemed more or less satisfied and left. Ixau apologized for the delay and offered tea. When Segodi accepted,

Ixau went to a small bathroom adjoining his office to wash a couple of chipped cups.

"What was all that about?" Segodi asked when Ixau returned.

"The woman?" Ixau shrugged, as he poured boiling water from an electric kettle on his desk into the cups. "She says someone has stolen one of her goats." He dropped a *rooibos* tea bag into each cup.

"And is that so?"

"Probably." He didn't seem to be very concerned about it, although the woman obviously had been. "I've been asking around about that man we found last week, Sergeant. I think I know who he is. His name's Heiseb."

Well, that's some progress, Segodi thought. "You had pictures of the dead man?"

Ixau nodded. "I took some while I was waiting for you."

Segodi wasn't sure if he should be pleased or annoyed. It seemed the man had initiative, which he didn't expect in a Bushman constable, let alone one posted to the middle of nowhere. He drained his tea. "Well, introduce me to these friends of Heiseb," he said.

"Well, they're not exactly friends of his," Ixau replied, "but they know him all right."

IXAU DROVE THEM in his beaten-up Land Rover away from the central group of modern buildings to the outskirts of the town, where there were a few roughly thatched huts that looked as though they'd been built overnight and might vanish as quickly. A small group of men of various ages was relaxing under some trees, drinking from a calabash that they passed around. Although it was still morning, it was obvious from the animated conversation that the calabash contained something alcoholic. The youngest of the group was just a boy, but he took his turn with the calabash. Segodi frowned. He can't be more than fourteen, he thought. He should be in school, not loafing around drinking.

Ixau walked over to them, introduced Segodi, and made himself comfortable in a sandy spot in the shade. In the absence of any chairs, Segodi reluctantly joined him on the sand and passed over the two packets of cigarettes he'd brought as gifts. These were enthusiastically accepted, and one packet was opened and distributed at once. There was a pause as the men lit up. Even the boy eagerly took a cigarette, begged a match to light it, and inhaled the smoke without coughing.

Segodi asked Ixau to explain in their language that the police needed their help with an investigation. This was met with silence, but it didn't seem hostile. Ixau went on to remind them about the dead old man and passed around the pictures that Segodi had brought with him. There were nods and some discussion, and two of the men seemed to have a disagreement and insisted on seeing the pictures a second time. At last, they too nodded. "Heiseb," said one firmly, and they all nodded.

"Ask them to tell us about him," Segodi instructed. Ixau translated that, and after a pause, the man who looked the oldest started speaking. He waved his arms and pointed so dramatically to the northwest that Segodi automatically looked in that direction. After a long speech, the man stopped for a gulp from the calabash and to finish his cigarette. Two of the others took over, but shut up again when the older man was ready to continue. Segodi hoped something useful was emerging from all this; again he had no idea what was being said. At last the man stopped, and Ixau turned to the detective.

"Detective Sergeant, he says that Heiseb was a very old man. He's been in this area for many, many years, but he was old when he came here, and before that he came from there." He, too, pointed to the northwest. "He never lived here in the town, but sometimes he spent a few nights here and told wonderful stories of our people and of things in the past. So he was always welcome. Sometimes he traded things that he found in the desert—"

"What sort of things?" Segodi interrupted.

Ixau translated. There was a moment of silence, and the men

muttered to each other. Ixau repeated the question, surprised by their reticence. He obtained a few comments and translated, "They say he found things in the desert, sometimes old things. Sometimes he brought plants and herbs. Some of these are good medicine. He would trade for cigarettes, maybe some food, or cloth. Not much. He said he didn't need much." Ixau looked around. The men showed no sign of understanding, but they no longer smiled.

After a pause, Ixau continued. "They also told of the subjects of the stories. Some from long ago. Some from the beginning of all things, when the gods walked at Tsodilo."

Segodi wasn't interested in that. "Ask them when they last saw him."

This created more disagreement. At last Ixau said, "Not for two moons—that's two months."

Segodi shook his head. He didn't believe them. Something else was going on here, and he meant to find out what it was.

"Was he alone?"

Once again there was excited discussion, but apparently no disagreement.

Ixau looked surprised. "They say he was with a white man." He asked more questions before he continued. "Apparently the man comes here sometimes. They say his name is Krisfer or something like that. Maybe Christopher?" He tried this out on the group, and they nodded enthusiastically. "The man came here before, asking who knew stories about the past. They used to tell him stories— some they made up—but when he met Heiseb, he stopped asking the other people. He would get his stories from Heiseb after that."

"Why was he interested in the stories?" Segodi asked.

No one seemed to know.

"Maybe he was a scientist or a historian or something?" Ixau suggested.

Segodi nodded. That was possible. "And no one's seen Heiseb for two months?"

The group all agreed that was the case, but again the reaction was muted. Heiseb came and went, once or twice with the white man, but neither of them had been seen recently. Segodi insisted Ixau tell them that, if they were holding anything back—either about Heiseb or his death—they would be in a lot of trouble. This was met with silence. Segodi asked Ixau to say it again, but no one volunteered anything more. The mood no longer had the friendly atmosphere that had been generated by the cigarettes.

Segodi was sure the men knew more than they were willing to share with the police, but realized it was time to give up. He stood up, tried to dust the fine sand off his pants, and turned to Ixau. "Can I get something to eat here?" He didn't feel like driving back to Ghanzi on an empty stomach.

LUNCH WAS SIMPLY *pap* with a sinewy gravy that was supposed to be goat, but could have been anything.

"Maybe it's that woman's goat," Segodi joked. "And if it is, I can understand why you weren't concerned that it was stolen."

Ixau smiled. "At one time, people would share. There was enough for everyone. Now one owns this and another owns that."

Segodi grunted. That was how things worked. He concentrated on his food, wondering what he was going to do about the dead Bushman. New Xade had been a dead end. Ixau could go on making inquiries, but nothing seemed to connect Heiseb with the people here. He was a nomad, just someone who passed through.

Keen to get back to Ghanzi, Segodi took his leave of Ixau, told him to keep his ears open, and walked to where he'd parked his vehicle under the trees.

The boy who had been smoking and drinking with the group was waiting for him on the far side of the car, out of sight of Ixau's office. He looked scared. "Rra, I talk?" he asked in halting Setswana.

"Of course. I'll get Constable Ixau. He can help us talk."

The boy shook his head at once. "You only," he said.

Segodi hesitated, then nodded, unlocked the Land Rover, and

told the boy to get in. He did so, leaving the door open, perhaps to let out some of the heat. Segodi did the same.

"What do you want to tell me?" he asked, being careful to talk slowly.

"Heiseb," the boy said. "They follow sometimes."

"Who follows him?"

The boy shrugged. "The men."

"Last week?"

The youth shook his head. "I not know last week. But they follow. Sometimes."

"Why do they follow him?"

"He *know* things. About plants. Special. For medicine. More than medicine." The boy shook his head, frustrated by his inability to explain clearly in Setswana. He said something in his own language, but it meant nothing to Segodi. What did mean something to the detective was that Heiseb had something other Bushmen wanted. That could be a motive.

"Why didn't they just ask him? Trade it from him like they told us he liked to do?"

The boy shook his head again. "Tried. He not give. He not trade. He say he has nothing. But we *know*. He *very* old!"

Ixau came out of his office and spotted that the detective's vehicle was still there. "Everything okay, Detective Sergeant?" he called, and started to walk over.

"Yes, I was just talking to . . ." Segodi glanced to the passenger side, but the Bushman youth was gone. "Myself," he finished. "I must be off. Thank you, Constable." And he started the engine and plowed his way through the sand back to the road, leaving Ixau looking puzzled.

ON THE WAY back to Ghanzi, Segodi had plenty of time to think.

The key was the footprints. He smiled. It hadn't been two people walking in the desert together after all. Ixau had been wrong. It had been Heiseb searching for his magic plants or whatever nonsense it was, and then later someone else followed his tracks. Maybe that person came upon him digging up the plants; maybe they walked together to the road, while the follower begged for some of the magic. Until, angrily, he tried to take it from Heiseb. And Heiseb's brittle bones had broken, leaving his shocked assailant with a dead man. Then the follower panicked and ran back along the road toward New Xade. Ixau must have been wrong about the direction; it had been impossible to tell from those smudges in the sand.

Had it been the boy? Segodi thought not. The boy was scared, but surely if he had been the culprit, the last thing he would have done was to volunteer any information to the police. No, it was one of the others. Alone. There had been only one other set of footprints. No witness. And it really was nothing more than a scuffle that had gone wrong.

I'll write my report tomorrow, he decided. I'll explain what happened: accidental death following a scuffle with a person unknown. The coroner will be happy to get rid of it. And so will I.

Despite the long drive, it had turned out to be a good day.

CHAPTER 6

It was with great reluctance that Samantha drove to Tlokweng to interview the wife of the missing witch doctor, Botlele Ramala. If Samantha had had her way, she'd have let him stay missing. To her way of thinking, a missing witch doctor was better than a found one, but not as good as a dead one.

Her intense dislike of witch doctors emanated from her childhood, when a friend of hers went missing and was later found dead, parts of her body having been harvested for *muti*—supposedly a particularly potent potion. This traumatic event was the spark that made Samantha want to join the police. And since doing so, she'd focused both on pursuing cases of missing girls, cases that were often neglected by the police, and on trying to make the police force less chauvinistic—a task of great difficulty, in which she'd had little success.

As much as she didn't want to find this man, who called himself the chief of witch doctors with powers to heal, to influence, and to prolong life, Kubu was right. It did provide an opportunity to question people, not only about Ramala's disappearance, but also about other cases where he might be involved.

SAMANTHA STOPPED IN front of the small house on Mmaseroka Road, not far from the police station, and went to the front door, which was standing open.

"*Dumela?*" she said loudly. "*Dumela?*"

There was no reply. "Mma Ramala, are you there?" Still no reply.

Samantha walked around to the back of the house. There she saw a woman hanging clothes on a piece of cord, one end attached to the house, the other tied to a scrawny tree.

"Mma Ramala?"

The woman turned around and glared at Samantha.

"Are you the policewoman?"

Samantha nodded. "Thank you for agreeing to see me. Can we talk inside?"

The woman finished hanging a pair of jeans, then walked inside, beckoning Samantha to follow her. She pointed to a chair. "Sit there."

"Mma Ramala, may I have your full name, please? For the record."

"I'm Dipuo Ramala."

"Are you married to Botlele Ramala—the man who is missing?"

"Yes. And why did it take so long for the police to do anything?"

"Mma Ramala . . ." Samantha tried to answer.

"I phoned three days ago to say my husband was missing, and you only come now. It's true what they say, that the police don't do anything."

"Mma, if we investigated every missing person report right away, the whole police force would be running around not paying attention to other crimes. In about—"

"If it was your husband missing, the police would do something right away."

"No, mma. About ninety percent of people reported missing return within three days. That's why we don't do anything right away."

"But my husband is an important person. '*Kgosi*,' they call him, because he is chief among witch doctors. When he goes missing, something bad has happened."

"Mma, it's because he's so important that we waited. We expect someone like your husband to be in great demand all over the country. We thought someone needed his powers, and he didn't have time to contact you." Samantha wondered if she was laying it on too thickly. "But now it's three days, we'll do all we can to find him and tell him that you're missing him and that he should return to his home."

Mma Ramala sat quietly for a few moments. "Would you like some tea?" she asked brusquely.

"That would be very nice, thank you."

AFTER MMA RAMALA had poured the tea, Samantha continued. "You told me on the phone that your husband left home on Thursday morning and didn't return home on Thursday night."

Mma Ramala nodded.

"Has that happened before?"

Mma Ramala paused before answering. "Sometimes, but not often."

"Where had he been? When he didn't come home?"

Another pause. "He said he was helping a patient."

"Did you believe him?"

"Of course I believed him!" she snapped. "Why wouldn't I?"

"Do you have a good relationship with your husband, mma?"

"What are you saying? That he's gone off with another woman?"

"Not at all, mma. All I'm doing is trying to understand your domestic situation. When he left on Thursday morning, what sort of mood was he in?"

"As always—very positive about what the day was to bring and the people he was going to help."

"And the two of you hadn't had a fight or something like that?"

"No. Everything was fine."

"Please tell me about your husband's work, mma. What does he do? Who are his patients? And so on."

"Well, he grew up near Shakawe. You know where that is?"

Samantha nodded.

"Then you know it's close to Tsodilo, which is an important place for the Bushman people. His father was also a traditional healer—Botlele prefers to be called that, rather than a witch doctor—and spent a lot of time with them to learn about the desert plants they use for healing and so on. My Botlele worked as an apprentice to his father and eventually became a well-known healer also. When he moved to Gaborone about ten years ago, many people came to him to ask for his help. They were successful in their careers, but wanted to remain healthy and live to be very old. That way, they could have money and be able to enjoy their grandchildren and great-grandchildren."

Samantha frowned, her anger at how witch doctors exploited people's desires and fears starting to well up.

"His father had told him of a plant that slowed down aging and allowed people to live much longer. For many years he wasn't able to find it, but about three years ago he found a source. Then his business grew quickly, and he became well known for it, and people started calling him *Kgosi* because of it—because he was the best of the healers and also because he was very fair in how much he charged for his medicines."

"Do you know what the plant was or where he got it from?"

"He never told me exactly, but he said once that he'd found another healer who had it. My husband said the man didn't know what the plant was for, so he was able to get it cheaply."

"Do you know who that person is?"

Mma Ramala shook her head.

"And did your husband ever make *muti* from human body parts?"

"Oh no! He would never do that! He said you couldn't be a real healer if you killed people." She shook her head emphatically.

Samantha wondered whether Mma Ramala was just saying that because it was prudent to do so, or whether her husband actually believed it.

"Mma Ramala, did your husband say where he was going or who he was seeing on Thursday?"

"No, but he did say he had a meeting in the afternoon that could make him a lot of money."

"You're sure he didn't say who he was meeting?"

"I'm quite sure, but he was excited about it."

"Have you tried phoning him?"

Mma Ramala nodded. "Of course. Many times. It goes straight to voice mail."

"Does he have an office or does he work from here?"

"He has a small office at the Africa Mall—I don't know the exact address, but you'll see his posters on the street poles. And the regulars there will also be able to show you."

"And one last question, mma. How did he get to his office? It's quite far. Did he drive or take a bus or taxi?"

"He drove. He has an old, white VW Golf. I thought you would ask, so I wrote the registration number down. And his cell phone number. He's with Orange." She handed Samantha a piece of paper. "I took a bus to the Mall yesterday to see if I could find him. His office was all locked up, and I couldn't find his car either."

Samantha thanked Mma Ramala and asked her to contact her if she heard anything. When she reached her car, she phoned the receptionist at the CID headquarters and asked him to alert all police patrols in Gaborone and the surrounding areas to be on the lookout for Ramala's VW. She also asked him to contact Orange to see if they could locate Ramala's phone and provide a list of all calls made and received over the past four weeks. That information could be very useful even if Ramala reappeared, she thought.

• • •

SAMANTHA'S NEXT STOP was the Africa Mall, a higgledy-piggledy collection of small shops and street vendors. And sure enough, many of the street poles had posters advertising *Kgosi* Ramala's proficiency and wares. At the bottom of each poster was an address and a telephone number—the one Mma Ramala had given her. She pulled out her mobile phone and dialed the number. As Mma Ramala had said, it went straight to voice mail. She left a message, asking for an urgent return call, but didn't expect to get one.

Then she walked to the address on the posters. The door to the small office was closed and locked. She knocked loudly but there was no response. She looked for a window, but there wasn't one.

"*Dumela,* rra," she said to a nearby street vendor. "Have you seen Rra Ramala today?"

The young man shook his head.

"When was the last time you saw him?"

"I think it was last Thursday—in the morning. He came in as usual at about nine o'clock. Then he went out again just before lunch."

"Did he say where he was going?"

The man shook his head. "He doesn't tell things like that."

"Do you know if he took his car?"

The man shrugged. "I don't know, but he walked towards where he usually parks it."

"Where's that?" Samantha asked.

"It must be up that road somewhere. That's the direction he comes from every morning and where he goes at the end of the day."

Samantha thanked the man and walked up the street. She spent about fifteen minutes fruitlessly searching it and surrounding streets for Ramala's white VW Golf. As she was walking back to Ramala's office, she saw a patrolling squad car and flagged it over. After she'd identified herself, she asked the two policemen in the car if they could help her open Ramala's office door.

One said he knew the caretaker of the building and would go and find her. About ten minutes later, the two arrived back, the caretaker carrying a large bunch of keys. She fumbled through them for a few minutes until she found the one she wanted. Then she opened the door.

It took Samantha a few moments to find a light switch. When she turned the light on, she wasn't sure whether she was disappointed or relieved—there wasn't a body. She walked over to the desk to see whether there was any indication of who Ramala was scheduled to meet on the previous Thursday afternoon. While fiddling through a pile of papers, she came across a calendar, with the whole month showing. There were several entries for the previous Thursday: Jacob Luma and Baruti Moremi in the morning, and Hair On in the afternoon.

Samantha wrote down the names of the two men, then puzzled over the meaning of "Hair On."

Surely that's not someone's name, she wondered. And it's not likely that Ramala was going to have a hair transplant or buy a wig.

She decided she'd need to check, just in case. Then she flipped back to the previous two months. Ramala certainly had a lot of customers. Only one caught her eye—a Christopher Collins. She wrote down his name too.

Odd that a white man came to see a witch doctor, she thought. At least his name sounds white. I guess they want to live forever too.

She poked around a little more but found nothing that gave her any clue as to where Ramala had gone the day he disappeared. So she asked the caretaker to lock the door and went to talk to the neighbors.

Just to the right of Ramala's office, three men were sitting on beer crates, smoking hand-rolled cigarettes. Cartons of Shake-Shake beer stood in the sand at their feet.

"*Dumelang borre,*" Samantha said as she approached them.

"*Dumela,*" they responded without enthusiasm.

"I'm Detective Khama from the CID." She pulled out her badge and waved it in front of them. They looked at her, but didn't respond.

"Your neighbor, Rra Ramala, has been reported missing. His

wife last saw him last Thursday. Do you remember seeing him then or since then?"

One of the men replied, "He was here on Thursday morning and left before lunch, but I haven't seen him since then." The others nodded in agreement.

"What was his business?" Samantha asked.

"*Aaii*. You don't know?" The man looked at the others. "He was a healer—an important healer. Perhaps the most important one in Gaborone."

"What did people come to see him about?"

"People saw him for many things, mainly sickness, and he was famous for his *muti*. In the last year or two, people came to see him because they wanted to live longer. They believed he had the power to push death into the future."

"What happened that he suddenly became famous for making people live longer?"

"He told us that he had found a magic ingredient for his *muti*," one of the men replied. "Soon many powerful people were here to see him—many politicians and businessmen. He must have made many pula."

"But he didn't show it," another chimed in. "He didn't like to show off. He stayed the same even after he became famous. Sometimes he would even sit with us and have a beer."

"Did he ever talk about what he found that made people live longer?" Samantha asked.

"No, he never talked about work." The man paused. "We'll miss him if he doesn't come back. Not everybody has a famous man next door."

The others nodded.

"Can you think of anything unusual about him or the people who came to see him? Something that was odd or out of place?"

The men looked at each other and shook their heads. "He was just an ordinary man," one said.

"What about his box?" another asked. "That was a bit strange."

"What box?" Samantha perked up.

"He always carried a small box. Looked as though it was made from stone. He had it when he arrived in the morning and took it home when he left at night."

"Even when he went out during the day . . ."

"Do you know what was in it?" Samantha asked.

"No . . ."

"But that was the only time we saw him angry."

"He was having a beer with us," another chipped in, "and I asked what was in it. I leaned down to pick it up. He lost his temper and shouted that if I ever touched it, I would die."

"We were all shocked. We'd never seen him behave like that."

"Did you ever find out what was in the box?"

The men all shook their heads. "Never," one said. "We were too scared to raise the subject again."

Samantha took out her notebook and noted their names and contact information. "Thank you all. Please could you write down who you remember came to see him. They may have some more information. I'll come back this afternoon to collect the names. Also, please contact me if you see him or hear anything about him." She gave each of them one of her cards.

She was about to walk off, when she stopped. "Did he have any unusual visitors recently that you noticed?"

All three shook their heads.

It seemed that Rra Ramala had indeed disappeared without a trace.

I hope he stays that way, Samantha thought.

CHAPTER 7

"Any word on that VW Golf?" Samantha asked the man at reception when she returned to CID headquarters.

The man shook his head. "Nothing yet."

"Please try to find phone numbers and addresses for these four people: Jacob Luma, Baruti Moremi, and Christopher Collins." She paused. "And someone whose name may be . . . Hair On."

The receptionist raised his eyebrows. "I'll phone you when I have them," he said.

Samantha nodded and went to her office.

It was only a few minutes later when the receptionist buzzed her with the numbers of the first two men who had seen Ramala the previous Thursday. However, there was no Christopher Collins in the phone directory or at directory assistance, and there was no person with the last name On, nor one with the name Hair.

"Damn!" Samantha cursed out loud, even though there was no one to hear her.

What did "Hair On" mean? she wondered. And was Collins just a gullible tourist?

She sat for a few moments, then picked up the phone and dialed the first number.

"Rra Luma? This is Detective Khama of the CID. Is this a good time to speak to you? I have a few questions."

Samantha explained why she was calling and, for the next few minutes, quizzed the man about his relationship with the witch doctor Ramala. He confirmed that he'd visited Ramala the previous Thursday to buy some *muti* that would make him live longer.

"Many of my friends swear that they're much healthier because of him," he said. "They all expect to live to over one hundred. I want to do that too."

"Do you know what's in the *muti*, Rra Luma?"

"No. He doesn't say."

"How did he give you the *muti*?"

"What do you mean?"

"Did you see him prepare it? Or was it ready when you arrived? What sort of container was it in? You know, that sort of thing."

"Okay. After I paid him, he took a small jar. It was painted black. He poured what looked like a little water into it from a glass jug. Then he opened another jar—it was much bigger—and added a little liquid to the water. Finally, he opened a little box and took something out with a teaspoon and put it into the jar. Then—"

"Was the box made from stone?" Samantha interrupted.

"Yes. It looked like it."

"Then what happened?"

"When he added the stuff from the box to the jar, he muttered something I didn't understand. As though he was casting a spell on it."

"Then?"

"Then he lifted it above his head with both hands and closed his eyes. After a minute or two, he opened his eyes and handed me the jar. He told me to take a tablespoon of the *muti* twice a day for a week."

"That's all you had to take?" Samantha asked, incredulous.

"Oh no. I have to repeat this every month for two years. Then it's finished."

"May I ask how much this costs?"

"I'm afraid I can't tell you, Detective. *Kgosi* Ramala gave me a special price. He asked me not to tell anyone because then everyone would want the same arrangement."

"I won't tell anyone," Samantha said.

"I promised not to tell. I'm afraid the *muti* won't work if I do. I can tell you it was expensive. But it's worth it."

Samantha rolled her eyes, happy that Rra Luma couldn't see her.

"One last question," she said. "We found another appointment on his calendar, for later on the Thursday you saw him, for a person whose name appears to be Hair On." She spelled it out. "Does that mean anything to you?"

"I'm sorry, Detective. I've no idea who that could be."

After she had hung up, Samantha repeated the process with Baruti Moremi, with the same results. Yes, he'd visited Ramala to get some of his anti-aging *muti*, and no, he had no idea who Hair On was or what "Hair On" meant. He, too, had been given a special price, not to be divulged to anyone.

Finally, she phoned Mma Ramala. She said her husband hadn't returned and she hadn't heard from him. When Samantha asked if she knew what the entry "Hair On" on her husband's calendar meant, she couldn't help.

"I'm told that he carried a box with him, possibly made from stone," Samantha continued. "Do you know what was in it?"

"Oh yes. That was where he kept the main plant for his *muti*."

"And that was the only place he kept it?"

"As far as I know."

Samantha realized there was little more to be learned and thanked Mma Ramala.

"Please do everything you can to find him," Mma Ramala pleaded. "I'm afraid another witch doctor may have killed him."

That idea had also crossed Samantha's mind. Perhaps Ramala had become too successful.

SAMANTHA WONDERED WHAT to do next. She hadn't made any progress at all. She thought of going to see Kubu for suggestions, but quickly rejected that idea. She wanted to show to him that she could handle a case, even if her heart wasn't in it.

After a few minutes she locked the door to her office, sat down, and put her feet on the desk. She leaned back and closed her eyes. Kubu had once told her, when she'd walked into his office and found him dozing in this position, that he often did this to let his subconscious work on a difficult problem.

She wasn't quite sure what to expect, but it wasn't long before she began to nod off, her mind wandering in and out of consciousness. She dreamed of old men drinking *muti*—the years slipping from their shoulders, their bodies straightening up and becoming active. She saw an apparition dressed in a leopard skin catching young girls and whisking them away.

Her body twitched.

Her mind went back to the horrible case of the witch doctor they had caught who had killed people so he could use their body parts in his so-called magic potions. He was wearing a leopard skin when they caught him.

Suddenly she was awake. That's what she could do, she thought. She could speak to the witch doctor who had helped them on that case—Mma Gondo. Maybe she could give her a lead or some insight into Ramala and his practice. Then she'd take a better look through Ramala's office—maybe there were other people on his calendar who could help her find him, and maybe she could find some information about unsolved murders of young girls along the way.

She lifted her feet off the desk and stood up.

It works! she decided. Kubu was right. And I thought he'd made up the story to disguise napping on the job.

· · ·

SAMANTHA WALKED UP to the nondescript house surrounded by nothing but sand and a few rocks marking the path to the front door. Nothing had changed since she'd been there several years before. The same elderly man sat barefoot on a milk crate outside the door, wearing long pants, patched at the knees, and an old sport jacket. Gray hair curled from underneath a brown fedora.

"*Dumela*, rra," Samantha said, standing several yards away. She was sure he hadn't changed his clothes since the last time she was there.

"*Dumela*," came the reply. Most of the man's teeth were missing and, when he spoke, there was a slight whistle.

"I am Samantha Khama, rra," Samantha began.

"I know who you are," the man wheezed. Samantha was shocked that the man remembered who she was. He struggled to his feet and shuffled inside.

"The policewoman is here to see you, mma."

She did not hear the reply, but a few moments later, the man returned.

"She will see you," he said, and returned to his milk crate.

Samantha walked into the house and stopped, letting her eyes accommodate to the darkness. Then she walked into an adjacent room, where she saw Mma Gondo sitting in the corner, wrapped in a blanket. She had white hair and a heavily wrinkled face.

"Sit over there." She pointed to a low wooden stool.

Samantha sat down and waited.

The old woman stared at her. Eventually she spoke in a husky voice.

"You want to know about Botlele Ramala—the man who calls himself *Kgosi*." It was a statement, not a question.

Again Samantha was shocked. How did the woman know that?

Samantha nodded. "That's right, mma. He is missing, and we're trying to find him."

The old woman sat quietly for a few moments, then spoke. "Ramala is not as powerful as he believes. His *muti* does not work like he says. Perhaps some man who paid him for the *muti* died, and his brother sought revenge. Perhaps he is dead."

"Do you *know* that something has happened to him?"

The woman took her time to answer. "I do not have information from this world. The spirits have told me these things."

"Do you know where I can find him?"

The woman nodded. "Where water plays, but plays no more. You will find him there."

Samantha frowned. I wish these witch doctors would say things clearly, not in riddles, she thought. *Where water plays, but plays no more.* Where the hell is that? she wondered.

"I don't understand where that is, mma. Can you explain it to me?" Samantha asked quickly. "Can you help me find Rra Ramala?"

"If you are clever, as they say, you will find him." The woman lifted her hand and dismissed Samantha.

Samantha stood up. "Thank you, mma. You are a woman of great wisdom," she said, and left the room.

I can't believe I'm saying these things, she thought. I'm getting as bad as them.

She paused for a few moments when she stepped into the sunshine. The old man was still on his crate, eyes closed.

"Thank you, rra," she said as she walked away.

The old man nodded slowly, but didn't open his eyes.

SAMANTHA WENT BACK to Africa Mall and found the caretaker, who let her into Ramala's office for the second time that day. "Do you know what has happened to him?" the woman asked.

Samantha shook her head. "We have no information at all, and we haven't found his car. I think he's driven to Kasane or Kazungula and forgotten to tell his wife. He'll show up one of these days, I'm sure."

"I hope so," the caretaker responded. "It's good to have a famous person here. It brings many people to the area. We like that."

Samantha thanked her and started going through Ramala's

office. She paged back through his calendar, she flipped through all his files, she studied a ledger of what seemed to be payments, but to no avail. She found nothing that could possibly tie him to the several unsolved murders believed to be connected to witchcraft. Nor did she find anything that indicated that he'd left town. In fact, it was as bland and uninteresting an office as she'd ever seen. There wasn't even a locked filing cabinet or safe that could hide incriminating evidence. Everything was open and accessible.

Samantha sat down in Ramala's chair, defeated. She'd learned absolutely nothing from her visit. She'd found no leads, not even any *muti* for forensic analysis. The office was completely clean.

She closed her eyes, and an image of Mma Gondo came into her head. The old woman was talking: "Where water plays, but plays no more," she said. "You will find him there."

Samantha still had no idea what that meant.

CHAPTER 8

Kubu arrived at his office on Tuesday, still thinking about the weekend. Because things were quiet at the CID, he'd taken Monday off to spend more time with his mother and to take her back to Mochudi in the afternoon. It'd been good to see the joy that she took in her grandchildren, and how much they loved her too.

It amazed him how important grandparents could be. He'd seen little of his own grandparents because his mother's parents came from Francistown, a long way north, and although Mahalapye, where his father's parents lived, wasn't as far away, Wilmon hadn't been really close to them.

The weekend had had a few rough patches. Amantle had felt uncomfortable with the children sharing their parents' bedroom and had eventually insisted that they spend Saturday and Sunday nights with her. Kubu realized that they had to consider a bigger house. One with three bedrooms would be good. Then Amantle could have her own room—perhaps she would even consider coming to live with them at some time in the future—and the girls would each have their own rooms when they were older.

But where was the money to come from? Policemen didn't earn much—certainly not the honest ones. Perhaps they could build on a room. Maybe he could do much of the work himself. After all, he'd practically built the garage on his own. But the more he thought about the idea, the less practical it seemed. The garage was separate from the house and had been a simple design. And he'd had a *lot* of help from his friends.

They had also been concerned about Nono. She hadn't been herself. The girl had started life hungry and had never quite lost her gratitude just for having enough to eat. For her to play with her food, leave dinner early, and wake up tired in the morning was unheard of.

Amantle had pushed for them to visit a traditional healer—which Kubu's father had been—but Joy was dead against anything that smacked of witch doctors. So she'd made an appointment with Nono's doctor for Monday morning, and they'd taken her together. Kubu thought the doctor had looked worried, but he'd made Nono laugh with his funny faces, and she'd let him take blood for the tests without crying. But when he'd told them to expect the results only in a couple of days, Joy had been very short with him, demanding that they do it quicker.

It was almost with relief that Kubu put the memories of the weekend aside and started concentrating on his email to see what new cases had come in on Monday. However, there wasn't much. If this carries on, he thought, they'll close the CID. They won't need us anymore. But, of course, he knew that wouldn't really happen. Human nature never changed.

The morning passed comfortably as he dealt with outstanding paperwork. He went out for a leisurely lunch, complete with a large steelworks, and returned feeling that a short rest with his feet up on the desk and eyes closed might be in order.

Before executing this plan, he checked his email once more, and there he did find something interesting, something that put sleep right out of his mind. It was an email from Detective Sergeant

Segodi, containing his report on the death of the Bushman near New Xade. Kubu was immediately intrigued. Would Segodi's findings help to resolve Ian's physiological paradoxes?

The report was quite brief, and Kubu's disappointment grew as he read it. It was nothing but a circumstantial theory, and even that didn't point to a killer.

As he reached the end of the report, the phone rang. It was the director's secretary, Miriam. Director Mabaku wanted to see him as soon as he had a moment. With a grunt, Kubu heaved himself out of his chair.

MIRIAM SHOWED HIM into the director's office right away, without the usual short wait. Perhaps the slowdown in Kubu's office had spread to his boss's as well.

Mabaku waved Kubu to a seat at his desk and uncharacteristically spent a few moments asking about Kubu's weekend with his family and his day's leave. Usually he got straight to the point. Something's up, Kubu thought. At last, Mabaku said, "The commissioner thinks we need better training for our young detectives, Kubu. Sort of on-the-job guidance. I'd like you to be in charge of that."

"Me? But I focus on the serious crimes. I haven't got time to start running courses. And I'm really busy at the moment—"

"With what?" Mabaku interrupted. He rapidly ran through all Kubu's cases, pointing out that they were either resolved or awaiting trial. "Busy with what?" he repeated.

Kubu had an inspiration. "That Bushman case. You know the one that Ian was so puzzled about?"

Mabaku shook his head. He hadn't really been following it. Kubu filled him in, emphasizing the factors that Ian found so puzzling, and then turned to Segodi's report.

"I just got a copy this afternoon. I asked him to keep me in the loop because of the forensic aspects. It's ridiculous! The best he could do was come up with an identification of the deceased. Otherwise, he's pushing the theory that someone followed this

Heiseb. Instead of the two sets of footprints being two people walking together, the second one is now supposed to be someone who came later, following Heiseb's tracks. Then this person came on Heiseb and tried to steal something from him, and his neck was accidentally broken in the scuffle. All very unfortunate. End of case."

Mabaku thought about it. "What's wrong with that?"

Kubu frowned. "Just about everything. Someone he doesn't even identify told him a story that other Bushmen used to follow Heiseb because he had something they wanted. There's no clarity on what that might be. Some secret Kalahari herb or something, perhaps. And Segodi's made no effort to find out *who* followed Heiseb. He didn't try because there is only one other set of tracks, so there can't be any witnesses! Even if this half-baked theory is right, Director, it's still manslaughter at least. The assailant was trying to steal something, and the victim died." Kubu shook his head. "I think Segodi isn't interested because the victim's a Bushman, and a very old one at that, and the crime took place almost a hundred miles from his office. It's too much trouble. But we can't just leave it at that. This is serious. I need to get involved."

Mabaku said nothing for a few moments. "Well, if you're right, it certainly sounds as though Segodi hasn't done a great job. I'll review it. If I'm not satisfied, I'll refer it back."

Kubu nodded, but Mabaku held up his hand to prevent any implicit agreement. "*But* that case is in Ghanzi's jurisdiction, and they'll be investigating. At the moment, it has nothing to do with us. Specifically, it has nothing to do with *you*. I know you're interested because of Ian's findings and because a Bushman is involved, but stay out of it." He paused. "And we need to report to the commissioner what we're doing about this training issue."

"Why do I have to do it?"

"Because the commissioner said he wanted the top man on it."

"That would be you, Director."

Mabaku brushed that aside. "You're a good mentor, Kubu. Look how far Samantha has come with your help. A weekly meeting to discuss techniques and so on will be fine. You can bring in Ian, Zanele, and other senior officers. It won't take that much time. And it will look good on your résumé when it comes to promotion."

Kubu could see no way out, but he wanted something in return.

"Okay, you can tell the commissioner I'm doing it. And you'll review the Bushman case? And bring me in if Ghanzi needs some help?"

"Absolutely," Mabaku agreed.

The deal was done.

PART 2

CHAPTER 9

The van arrived at two a.m. and drove slowly through the hospital grounds so as not to attract attention. The night guard saw it, but things happen all day and all night at large hospitals and, when it headed around the back, he guessed where it was going and took no further notice.

The van pulled up opposite the morgue, and three men jumped out. There was no talk; they knew what needed to be done and who would do it. One carried a pair of heavy bolt cutters and other tools; one a powerful flashlight and a folded body bag; and the third, as soon as he was out of the vehicle, faced back the way they had come, hand on the butt of a pistol, his eyes missing nothing. The men had no intention of being caught.

The main door was secured by a heavy bolt with a padlock. Witch doctors would pay well for human body parts, and Ian MacGregor knew that. He wanted the morgue well protected. However, one of the men had been here earlier and knew what to expect.

They didn't try to cut through the padlock; padlocks are made of titanium-reinforced steel to withstand precisely such attacks.

However, the mounting was made of less stern stuff and surrendered to the bolt cutter without much resistance. There was still the Yale lock, but they levered the door open with a heavy screwdriver. There was a noise when the jamb broke, and they waited for half a minute to see if there was any response.

Once they were sure that there would be no interference, the men who had forced the door donned latex gloves and disappeared into the morgue, leaving the man with the gun on watch. There were only a dozen refrigerated drawers, but checking the dead bodies was an unpleasant job, and they muttered to each other as they worked. The sixth drawer contained what they wanted. They bagged the body, zipped the bag closed, and carried it out between them.

The man outside had already opened the back doors of the van, and he waited while they loaded the body bag. Then he covered it with empty cartons while the others went back into the morgue. One returned with a box loaded with the items of interest they'd spotted in the autopsy room, and the second with a desktop computer. The third man waited until everything was closed up and the vehicle was running before he climbed in.

They drove back the way they had come, left the hospital, and headed into the night.

KUBU WAS ENJOYING his first cup of tea of the day and a cookie or two to make up for a hurried breakfast, when the phone rang. It was Ian MacGregor, who was so angry that Kubu could hardly understand him through the Scottish burr.

"They've broken into my mortuary, Kubu! Bastards! After body parts. It's outrageous!"

"Calm down, Ian. Who's broken in and what's been stolen?"

"Who? How would I know? Isn't that what your people are supposed to find out? Heaven knows what's been taken, but certainly my organ samples are gone. And my computer! There's no mess in the morgue itself, but I'll bet they've stolen the bodies too. I didn't want to touch anything in there."

"Quite right, Ian. I'll get forensics over right away."

"Good," Ian responded, mollified. "And come yourself, Kubu. I'm very upset."

"On my way."

KUBU FOUND THE pathologist sitting at his desk, sucking his unlit pipe. It seemed to have calmed him down somewhat. Zanele, the gorgeous head of forensics, was already working with her people in the morgue—an assignment they were clearly not enjoying.

"Hello, Kubu," Ian greeted him. "Well, let's find out what's missing. If Zanele doesn't chase us out, that is. I'm sure it'll be the bodies they were after."

They soon determined that Ian was right, or at least partly right.

"Just the body of the Bushman. Why that one specifically? I was sure they would've taken the body of that young girl in number three. The hit-and-run victim," Ian said, puzzled.

"And nothing else?"

"Well, I had a number of organ samples from the autopsies in there. Some from the Bushman and some from the man in number eight. Those are all gone."

Kubu's heart sank. This certainly seemed to be an organ hit. Where would he start? The witch doctors who made potions from human remains were a secretive group. He wasn't likely to catch the perpetrators, and if he did, they would never divulge who was behind the thefts. They were far too scared of the powerful black magic for that.

For a moment he wondered about the missing *Kgosi* Ramala. Could this somehow be linked? Could the witch doctor have dropped out of sight to pull off this robbery?

"I suppose we should be grateful that they stole body parts from someone who's dead," he commented. "The ones who murder people for what they want are far worse."

"It's all the same principle."

Kubu nodded. "Is everything from Heiseb gone?"

"Heiseb?"

"That was the Bushman's name. That's really about all we know about him so far."

"Well, I have my notes, of course. They're on my computer at home. I back up everything through the cloud." Kubu wasn't sure how a cloud was involved, but he didn't interrupt. "And there's this." Ian dug in his top desk drawer and produced a pillbox. He opened it to display three brownish molars. Kubu wasn't sure if the cloud or the teeth was the more confusing.

"Teeth?"

Ian nodded. "Luckily, I extracted them yesterday. I'm going to send them to Denmark." Seeing Kubu's expression, Ian laughed for the first time that morning. "Remember we wanted to know how old he was? Well, I did some research, and it turns out there *is* a way to find out. Do you know about carbon-14 dating?"

"That's used to check how many years something's been dead, isn't it?"

"That's right. While an organism is alive, it keeps replacing its cells with new ones, and the carbon it uses to do that is a mixture of different isotopes that occur naturally in known proportions. Once the organism dies, the radioactive carbon-14 isotope continues to decay, and so there's less and less of it as a percentage as time goes on. So, when one measures that proportion, you can estimate how long the creature has been dead." Ian paused.

"Now the trouble with estimating how long someone was *alive* is that the carbon keeps getting replaced—except for the lens in the eye and the enamel in the teeth. Molars are developed at around two years of age, and the enamel is then sealed. So, from the teeth, you can make an estimate. It's a lot more complicated than that, but there's a lab in Denmark that reckons they can get the estimate to within a few years."

"Interesting. Will they do it?"

"I spoke to a Professor Dinnesen yesterday. He said they'd try."

Kubu shrugged. "Well, it probably won't help us with either the murder or the robbery, but it'll be interesting to know if you were right about him being so old. Did you get anything back about the bullet?"

Ian nodded. "Well, it's something like a forty-five caliber, but that doesn't say a lot. A hunting bullet they think."

"That doesn't help much."

"No, but I have another idea. I did some searching on the internet. I wonder if it could be a Mauser forty-three bullet."

"A German one? Do they still make those? They go back . . ."

"More than a hundred years. Yes."

"You still think he could be *that* old?"

Ian shrugged. "It's just interesting. Those guns are still around today. But they use black-powder cartridges. I've asked the ballistics people if there's any way to tell if it was that sort of cartridge from the old bullet. They're looking into it."

Kubu felt Ian was going a bit overboard with his theory, but at least it was taking his mind off the burglary.

"Well, I'll get onto investigating the break-in. Maybe someone at the hospital noticed something. At least, they must have a night guard. And you'll need to talk to them about better security."

"I certainly will. Damn body snatchers!"

Kubu headed off to hospital reception. He was disgusted, but not surprised, by the lengths to which witch doctors would go to get what they wanted. But there was a niggle in the corner of his mind. Why leave the body of the girl? Surely a young female corpse—perhaps a virgin—was a more valuable prize than the wizened Bushman? Somehow, it didn't quite add up.

CHAPTER 10

When Kubu returned to his office at the CID, he was still mulling over the events of the morning. He had little recollection of the drive back from the hospital; his mind had been elsewhere, and the driving had been on autopilot. When he arrived, he wasn't surprised to receive a message that Director Mabaku wanted to see him. News of the break-in at the morgue would already have reached him.

The director waved him to a chair. "What the hell happened at the hospital? I thought the morgue was supposed to be secure."

Kubu shrugged. "They cut the mounting for the padlock and forced the door. That would have made a noise, but no one seems to have heard anything. I spoke to the night guard. He remembers seeing a black van heading round the back of the hospital sometime after midnight. He thought it was going to the morgue to leave a body there, not remove one. He didn't take much notice and didn't get the license plate number. He's about as useful as a blind man watching over goats."

"Motive?"

"Ian thinks the witch doctors are behind it. After body parts for their potions."

"And what do you think?"

Kubu hesitated. "It makes sense."

Mabaku knew him too well. "But . . . ?"

"But they only took the body of the Bushman. Why leave the others? One was a young girl."

Mabaku frowned.

"However, there might be a link with Samantha's case," Kubu continued. "She's following up on a witch doctor who was reported missing last Thursday. He calls himself *Kgosi* Ramala and claims to have the power to prolong life. If he heard about the very old Bushman, it would make sense for him to want the body to make life-extending *muti*. Makes sense from his perspective, that is."

Mabaku nodded. That was the way *muti* was supposed to work, he thought. Take the genitals of a virile man to make a potion to improve sexual performance; take the breasts of a girl to help a woman conceive. It was disgusting, but many people believed in it, at least to some extent. And such things can be self-fulfilling: if you believe that your sexual prowess is enhanced, it may become so.

"So you think this Ramala disappeared to arrange or pull off this body snatch for *muti* for his clients?" he asked.

"That's one possibility. Of course, the question is how he knew about Heiseb in the first place." Kubu hesitated. "Ian told me that a visiting professor from the US was talking about something similar at the university."

"I don't think witch doctors spend a lot of time at the university."

"Maybe not. But the story could've reached ears with different interests. Maybe someone else wanted to study the corpse, perhaps to try to find the secret of the Bushman's extreme old age and what caused it. The thieves took everything connected with him—the organs that Ian had removed, the computer with all the records.

Fortunately, Ian has the records backed up, and he still has three teeth."

"Teeth?"

Kubu explained about the age assessment. If the Bushman was as old as Ian thought possible, that would be enough to make the body of real medical interest.

"This is beginning to sound like science fiction, Kubu. Radioactive dating of teeth and medical conspiracies. Stick to the witch doctor theory. That makes a lot more sense. They just took the computer to sell, not for the data. And, of course, they wanted the organs; that's where the strongest power is supposed to lie. The best idea is to try and pick up some information out on the street. They're going to want to sell the bits and pieces once they've cut the poor devil up. That's the way to catch them."

Kubu nodded. It was a reasonable approach, and he wouldn't be at all surprised if Ramala's fingers were in this pie. Then he had an idea. "Let's set a trap. Why don't you put out the word that you're looking for an anti-aging potion, Jacob?" he asked. "I'm too young. But you could do it. Not that you're old, of course," he added hastily.

Mabaku sat and thought for what seemed a long time, but at last he shook his head. "It's not a bad idea, Kubu, but I'm not going to do it. I have a wife and children and grandchildren. Of course, I don't believe in this magic nonsense, but I'm not going to take any chances with it."

Kubu was stunned for a moment. Was Mabaku suggesting there might be something in the black magic of these abominable witch doctors? But then he realized Mabaku was thinking about belief. No one knew what people carry in their heads from childhood. Suppose Mabaku's wife believed in the powers of witch doctors. What might happen to her? For that matter, I wouldn't want a witch doctor putting a spell on my mother. If Amantle knew about it, anything could happen. At last he nodded, accepting that they needed to keep their distance. "You're right, Director," he said. "I'll talk to some informants on the street and see what turns up."

Mabaku nodded and glanced down at his paperwork, but Kubu remained seated. "There's another possibility too, and not a nice one," Kubu said. "Maybe there's something about the body that points to the murderer. Something we've missed. Perhaps some subtle poison? But then, why break his neck? I've really no idea," he added quickly, forestalling Mabaku's objection. "Anyway, if that's the case, we're not going to find the body. The murderer will make sure of that."

"But the autopsy has been done," Mabaku said, "and the body's been carefully screened by forensics. We would've released the body for burial soon anyway. Why wouldn't the murderer just wait for it to be safely underground?"

Kubu thought about it. "Maybe the murderer doesn't realize that. And maybe he's worried that something will turn up to make us search deeper."

Mabaku shrugged irritably. "Okay, follow up all these ideas, but witch doctors make the most sense to me."

"Of course, the last possibility means I need to investigate Heiseb's death. If there's a secret, it lies there."

"Yes, yes, do that. Just don't stand on Ghanzi CID's toes. Just concentrate on those damned witch doctors."

The director turned his attention back to his paperwork, and this time Kubu took the hint. He intended to get to the bottom of Heiseb's death, as well as the subsequent theft of his body. Although he had no evidence whatsoever, Kubu had a hunch that the two crimes were somehow connected.

AFTER LUNCH, KUBU called Ian to bring him up to date with developments, or rather the lack of them. Expecting the same reaction as he'd received from Mabaku, he mentioned the idea that it was the Bushman who was the target of the raid, rather than human corpses in general. After he'd finished, Ian was quiet for so long Kubu thought he'd lost the connection.

"I don't know, Kubu," Ian said at last. "It seems pretty far-fetched, but there was something very odd about that man. I got the report back on that bullet I found in him. They believe it did come from a black-powder cartridge. They stopped making those a hundred years ago."

"Are you saying he was shot before World War I?"

"Well, we can't really deduce that. There's always an awful lot of surplus ammunition after any war. It was probably all over the place for decades, particularly in out-of-the-way places like South West Africa."

Kubu thought about it for a few moments, but there didn't seem to be any more to say, so he thanked Ian and was about to hang up when Ian said, "By the way, I remembered his name—that anthropologist from the US. It was Collins, Christopher Collins." Kubu thanked him again and said good-bye.

The most likely scenario was still the witch doctors, and the most likely witch doctor was Ramala. He'd need to find out if there was any link between him and Heiseb. All he knew at the moment was that Heiseb had been seen with a white man near New Xade, and he wondered if Collins might have been that man. It seemed a good place to start.

He phoned the university and, after some effort, discovered that the right person to talk to was a Professor Thabo in the Department of Sociology. The department's secretary informed him that the professor had already left for the day, so Kubu made an appointment to see him the next morning.

He scrabbled in his drawer and popped a cookie into his mouth. Play *what if*, he thought. Was there something about the body that might point to the murderer? Something Ian had missed? Kubu thought it unlikely. Ian had done a very thorough job, and Kubu had great respect for his work. Still, it was worth checking, and if someone wanted the body destroyed, there was an obvious way to do that. Kubu phoned the undertaker who dealt with cremations in Botswana, but drew a blank. There were no recent requests. Local people seldom chose that way of disposing of a body.

On the other hand, suppose someone wanted the Bushman's body for analysis or dissection or whatever. What would they do with it? Put it in a chest freezer somewhere? But then what? They wouldn't be able to work on it safely in Gaborone. There was too much chance of being discovered.

On impulse, he picked up the phone and called customs. Once he found the right person, a Rra Tole, he got a quick answer to his question.

"Yes, as a matter of fact there was a dead body repatriated this morning. All the paperwork was in order. Is there a problem, Assistant Superintendent?"

"Who was it? Who was the dead man, and where was the body taken?"

"A young woman, actually. A Chinese girl who died of malaria up north. The father went back home with her. Terrible. The girl was only thirteen. It was a charter to Johannesburg, and then they were changing to a scheduled flight to somewhere in China— Beijing first, then on to somewhere else."

"Anyone else? Any papers filed for the next few days?"

"No, that's all. It doesn't happen often, you know. If you give me your number, I'll call you if we get another request."

Another blank. Well, it had been a very long shot. Kubu thanked the man and hung up just as his cell phone started playing the march from *Aida*. He saw it was Joy.

"Oh, Kubu, I heard from the doctor. Nono's viral load is way up. I'm so worried about her." She sounded close to tears.

"But the ARVs . . ."

"The doctor thinks her body's rejecting them. As though she's become allergic. I don't really understand it. He thinks that's what's causing the nausea and listlessness. Anyway, I'm not sure I trust him anymore, so I'm taking her to a specialist on Friday." There was a crash in the background, and a child started to cry. Kubu recognized one of the regular small crises of the day-care center where Joy worked.

"I have to go, Kubu. We can talk this evening."

For the second time that morning, Kubu sat stunned. He'd always assumed that as long as Nono took her ARVs, everything would be fine and she would lead a normal life. He knew about potential physiological and psychological problems, and he knew that no one really understood what would happen to HIV-positive children as they grew to adulthood and beyond, defended only by ARVs. Both he and Joy knew these things, but both believed good nutrition, a disciplined regimen of ARVs, and lots of love would keep Nono healthy.

He took several deep breaths and, after a several minutes, he sat back, feeling calmer. This wasn't about some anonymous child. This was about Nono. Whatever it took, she was going to be okay. He and Joy would make absolutely certain of that. Whatever it took.

CHAPTER 11

Festus Moeng pulled his truck into the parking bay outside Gaborone's 4x4 4U Car Rental, climbed out, and slammed the door, not bothering to lock it. He walked into the office and was pleased to discover that it was empty except for a bored-looking clerk, who glanced up at Festus and then returned his attention to his computer screen.

Festus walked over, spread his large hands on the counter, and announced, "I need some assistance here."

The man looked up. Festus was pleased to see his expression become more respectful as his eyes scanned up Festus's six-foot-six height with breadth to match. Still, the man held the home ground. "How can I help?" he asked casually.

"I need some information about a vehicle rented by a Dr. Christopher Collins." He shoved a printout of an email across the counter. "Here's the reservation confirmation. We need to know where the vehicle is now."

The receptionist picked up the email and glanced at it. "And you are?"

"My name is Festus Moeng," he replied. "I work with Dr. Collins. He usually communicates with us regularly by satellite phone, but we've been out of touch for several days. We're concerned that something might be wrong. A breakdown or something. So we need to find his location and get someone out there to check on him."

The clerk looked doubtful, but he turned back to his computer and rapidly entered information on his keyboard. Half a minute later he nodded. "Yes. Dr. Collins—Toyota Land Cruiser set up for camping. He picked up the vehicle on the eighth. He has it rented for four weeks. Here's the reference number." He wrote a string of letters and digits on a slip of paper. "That's all I can do for you without a formal request."

Festus leaned across the desk, glaring down at the clerk. "This *is* a formal request! You have satellite tracking systems on these vehicles. Activate it and find out where that Land Cruiser is."

The clerk moved back in his chair, but didn't give any ground. "I can only do that if we get an official report that the vehicle is stolen or a request from the police or—"

"Just activate it and say it's a test. A man's life could be at stake here!" Festus allowed his voice to move from insistent to angry.

"There's a cost to doing that. I can't—"

Again Festus interrupted. "A cost? How much?"

The man hesitated, then glanced down at his desk. "Hmm, two hundred pula, I think."

Festus took out his wallet, removed five one-hundred-pula notes, and spread them on the desk. "That should cover it," he said. "Now get the information. Right away."

A FEW MINUTES later Festus jumped into his truck and powered up the GPS. He punched in the coordinates from the tracking system and waited for a view of the area to come up. When it did, he saw that the indicated point wasn't on a marked road, but that didn't surprise him. There were lots of dirt tracks that didn't make it onto GPS maps, even those for 4x4s. He zoomed out too quickly, and the image became a low-resolution map of Ghanzi province. After he'd slowly zoomed in again, he estimated that the vehicle's location was in the desert, some twenty miles northeast of New Xade. He sighed. It could be a lot more than twenty miles if he had to pick a way through the scrub.

I better stock up with food and water and fuel and get going, he thought. If I get three or four hours' driving in tonight, I can get to New Xade tomorrow morning and start searching.

CHAPTER 12

"Detective Khama? Constable Malaka here. We've found the white VW Golf you're looking for." Malaka's voice was excited.

"Where are you?" Samantha asked.

Malaka explained that they'd found the car in the parking lot at Game City, not far from the Wimpy. "We have to thank one of the security guards. He told us that he'd noticed a couple of kids hanging around a car, looking into it, then looking around. He told them to move on a couple of times, but they came back, so he called us. When we looked into the car, we saw why the kids kept coming back. There was a new, big-screen iPhone 6 lying on the passenger seat. It was just luck that we remembered the APB about the VW Golf."

"That's excellent news. Thank you. Please secure the area. I'll be there in fifteen minutes." She hung up.

This is not good, she thought. If Ramala's in town, why would he leave the car at Game City? And if he's left town, it's the same question. And why leave an expensive phone lying in plain sight? I don't have a good feeling about this.

Then Samantha dialed forensics and asked for Zanele. When she answered, Samantha explained the situation and told her where the car was. "I don't know if there's anything of use there, but we need to check," she said.

"Of course. My team will leave right away," Zanele said. "See you in a few minutes."

SAMANTHA COULD HAVE walked to Game City from her office at Millennium Park, where the Criminal Investigation Department was housed. However, she decided to drive, in case there was something to bring back to the office. And, truth be told, she was always a little nervous of the troop of baboons that occasionally came down the hill, hoping to find open windows and available food. Several people in the complex had been terrorized by the impudent animals, particularly when fruit was left lying around.

Samantha arrived before Zanele and spoke to the two policemen who had called in the vehicle.

"Good job in remembering about the APB," she said. "Did the security guard tell you when he first saw the car?"

"We didn't ask."

"Constable Malaka, please go and ask him. Also see if there's CCTV footage of the parking area. If there is, please get all the tapes since last Thursday morning."

The constable nodded and headed toward the mall.

"Did you try to open the doors?"

The other policeman shook his head. "We didn't touch a thing," he said.

"Excellent. Well done," she said.

Then she inspected the car. When she saw the iPhone, she cursed Orange's tardiness in responding to her request to track it. Had they been on the ball, they might have found the car a day earlier.

Again she had a bad feeling about the case.

Then she walked slowly around the car. The license was up to date; all the windows were closed; there was some mud in the wheel wells—not unusual when half the roads in the city weren't paved. And there were a few colorful advertisements and other papers on the backseat.

Just then, Zanele arrived with her team.

"Anything suspicious?" Zanele asked.

"Hard to say. There's a new iPhone 6 on the passenger seat. It's strange that someone would leave it there. For the rest, I hope you can pull some prints off the car or find something else we can work with."

"Okay. I'll give you a call as soon as I have something."

Samantha nodded, experiencing her normal frustration that nothing happened quickly in an investigation.

"Thanks, Zanele. Speak to you later."

As she walked back to her car, Constable Malaka walked over to her.

"The security guard says he only noticed the car this morning, when the kids started hanging around it, but he has no idea when it was parked here. The good news is that there are CCTV tapes on a seven-day rotation. The management is happy to get the last week's to you. They'll deliver them this afternoon. I told them where your office was."

"Thanks very much. Maybe we'll learn something from them," she said, and headed to her car.

As she drove back to the CID, Samantha thought about what Mma Gondo had said: *Where water plays, but plays no more.* That certainly didn't describe the Game City Mall parking lot!

She grimaced. She hated to admit that she was actually paying attention to the old woman's nonsense. *Where water plays, but plays no more.* She had no idea what it meant, if it meant anything at all.

IT WAS NEARLY five o'clock before Samantha was able to bring Kubu up to date on the Ramala case.

"Have you had a chance to look at the surveillance tapes yet?" he asked when she'd finished the story.

She nodded. "I worked backwards from when the security guards first noticed Ramala's car. It arrived at ten thirty-one on Monday morning, using the entrance from the Kgale Hill road. One person got out and walked back towards the entrance. It's very difficult to tell from the tape, but it looks as though the person got into a *bakkie* that was parked just outside the mall area."

"Can you see the person's face from the tapes?"

"No. He or she was wearing a hoodie and never looked towards the mall. And I couldn't see the number plates either. The color of the *bakkie* was probably white or, at least, something light."

"What about cameras at any of the businesses near the entrance?"

"I checked, and the only one there showed the person walking towards the entrance, but the face was covered. It didn't show the car outside."

"Anything from any of the buildings across the road? Maybe from *The Gazette*'s offices?"

Samantha shook her head. "There are some cameras on those buildings, but all look away from the mall into the Park's parking areas." She paused to see if Kubu had a comment. When he remained quiet, she continued. "I called Orange two days ago and asked them to put an urgent trace on Ramala's phone and where it had been since Thursday afternoon. They said it would take a few days to get the results. Perhaps you could add some pressure—they don't know me. Or perhaps the director could call them."

Kubu nodded. "I'll see what I can do." He paused, then continued. "I'm sure you've heard about the old Bushman who was found last week, and that he was murdered."

Samantha nodded.

"And that Ian was puzzled by how old he seemed, yet had a young man's organs, as well as having a bullet embedded in a muscle with no obvious entrance scar."

"Yes, that's really weird."

"Well, last night his body was stolen from the morgue. No others were taken, just his. I don't think it's a coincidence that the body of a Bushman who appears to have been extraordinarily old and a witch doctor who promised people near immortality have both disappeared at about the same time. There has to be a link, but I've no idea what it is at the moment. Let me know when you find Ramala, alive or dead."

"You think he's dead?"

"I've no idea. But this whole thing is just so strange that anything is possible."

Samantha thanked Kubu and returned to her office to catch up on paperwork.

She was about to leave for the day when the phone rang.

"Samantha, it's Zanele."

"That was quick," she exclaimed.

"Don't get too excited. I haven't got much for you. But there is one piece of important information I thought you should know immediately. The phone didn't belong to Ramala."

"Didn't belong to Ramala? Who did it belong to?"

"That's the bad news. We don't know—the SIM was unregistered. The phone has a couple of clear prints, but we'll have to check if there's a match in the database. They're not Ramala's."

"What about calls made or received?"

"Half a dozen calls to another unregistered number and three to Ramala, including one at two on Thursday afternoon. Of course, I've asked Orange to trace where it had been since Thursday. Maybe we'll learn something from that."

"I did the same for Ramala's number, but they said it would take several days."

"What's Ramala's number?"

Samantha opened her notebook and read the number to Zanele.

"We'll have the results tomorrow," Zanele said.

"How . . ."

"I know a guy in their technical department. He's single."

"Zanele!" Samantha exclaimed.

"We're just friends," Zanele responded. "And he sometimes needs a date at company functions."

"I don't want to know any more! Anyway, thanks. Please let me know as soon as you've anything else."

After she'd hung up, Samantha groaned. What bad luck that the phone wasn't Ramala's, she thought. But after a few moments, she realized that perhaps she'd just received some good luck. If she could track the movements of the mystery phone, perhaps it would lead to whomever Ramala was planning to meet.

Encouraged, she tidied her desk and went home.

CHAPTER 13

Kubu knew the University of Botswana well. He'd spent three years studying criminology there on a scholarship from the Botswana Police Service and had been back often. He liked the yellow fever trees, the views of Gaborone from the upper stories of the buildings, and the general bustle of the students.

Tumi and Nono will be here one day, he thought.

He smiled. His little girls were only four! But time moved quickly.

Professor Thabo's office was in the social sciences complex.

On the top floor, of course!

Kubu didn't exactly rush the stairs, but took them one by one. Still, he was out of breath when he reached the third floor.

The professor wore an open-necked shirt with a jacket and sported a carefully trimmed beard. He seemed more puzzled than disturbed by a visit from a CID detective. They shook hands, and he invited Kubu to sit.

"So how can I help you, Assistant Superintendent? The secretary mentioned something about Dr. Collins. I haven't seen him for some time. What's this all about?"

Kubu wished he knew the answer to that. "There's been an incident with a Bushman near New Xade," he replied. "We think Dr. Collins may know him or know of him."

The professor rubbed his beard. "Well, he's been on a number of research trips to that area. He came through and introduced himself earlier this year. I invited him to give a seminar, but I rather regretted it. He was very keen to push his theory, and spent rather more time than I wanted discussing it with me. I wasn't really convinced."

"What was this theory?"

"He believes the Bushmen—or at least the group he was studying—have a sort of oral memory, a method of passing on their history to the next generation through stories. That happens with peoples who don't have a written language, you know. He believes that some individuals are selected to almost live the history themselves, that they would see themselves not as narrators but participants in the actual events. Possibly these visions of the past, as he called them, are facilitated by hypnotic dancing or hallucinogenic plants. I was particularly interested in that aspect because some of my own work is around the societal significance of medicinal and recreational local plants. Anyway, he thought he'd met a Bushman who did exactly that, so he was very excited, of course."

Kubu nodded; this was pretty much what Ian had told him. "What was the name of this Bushman?"

Thabo shook his head. "He didn't tell me, and he refused to answer that question at the talk. He said it was a matter of making sure no one stole his work, and also a matter of protecting his subject's privacy. The feeling I picked up from people after the seminar was that they thought he was much more concerned about the former than the latter. Without any corroboration, people were pretty suspicious of the whole hypothesis."

He frowned, and Kubu deduced that Thabo had been annoyed about not being taken into Collins's confidence.

"Collins did give me a transcript of one of the stories the man told him," Thabo continued. "I could let you have a copy."

Kubu accepted, grateful for anything that could provide some insight into Heiseb, assuming that, indeed, Heiseb was Collins's subject. The professor scratched around in a filing cabinet and handed Kubu a stapled bunch of A4 pages. Kubu glanced at the front page and was disappointed that it was titled "Story of a Raid in South West Africa as Told to C. Collins by Subject X." The date was blank.

No name for X. No date. No location. He read the first paragraph.

It was Wind who told us they were coming. Wind brought us the sound of the horses' hooves and the smell of the men. Smells not part of our world, smells of unnatural things. We spread out quickly to hide. These men didn't see, but their horses might smell. I had my bow and the arrows that bring death, but they had guns. So we spread out and hid . . .

Kubu sucked in his breath. Even if this was just a story, he felt its power. He was drawn to the past, drawn again to the Bushmen, angry at their appalling treatment then and now. Thabo nodded. He saw Kubu's reaction but didn't comment.

"Do you know where Dr. Collins is now?" Kubu asked.

Thabo shook his head. "He visited me a few times, discussing his theory, showing me stories like that one. One was about what happened to the Bushmen in the war—the war between Germany and South Africa in South West Africa. He went up to Windhoek to see what they had in common with the white settler records." He paused. "The last time I saw him was about a month ago. He told me he was returning to the US to write up his research." He hesitated again, but seemed to have more to say. Kubu knew the way to handle that was to let the silence stretch.

After a few moments, the professor continued. "It was quite strange. He seemed to have changed. He wasn't pushing his theory the way he had before. And he prevaricated when I asked him when he would be back. I had the feeling that he wasn't as concerned about the oral history theory anymore. Something else was interesting him."

"Did he give you any hint what that might have been?"

Thabo thought for several seconds. "Not really. But there was one thing he said that struck me as strange. I told you he'd been trying to verify the facts of the stories he'd been told?" Kubu nodded. "Well, he said that all the facts in X's story agreed with records he'd found—at least if you made an allowance for the perspective to be changed to that of the Bushmen. I congratulated him and said that supported his theory. He looked at me for a moment and said, 'Perhaps not,' but didn't elaborate. That wasn't like him at all."

Kubu was intrigued, but his immediate need was to find this man, Collins. "What university is he with in the US?"

"University of Minnesota—the main campus in Minneapolis. They should know how to get in touch with him."

Kubu thanked the professor and rose to leave, but Thabo stopped him.

"Do you know the name of this Bushman who was killed?"

"I didn't say anyone had been killed."

Thabo hesitated. "Perhaps you didn't. I just guessed that if the CID was involved, it would have to be pretty serious."

Kubu accepted that for the time being. "We believe his name was Heiseb. Does that ring any bells?"

The professor quickly shook his head, but not before Kubu had detected a flash of recognition. He allowed a few moments for Thabo to reconsider his response, and then wished him good day. Since the professor showed no sign of leaving his desk, Kubu let himself out.

Thabo sat deep in thought for several minutes. At last he came to a decision and reached for the phone. Quickly he punched in the number he wanted and then waited impatiently for a reply. The answering voice, which Thabo recognized at once, asked who was calling and what his business was.

"Good morning, rra. This is Professor Thabo here," he said. "I have some news for you. I think it may be quite important."

CHAPTER 14

Festus Moeng stayed overnight in Kang, about halfway to New Xade. He had a short night's sleep and a light breakfast, then made an early start. It took another two and a half hours along the main road to Ghanzi before he reached the turnoff to New Xade. Then the road became worse than he'd expected, and when he neared Collins's reported position, it took a long time to find a track to get there. The last mile was through the bush, some of it dense, forcing him to make some long detours. Finally, when he reached the location the rental car man had given him, there was nothing. He was in the middle of nowhere, with no car in sight and no wheel tracks. He cursed. He knew coordinates could be off by as much as a hundred yards, which meant he had several acres to search. To make matters worse, he was surrounded by man-high shrubs.

He plowed ahead for a couple of hundred feet, keeping a lookout for tire tracks or bushes knocked down by another vehicle. After fifteen minutes, he looped back toward his starting point, but found nothing. As he set out in a different direction, he hit an aardvark hole and the truck pitched forward. Low range and diff lock got him out, but the vehicle crashed back into a tree root, and soon he realized he had a puncture. Cursing and sweating in the midday heat, he changed the wheel, grateful for the two spares he always carried. He was beginning to wonder if the rental agent had given him the wrong coordinates. If so, the man would be lucky to get off with a broken jaw.

On a whim, he climbed up onto the hood and looked around. Almost at once, fifty feet away, he saw a fairly straight slash through the bush, probably a firebreak separating one part of nowhere from another. It would be easy to drive on that. He jumped down, started the vehicle, and headed toward it, stopping just before he reached it. He climbed out, walked to the cleared area, and was pleased to see several vehicle tracks working their way along the cutting. Glancing up the firebreak, he could make out a yellow vehicle a hundred yards away, pulled off to one side and parked under one of the larger trees.

His instincts told him there was a problem, and he wasn't going to take any risks. He worked his way back to the truck and fetched his nine-millimeter automatic and a couple of extra clips, which he stuffed into his pocket. Then he started to circle through the bush to approach the other vehicle from the side opposite where his own was parked. If Collins was alone in the Land Cruiser, his attention would be on the direction where he'd heard the truck. Of course, if there were several people, it wasn't going to be so easy.

From time to time, Festus stopped and listened, but all he could hear was a variety of insect chirps. It was too hot even for birds. He wiped the sweat out of his eyes and moved closer, carefully stepping on bare sand patches to avoid making noise. At last he saw the vehicle through the bush and crouched, waiting for any signs of life. Nothing. Slowly he moved forward, alert for any reaction. Finally, he was close enough to see that no one was waiting for him, unless they were hiding in the vehicle. He crouched and made his way to the bush side of the car, where he could approach without being exposed. Standing up carefully, he had a good view into the Land Cruiser. It was empty.

Well, that wasted half an hour, he thought. But it's those half hours of extra caution that keep you alive.

He tried the passenger door and found it unlocked.

Was that because Collins was coming back soon, he wondered, or because the vehicle had been abandoned?

He left the door ajar and went round to the driver's side to examine the firebreak. He was pretty sure he had the answer then. He could distinguish two sets of tire tracks. One ended at the Land Cruiser. The other made a loop and headed back. Two vehicles had reached this point; one had returned. The question was, where was Collins?

There was the possibility that Collins had left his vehicle before the other one had arrived. Festus checked for footprints leading into the bush, but all he found were the tracks he'd made himself. Next he looked for footprints from the driver's side of the Land Cruiser, angry with himself for not checking before he'd walked there. However, it turned out not to matter. Although they were scuffed by his heavy boots, Festus could make out only one other set of footprints, leading from Collins's vehicle to where the other vehicle had been parked.

He cursed.

It looks as though Collins set up a rendezvous and just abandoned the Land Cruiser, he thought.

Festus spent the next half hour searching the vehicle but found very little of interest. There was typical camping gear—a stretcher, the tent, canned food, bottles of water, and a freezer, which was no longer running. Festus lifted the lid and was hit by the stink of rotting meat. He slammed it shut. Obviously the Land Cruiser had been abandoned quite a while ago. Probably pretty soon after Collins's last call, he thought. There were also some clothes, but no notes or anything Collins may have collected in the desert. Festus cursed again. It seemed that Collins had given him the slip.

Festus drove back along the firebreak, following the tracks of what he now thought of as Collins's getaway vehicle. At least this was easy, and he could drive with the windows closed and the air conditioner running at full blast. After about half a mile, he came to the main road between New Xade and the Central Kalahari Game Reserve. He realized he could have saved himself several hours if he'd found the firebreak earlier, before he'd headed into the bush. Well, no point in thinking about that now. The tracks he was following turned right toward New Xade. And toward Ghanzi, and the rest of Botswana, South Africa, and Namibia.

Festus found a patch of shade, pulled over, and drank half a liter of water. It was well past lunchtime, and he was hungry, so he dug out the sandwiches he'd bought the day before and ate them, ignoring the staleness of the bread.

While he washed them down with the rest of the water, his mind was working on what to do next. He checked his cell phone but, as expected, there was no reception. Angrily, he tossed the phone on the passenger seat. He knew Collins had been with a Bushman guide, so he'd be known in New Xade. Maybe he could find someone there familiar with the area and what Collins was looking for out in the desert. Maybe, once he knew that, it would give him a clue to where Collins had headed.

He started the truck and drove off.

FESTUS'S REACTION TO New Xade was even less enthusiastic than Detective Sergeant Segodi's had been.

What a dump, he thought. The village is well off the road to the game reserve, so even the tourists will pass it by.

As he entered the village, a few people watched his car and sullenly returned his greeting. He realized he needed help. He needed someone who could translate for him and who would know of the people who came through the village. The police station was the obvious option, but he didn't particularly want the police knowing what he was up to. His story about being Collins's coworker wouldn't stand up under scrutiny, and he didn't want the police on his case. No, he wasn't going there.

Then he saw a neat sign pointing ahead. SAN ARTS AND CRAFTS. No doubt something for tourists, and that meant someone there would speak some English or Setswana. He followed the bumpy track a short way until he reached a peculiar building that looked like a miniature church, complete with a covered porch. The building was surrounded by a fence and was obviously locked up.

Not a lot of passing traffic, he thought.

However, the sign at the gate had a telephone number, which he dialed. After a few moments it was answered.

"*Dumela*," he said. Then he asked, in Setswana, "Do you speak Setswana or English? I'm at the arts and crafts shop."

A woman replied in Setswana, "Yes, I'm coming. Please wait a little while."

Festus found some shade for the car and waited. He wondered how long "a little while" might be in New Xade.

After about fifteen minutes, an elderly Bushman woman came walking briskly up the road and approached the car.

"I am Mma Kang," she introduced herself. "I manage the San Culture Trust here. This is our shop," she added with pride. "It was donated to New Xade by the European Union."

"Yes, it's very . . . impressive," Festus replied. "My name is Festus. I'd be very pleased to see the shop."

"Yes, of course." Mma Kang fiddled with the lock on the gate and led him up the steps to the porch. She opened the door with some difficulty and switched on the light.

The place was a single large room with a table at one end, covered with trinkets. Four pictures hung on one wall, and Festus went over to view them. They appeared to be abstract representations of desert plants and animals, with no attempt at coherence or perspective. To Festus they looked like something a child might draw. A picture, he felt, should be attractive, and the subject immediately identifiable. Nevertheless, he looked at each one carefully.

"Interesting," he said at last.

The woman smiled and nodded. "I worked for years in the

museum in Gaborone before I came here. There we have pictures by Dada. She is a very great artist. But these are good, too, and much less expensive."

She probably worked there as a cleaner, Festus thought.

"Do you have any craftwork?" he asked. "I'm more interested in something like that."

"Of course," she said, and showed him a variety of ostrich eggshell necklaces and bracelets, as well as long strings of seedpods that rattled when shaken. Festus settled for an eggshell bracelet.

As he paid her, he said, "I'd like to hear more about the artists here." She was happy to oblige and, for the next few minutes, Festus listened and asked questions. As he thought it would, an eventual lull led her to ask what brought him to New Xade.

"I'm trying to contact a Dr. Collins, who I believe is doing research around here with your people. The university he works for said that he was often in New Xade. Did you meet him, perhaps?"

She nodded. "Oh yes. He visited here once, and we had a good talk. He is interested in how the Bushmen pass down their history through stories—particularly the Bushman group from this area. He was talking to everyone here at one time but, after he met Heiseb, he spent most of his time with him."

"Is it possible to meet this Heiseb? Does he live around here?"

Kang shook her head. "He was found dead a week ago. He was very old—much older than me—but still healthy. There is a rumor someone killed him."

"That's very sad," Festus said. "Do they know who did it?"

Kang shook her head again and looked down at her desk.

Well, well, he thought. I wonder if she thinks our Dr. Collins did it.

"Are the police investigating?"

"There was a detective here from Ghanzi a couple of days ago."

Festus shifted in his seat. That was bad news. If the police were also after Collins, he'd like to find him before they did. Suddenly, he realized he'd made a stupid mistake at Collins's vehicle. His fingerprints would be all over it. The police might jump to conclusions.

"Is there anyone else who might know more about Dr. Collins and Heiseb?"

She hesitated. "There is N'kaka. He is old too. Older than me, but not as old as Heiseb. He used to talk to them. To Heiseb and Dr. Collins. But he does not speak Setswana."

"Would you help me? It's really quite important. I could make a donation in exchange for your time."

She hesitated, but then nodded. She closed up the shop, told Festus to follow her, and headed off along a footpath. Festus was soon sweating, but the sun didn't seem to bother the old woman as she walked briskly along the sandy track.

Eventually she reached a small house made from concrete blocks, with a corrugated iron roof. Nearby was an acacia tree with a few plastic chairs sheltering in its shade. An old Bushman was sitting there alone, with a bottle of St. Louis beer stuck in the sand next to him.

It must be the temperature of soup, Festus thought.

Kang introduced N'kaka, who looked at Festus with suspicion and didn't respond to his greeting, but didn't object when they sat with him. A long dialogue followed between the two Bushmen. At last, Kang turned to Festus and said, "N'kaka wants to know why you are interested in Dr. Collins and Heiseb."

"Please tell him I work with Professor Collins. That I'm searching for him. That I'm afraid he may be lost in the desert." Another exchange followed, but N'kaka didn't look any more sympathetic. Kang turned to Festus with a shrug and said, "He refuses to talk about them. He says they have brought trouble to New Xade. They were greedy men."

Festus pounced on the last sentence. "Why does he say they were greedy?"

She asked him, but N'kaka brushed it aside with his hand as though he were waving off flies.

The heat, the irritations of the day, and now this intractable old man proved too much for Festus. Losing his temper, he grabbed the man's thin arm, yanking him forward. "Answer me, damn you!" he yelled. "Or I'll break your arm."

Turning his head to Kang, he added, "Tell him!"

Instead, she screamed at Festus, "Let him go! He is an old man. You cannot treat him like that!" She tried to pull him away, but he ignored her.

"Tell him!"

She gabbled something to N'kaka. His face indicated the pain, but he said nothing.

Festus cursed and let go so suddenly that the man fell backwards off his chair. "He knows nothing. Idiot!" he shouted.

He stood up and said to Kang, "Do you know anyone else who can help me find Collins? I'll give you money."

She shook her head. "I do not want your money. I do not think you are a friend of Dr. Collins at all. You are not a good man." With that, she turned away and headed off into the village.

Festus stared after her.

Stupid woman! he thought. If she'd got some answers out of N'kaka, she'd have made a bit of money. But she's just a stupid old woman who sells scam artworks to gullible tourists.

He snorted, turned his back on the old man, who was nursing his wrist, and walked away in the direction of his truck.

He decided that he might as well head for Ghanzi. Maybe a few discreet inquiries there would turn something up.

CHAPTER 15

It was "Grand March" from *Aida* emanating from his phone that woke Kubu from a deep sleep, and it took him a few moments to orient himself. Eventually he sat up and staggered out of bed, putting one hand down on the covers to balance himself. He vaguely recalled that his mobile was in one of the pockets of his trousers, which were draped over the back of a chair in the darkest corner of the room. However, before he could move toward the chair, the ringing stopped.

Kubu shook his head, trying to wake up, and sat down on the edge of the bed to gather his wits. He turned on the bedside light, which caused Joy to grunt and roll over. Again Kubu stood up, and he walked carefully over to the chair to retrieve the phone. Just as he was about to see who had called, the phone rang again, startling him.

"Assistant Superintendent Bengu." His voice had a deep, disjointed texture to it. He cleared his throat and repeated the salutation.

"I hope this is a good time to call, Superintendent Bengu." The person speaking was obviously an American woman.

Kubu grunted.

"This is Petra Collins in Minneapolis. I got a message from the University of Minnesota asking my husband to call you as soon as he could." She paused. "Actually, he's in Botswana at the moment."

"Do you know where?" Kubu asked as he opened the bedroom door and went to sit at the dining room table. "We've had an incident here involving an elderly Bushman we believe he knows, and we thought he might help us with some of the details. One of his colleagues at the university here told us your husband had returned home to the States about a month ago."

"Yes, he was here for about ten days, then he went back."

"When was that?"

"Well, today's Thursday the twenty-second, and he left two weeks ago last Monday. So that would make it Monday the fifth. He sent me a text message when he arrived in Botswana, late on the sixth, and we spoke briefly the following day. He said he was heading out into the Kalahari the next day." She paused. "I haven't heard from him since, but that's not unusual. He often doesn't contact me until he gets back to Gaborone."

"Do you know what he's doing in Botswana?"

"Of course," she said. "He's been to Botswana several times over the past year or so, trying to prove a theory he has about how Bushmen pass down their oral history. He's convinced that, rather than just telling stories of things that have happened in the past, they pretend to have been part of the stories. He was very excited when he found a Bushman who appeared to do exactly that."

Kubu said nothing.

"That's why he went back. He wanted to talk to the Bushman some more."

"Do you know the Bushman's name?"

"If I remember correctly, it was something like Hossip or Hysip."

"Do you know where he was going to meet him?"

"All I know is that Chris goes to a town on the west side of the country—New something or other. It has a click in it. Then he heads into the desert."

Kubu perked up. "It's probably New Xade. There are a number of Bushman groups in the area."

And it's close to where Heiseb's body was found, he thought.

"Mrs. Collins, where does your husband normally stay when he's in Gaborone?"

"I think it is a hotel called The Palms or The Grand Palm or something like that."

"That would be The Grand Palm—it's a good hotel. I'll contact them, and if I find out anything useful, I'll let you know."

"I'd appreciate that."

"Thank you very much for contacting me, Mrs. Collins. If you hear from your husband, please ask him to contact me immediately."

As SOON AS the call with Kubu had ended, Petra dialed another number.

"Ross Pharmaceuticals."

"Brian Ross, please."

"Hold the line."

A few moments later, Ross came on the line.

"Brian, this is Petra. Have you heard from Chris? I'm really worried. On Monday I got an email from him saying that he's going to Namibia and that I shouldn't tell anyone. And I just got off the phone with someone in the Botswana police. They're looking for Chris. It sounds as though something's going on with that Bushman he's been working with, and they want to get some information from him."

"The Botswana police? Did they say what it was about?"

"No. That's all they said."

"And they didn't know where he was?"

"No. They thought he was here."

"When did you get the email? Can you read it to me?"

"It came in at quarter past seven in the morning and said, 'Hi darling, I'm going to Namibia and don't want anyone to know. Please don't tell ANYONE. I'll be out of touch for some time but don't worry. All's well. I love you, Chris.' The 'anyone' is in capital letters."

"Well, I don't think it's anything to worry about."

"It's also a bit strange. He never says 'I love you.' He usually just says 'Love.'"

"I'm sure he was just in a rush. I have a contact in Gaborone. I'll have him see what he can find out. Please let me know when you hear from him."

"And you do the same. Thanks, Brian."

Ross put down the phone and sat quietly for a few minutes.

Shit, he thought. Has he reneged on our deal?

Then he found a number in his Contacts folder and dialed it. Eventually it was answered by a very sleepy voice.

"Yeah?" it mumbled.

"Festus. It's Brian Ross from the States. How're you doing with the Collins thing?"

"Um. Give me a minute. I was fast asleep." He coughed. "Okay, I'm here. I found his four-by-four yesterday in the desert, but there was no sign of him. From some tracks I found, it looked as though he met someone in the desert and left with him."

"Were you able to follow them?"

"No. It was impossible. But I went into the nearest town, which is a Bushman community. They knew who Collins was—he used to spend time with an old Bushman in the area."

"Did they know where he was?"

"They hadn't seen Collins for a month or two, but they also said that a Bushman Collins had been speaking to had been murdered. And that the police were looking for Collins."

Shit, Ross thought. I can't believe Chris would do this to me.

"I think he may be in Namibia. Do you have any contacts there?"

There was a pause while Festus absorbed that. "Namibia?

Namibia's a huge area, Mr. Ross. Do you have any idea where he would have gone there, or why?"

"Maybe he needed to get out of Botswana."

"I have a contact in Windhoek, but—"

"Okay," Ross said. "I'm going to come over there to see what's going on. In the meantime, keep looking, but don't speak to the police about it. Let's keep them out of it."

"When will you get here?"

"I'll let you know. Probably on Monday or Tuesday."

After he hung up, he pressed the intercom line to his secretary. "Joe, please book me a flight to Botswana. I'll leave on Sunday if that's possible. And get me a decent room in Gaborone for four nights, preferably at the same hotel you booked Collins in at."

KUBU ARRIVED AT the office a little late the next morning, still feeling a bit groggy from the interruption of his sleep. He immediately contacted immigration and asked them to dig into their computers and come up with Collins's movements over the past eighteen months.

He was just about to settle down to the dreaded paperwork, when his phone rang. It was Joy.

"Kubu, I've just got back from the specialist. She wants her to go into hospital for a few days for tests and observation. They're going to try some different treatments. I'm so worried. I don't think the doctors know what they're doing."

"Darling . . ."

He stopped as he heard Joy shouting at somebody to stop making a noise.

"Sorry," she said. "These kids are getting to me today. Anyway, Nono's getting worse. She hardly ate anything this morning, and she's got no energy. All she wants to do is sleep. It's so unlike her."

Kubu felt as though a wet blanket had wrapped itself around his body. Nono was HIV positive, but there'd never been any sign of it becoming AIDS—until now, it seemed.

What could have gone wrong? he wondered.

"Of course, dear. Is she with you at the day-care center?"

"Yes."

"I'll meet you at home in half an hour. Then we can go to the hospital together."

WHEN HE ARRIVED at home, Joy was already there. As he walked onto the veranda, she came out of the front door, her face full of fear. "I'm so worried, darling," she said.

Kubu walked over and put his arms around her.

"The specialist thinks that she's developed a reaction to the antiretrovirals," she continued. "But she's quite optimistic that they'll be able to find a treatment that works."

Kubu hugged her tighter. "They'll find one. Don't worry."

"And if they don't?"

"My love, we'll deal with whatever happens. Now we need to give her all our love and support. Let's take her to the hospital and get her settled."

Kubu walked into the house and went to the girls' bedroom. Nono was there, sitting on the bed. Next to her was a small suitcase, with clothes and a few books.

"How are you feeling?" Kubu asked as he sat down beside her.

"I'm tired," Nono replied. "I want to go to sleep, and my head hurts."

Kubu put his arm around her. "The doctor thinks the medicine you're taking may be making you tired. She wants you to go to hospital for a few days, so she can find a better one."

Nono nodded but didn't say anything.

"Have you got your nightie?"

Nono nodded again.

"And your toothbrush and some books?"

"Yes. Mama put them in the case."

"Okay. Let's go. Next stop, the hospital."

• • •

AFTER MAKING SURE that Nono was comfortably settled, Kubu left Joy with her and returned to the office, where he found a note on his desk to see the director. He groaned—he didn't feel up to a meeting with Mabaku.

As he waited outside Mabaku's office while the director was on a phone call, Mabaku's assistant, Miriam, handed Kubu a fax.

"It's from immigration, and apparently for you," she said. "I gave it to the director because it didn't have your name on it, and he wants to know what's going on."

"Well, it's going to be a short meeting," Kubu retorted dryly. "I don't know much of anything."

Kubu glanced at the fax, which gave the details of Christopher Collins's comings and goings for the past three months. The only items of interest were that he'd left Botswana, as Professor Thabo had indicated, just over a month earlier and had returned on the evening of the sixth, just as his wife had said—just a few days before the Bushman had died.

Where is he? he wondered. Is he still in the middle of the Kalahari or has he skipped the country?

He glanced at the fax again.

No record that he's left Botswana, but their information might not be completely up to date. I must tell them to watch for him at the border posts.

Miriam interrupted his thoughts. "You can go in now."

Kubu walked into the director's office, and Mabaku waved him to a seat.

"Who's Christopher Collins?"

Kubu just managed to refrain from rolling his eyes at his boss's social skills.

"Director," Kubu started. "As you know, the body of the old Bushman, who we think was murdered, was stolen from the morgue. We've recently obtained information that an American anthropologist—a Christopher Collins—has been hanging around the Bushman on and off for the last several months, apparently using him as a research subject. He went—"

"I told you anything to do with the Bushman case was Ghanzi's responsibility."

"And what have they done?" Kubu asked sharply. "Nothing! And you told me I could look into different possibilities about the theft of the body. It's quite possible that Collins was the last to see the Bushman. He could even be a suspect!"

Mabaku glared at Kubu.

"Have you reviewed Segodi's report yet, Director? If you did, you have to admit it was third rate at best."

Kubu could see Mabaku clenching his teeth. He wondered if he'd pushed his boss too far.

Eventually Mabaku took a deep breath. "What's this Collins researching anyway?"

Kubu relaxed. "He's looking at the oral history tradition of Bushmen."

Mabaku snorted. "Another Professor of Bullshit—wasting taxpayer money on something totally useless!"

"I spoke to his wife last night," Kubu continued, ignoring Mabaku's outburst. "She returned my call at one in the morning. She told me that he's back in Botswana."

Mabaku frowned.

"And this fax shows he was in the country when the Bushman was killed."

"So why don't you pull him in for questioning?"

"That's the problem. No one seems to know where he is. His wife says she hasn't heard from him for two weeks, but she isn't worried because that's normal when he's in the Kalahari."

"This is getting out of hand." Mabaku brought his fist down hard onto the desk. "A Bushman is murdered, and our great Scottish pathologist thinks he was a hundred and fifty years old. Then a witch doctor disappears, who's famous for selling people anti-aging *muti* at exorbitant prices. Now an American researcher, who probably knows the Bushman better than anyone else, can't be found! Is the world going mad?"

"You have to admit, Director, that it would be an amazing co-incidence if these things weren't connected somehow."

Mabaku let out a sound that reminded Kubu of a geyser blowing.

"Well, you'd better find out."

"We're working on it, Director."

"Call me at home tomorrow afternoon and let me know how you're progressing."

"Yes, sir," Kubu said, groaning inwardly. He had enough on his mind without having to report to his boss on a Saturday.

CHAPTER 16

"I'm sorry to call so late on a Friday, Samantha, but it's been diffi-cult to get the tracking information from Orange. Can I come over and show you what we've found? You'll need to see it." Zanele's voice sounded excited.

"Of course. You know where my office is."

Samantha took advantage of the time to tackle her paperwork—something, it seemed, all detectives disliked. She'd nearly finished when there was a knock on the door. Samantha jumped up and opened it.

"Let's go to a conference room," she said. "There's more room there to spread out."

After they sat down, Zanele spread out a laminated map of Gaborone with various colored lines drawn on it.

"The black line is where Orange tells us Ramala's phone moved from Thursday morning." She pointed at one end of the line. "This is Ramala's home. He left there and went to his office, as we know. Then it traveled to the Riverwalk Mall at one fifteen, where it stayed for about an hour. After that it traveled down the A1 toward Lobatse, past the Mokolodi Nature Reserve turnoff, then turned left and was at one location for about an hour, then disappeared."

"How do you mean, 'disappeared'?"

"Orange says that either the battery was taken out, which is unlikely since the phone was an iPhone and you can't easily remove the battery, or it was destroyed."

"But it must have disappeared at its last known location, right?"

"That's right."

"Have you been there yet?"

Zanele shook her head. "No, I just received this information, and I thought you'd want to come out with us."

"I would." Samantha felt a tingle of excitement. It might be the beginning of a trail.

"The red line shows the journey of the phone we found in Ramala's car," Zanele continued. "There's no trace of it before the Thursday Ramala disappeared. As you can see, on that day it started at the same location where Ramala's later disappeared, then traveled into Gabs to Riverwalk Mall—where it arrived at about one o'clock, by the way. Then it went back to where it started, at exactly the same time as Ramala's—maybe even in the same vehicle, but not necessarily so. Then on Monday morning . . ."

"At ten thirty-one . . ."

"How did you know?" Zanele asked.

"We have it on CCTV from Game City."

"So you know the rest."

Samantha nodded. "Any luck with prints on that phone?"

Zanele shook her head. "There's no match with anything on our database."

"Never mind," Samantha said, standing up. "We're going to find a magistrate to get a search warrant."

"I've taken care of that already. It took a bit to persuade her to use this Orange tracking as the basis of the address. But she did. My team's ready when you are, and I've got a sergeant and some constables on standby, as well."

"I'll let Kubu know what you've found, then we can leave."

"I did that already. I was talking to him about something else and he asked."

Samantha shrugged, a little put out.

"Kubu says you're in charge of the case. He went home a little early because his daughter's not feeling well."

"Okay, let's go."

THE LITTLE CONVOY of two police cars, the forensics van, and Zanele's car stopped shortly after it turned off the A1. The sergeant walked over to Zanele and Samantha.

"Better you and the van stay here until we've cleared the area. We'll radio you when you can come."

Zanele handed the sergeant the search warrant. "I checked Google Maps and Google Earth, and it seems there's only one building down that road. But if you aren't sure where to go, call us down and we can make a decision."

The man nodded and returned to his car.

About five minutes later, Zanele's radio crackled. "Cruiser One to Forensics."

Zanele grabbed her microphone. "Go ahead, Cruiser One."

"You can come down. There's only one residence—a house and a detached garage. No one at home."

"Okay. We're on our way. Secure the area and don't go inside either building. And if there's a plot number, please contact Detective Edison Banda at CID so he can find out who the owner is."

"Ten-four. Out."

"I wonder what we're going to find here," Samantha commented as they moved forward. "I hope it's not Ramala's body."

"At least if we find it, we'll know what's happened to him. If we draw a blank, we're no worse off than before."

THE TWO CRUISERS were parked just before a rickety gate, about fifty yards from the house.

"Smart move," Zanele commented. "We'll be able to see any tire tracks that are on the property."

When they arrived at the house, the sergeant told Samantha and Zanele that there was no sign of a break-in at the main residence, but that a window was broken at the back of the garage. It would be possible for someone to climb in and open the garage door, which was electrically operated.

"Let's check the garage first, while there's still some light," Samantha said.

First they walked to the front of the garage, carefully avoiding tire marks and footprints clearly visible in the sand. "Secure this whole area with tape, please," Zanele said to one of the constables. "We'll want pictures of all this."

Then they went to the back of the garage where the window was broken. The sergeant pulled on some gloves and opened the window catch.

"It would have to be someone small to get in," he commented. He called the smallest of the constables over. "Okay, climb through, then see if there's a button inside to open the door. If there isn't, there's usually a release so you can open the door when the power goes out. Be careful where you walk."

The constable wriggled through the opening and, a few seconds later, shouted that he was opening the door.

Once her eyes had accommodated to the low light, Samantha was disappointed. The garage was, for all intents and purposes, empty. There was no car, no body, no apparent signs of blood. There was a broken bottle under the window, a ladder standing in the corner, and a variety of gardening tools—a hoe, a rake, a shovel, a hand trowel, and a hose wrapped around a yellow plastic spool on the wall.

The owner obviously enjoys tending the vegetable garden, Samantha thought, recalling the fenced area near the gate. She'd noticed a number of new plants pushing their way through the soil into the sunshine.

"Gather round, please." Zanele walked to the side of the garage. Samantha and the forensics team followed her. "This is how we'll proceed," Zanele said and, for the next few minutes, laid out the strategy for checking the garage. She allocated tasks to the various team members—checking for bloodstains, dusting for prints, checking for footprints, and so on. Then she turned to Samantha. "You can stay if you want, but I can't have you in the garage until we're finished. I suggest you go and enjoy your Friday evening, and we'll call you if anything of interest turns up."

"I've nothing planned," Samantha responded. "I tell you what. I'm going to take a look around the main house. When I've finished, I'll check with Edison to see who owns this place, then get hamburgers and cold drinks for everyone from the Wimpy at Game City."

"How are you going to get into the house?" Zanele asked.

Samantha grinned and pulled a small leather pouch out of her pocket. "My picks. I can get into almost anything."

Zanele shook her head. "You're amazing."

"I'll be back in an hour or so. Then you'll have a better idea if anything happened in here."

The plan appealed to everyone, and Samantha walked over to the main house.

WHEN THERE WAS no response to her banging on the front door, it took Samantha less than a minute to open it. First, she walked through the house to get a sense of its layout. Then she returned to the room that was being used as a study and spent nearly fifteen minutes looking through drawers, the filing cabinet, and various papers stacked neatly on the desk. Nothing attracted her attention as being suspicious.

Next she went to the living room and glanced at the books stacked on a makeshift bookcase under one of the windows. It was a typical mix of titles: business, finance, and bookkeeping; guidebooks to the flora and fauna of Botswana; travel books to the

Okavango Delta, Moremi, and Chobe; gardening books and books on indigenous plants; cookbooks; and a variety of mysteries and thrillers.

She opened cupboards in the kitchen, only to find sparse pickings, and there were two pizzas in the freezer. It was obvious that the occupant wasn't a gourmet cook.

Finally, she checked the bedrooms carefully. The only interesting thing she found was a safe in a bedroom closet behind some hanging shirts. That was one door she couldn't open.

WHEN SHE RETURNED an hour later, the garage was bathed in light from a set of portable floodlights powered by the forensics van. As she walked up, arms full of Wimpy packets, Zanele came over to help. "A lot's happened since you left. Let's get everyone together and tell you what we've found."

A few minutes later, the group was sitting on the veranda of the house, tucking into their hamburgers.

"First," Zanele said, turning to Samantha, "what did you find out?"

"The house belongs to a Jonah Gampone. Edison says he's in the import/export business. He spoke to someone at the company, who said that Gampone was out of the country, but didn't know where, or when he'll be back. Edison's trying to find out."

"Okay, thanks. On this side, it looks as though parts of the garage floor have been recently cleaned, but we found traces of blood on the floor towards the back. We're trying a new product at the moment that allows us to test immediately whether the blood is human. The test came back positive. We'll have a DNA test done on it as soon as we can to confirm that. Second, there's a bottle at the back of the garage that appears to have been broken very recently. There's little evidence of dust on any of the edges. Also pieces were swept to one side, probably with a hand, because we found some blood on one piece. Again it tests as human blood, but we can't tell whether it is from the same source as the first traces.

We'll take all the pieces back to the lab and test for prints." She paused to take a bite from her hamburger.

"Also, the shovel has been used recently, and the soil remnants on it look different from the soil in the vegetable garden, but we haven't had time to check further."

"I wonder if he was digging a grave," Samantha said.

"Maybe," Zanele replied. "We'll take a look tomorrow morning. I'll have the canine guys bring out a couple of dogs."

THE GROUP MET at Gampone's house at eight the next morning. The forensics team continued their scrutiny of the garage while Samantha picked her way carefully around it, looking for tracks or any signs of a burial. She was halfway along the third side when she spotted footprints heading into the scrub and, not far from them, others returning. She followed the ones leaving the garage until they reached what looked like a public path worn into the sand. There the footprints disappeared, blending into the hundreds of others.

She walked down the path for several hundred yards, hoping she'd see two sets of prints leave the path and continue into the bush, but she was disappointed. Then she retraced her steps and repeated the exercise in the opposite direction, again without success.

She decided to return to the garage, hoping that the tracker dogs had arrived. And indeed they had. There were two constables with dogs, waiting near the house. One constable introduced himself, then pointed to the dog. "That's Snoop. She's our tracker dog." Then the other constable introduced himself and said his dog's name was Hamlet.

"Hamlet?" Samantha laughed. "What sort of name is that for a dog?"

"He's our cadaver dog. He's just arrived from South Africa," the constable said.

"Cadaver dog? What on earth is a cadaver dog?"

"He finds buried bodies."

Samantha's smile disappeared, and she gestured to Snoop's handler to follow her to the garage.

"We don't have a lot to go on," she said. "We think the spade was used, maybe to bury a body. Can Snoop pick up a trail from that?"

"Maybe."

"I've picked up two sets of footprints. I'd like Snoop to follow them if possible."

After Snoop had sniffed the spade, her handler took her to the footprints Samantha had found.

"I followed them to a public path," she said, "but then I lost them. I'm hoping Snoop can help us track them after that."

"Let's go, Snoop," the constable said, scratching the dog on the head.

The dog pulled its handler along, following the two sets of footprints. When it reached the public path, it stopped. After a moment, it walked up the path for a few yards, sniffing intently. Then it turned and went back and sat down.

"She's lost the scent here—who knows how many people have walked along the path since the men you're looking for. I'll walk along the path both ways to see if Snoop finds something."

Samantha nodded.

"Come along," the handler said to the dog. "Let's try this way."

The two walked slowly, with the dog sniffing on and around the path. After about five minutes, the handler pulled the dog up. "It doesn't look as though there's anything this way. Let's try the other side."

They walked back to where the tracks had disappeared, then continued in the opposite direction. Again the dog sniffed on the path and at both sides. Again there was no reaction, until, after three or four hundred yards, the path did a little jog to avoid a tree. The dog pulled at its leash, dragging the handler headlong into the bushes. Following behind, Samantha could see tracks ahead of the dog.

Not good, she thought. There's only one reason to go into these bushes.

After a minute, the dog stopped and looked around. The handler led it in a circle around that point, but nothing attracted the dog.

"That's strange," the handler said. "The tracks seem to disappear into thin air."

"No," Samantha said. "Look at the sand. It looks as though it's been swept—quite a big area too." She looked around. "There," she said, pointing. "They used that branch." She shook her head. "It makes no sense. Nobody is likely to come down here."

She took out her radio and asked for the cadaver dog to join them.

When Hamlet and his handler arrived, Samantha pointed out the swept area and asked them to check it all out.

The handler nodded and led Hamlet around the edge of the area. When they reached the starting point, they moved about two yards into the area and repeated the sweep. And then they did it again. Suddenly the dog stopped.

"Over here," the handler shouted.

When Samantha arrived, the handler pointed to an area of newly turned soil. "This has been recently dug. See that soil there?" He pointed to small areas of sand that were darker than the rest. "That's not surface soil. Probably never seen the light of day before." He stepped back and gazed at the area. "Whoever did it knew what they were doing. When a body's buried, there's not enough room for all the sand to fit back in the hole, so there's usually a slight mound above the body. There isn't one here, so they must have spread the sand around to prevent it from showing."

He scratched Hamlet's head. "Good boy, Hamlet. Well done."

Again Samantha pulled out her radio.

"Zanele," she said, "I think we've found where the body is. Please call Dr. MacGregor and have him come as soon as possible. Then, could you also take a look around for clues, and bring one of the constables to keep the area secure?"

"Will do," Zanele answered.

• • •

ZANELE HAD COMBED the entire swept area but had found nothing useful. So she returned to the garage to continue her search
there.

When Ian MacGregor arrived, he was disappointed that there
was no mound. "Now we have to find where the body's lying," he
grumbled. "Let's hope it's where the dog stopped. Get some gloves
on and let's get digging."

They pulled on their gloves, and Ian instructed her to kneel
next to where Hamlet had stopped. He kneeled down opposite her.
Then they slowly swept the sand away.

It didn't take long before Samantha felt something solid. She
pulled back her hand.

"Found something?" Ian asked.

She nodded. "Maybe a shoe."

She continued to sweep, and soon the whole shoe was visible.
"It's loose," she said. "It's not on his foot."

"Must have come off when they threw him in here," Ian muttered.

Shortly after, Samantha unearthed the second shoe, also not on
a foot.

She frowned. "That's really odd. Why would they take his shoes
off?" she asked.

Ian just shook his head.

They both continued, until suddenly Ian told Samantha to stop.
"There's no point in continuing," he said. "Look here."

He pointed to the hole they'd excavated. "We've reached the
bottom. It hasn't been dug any deeper."

He leaned over and inspected the soil. "That dark area looks as
though it could be blood. Seems someone was buried here, then
dug up." He stood up. "I've never seen that before except when a
body is exhumed."

"I'd better get Zanele back again," Samantha said, pulling out
her radio yet again. She stood up and explained to Zanele what
they'd found.

"She'll be here in about twenty minutes. They're just wrapping up in the garage," she said to Ian. "In the meantime, I'm going to take a look around to see if I can find any traces of who did this. I'll be back shortly."

She walked around the perimeter of the swept area, then repeated the exercise, except ten yards farther out. The third time she repeated the circle, she broke out of the bushes at the edge of Gaborone Dam—at least it had been the edge when the dam was full. Now the water was a long way from the edge. Just to her right was what looked like a small abandoned jetty—of no use since the water receded several years before. And leaning against the tree was a board with loops of rope next to it.

One of those boards that get pulled behind a motorboat, she thought.

Then it struck her what the old witch doctor had said: *Where water plays, but plays no more.*

Could this be where she meant?

A shiver went down Samantha's spine, and she turned and left.

CHAPTER 17

Kubu, Joy, and Tumi arrived at Nono's hospital ward at about nine o'clock on Saturday morning. Tumi had wanted them to stop and buy an ice cream for Nono, but Joy had persuaded her to wait to see if Nono was feeling well enough to eat it.

"She always eats ice cream," Tumi protested.

"What if she's sleeping?" Joy asked. "The ice cream will melt."

"Then I can have it," Tumi said. "Let's buy her an Eskimo Pie."

"No, darling," Joy said. "We'll all have ice cream when she's feeling better."

As they walked toward Nono's ward, they could hear that it was already full of friends and relatives of the other patients. Kubu thought it was the sound of false cheer.

"How are you feeling, my darling?" Joy asked as she took Nono's hand.

"A little better, but I'm still tired all the time."

"I asked Mama to buy you an ice cream," Tumi said as she climbed onto the bed. "But she said we'll all have some when you're better."

Nono just lay there, her eyes closed.

Kubu went to the other side of the bed, squeezing past a couple talking to their mother, who looked to be very old. He leaned over and kissed Nono.

"The doctor says the medicine you've been taking doesn't like you, so she's changed it. She wants you to stay here a few more days, so she can keep an eye on you. She thinks you'll be home in two or three days."

Nono nodded, but didn't say anything.

Joy looked at Kubu, worry showing in her face and eyes.

"She says you'll start feeling better tomorrow," Kubu continued, trying desperately to cheer her up.

Again she nodded.

"And look what I've brought you," Joy said. Just as she opened her bag, Kubu's phone rang.

"I wish you'd change that stupid ring to something that sounded like a phone," she snapped.

Kubu pulled the phone from his pocket and looked at the screen. It was Samantha. He shrugged and left the room to take the call in private.

Samantha told Kubu what they'd found.

"You think they buried him, then dug him up again?" Kubu was incredulous.

"That's what it looks like," Samantha responded.

"I don't know what's going on here, Samantha," Kubu said. "That's the second body that's disappeared—both somehow connected with longevity."

"Can you come here and take a look around?"

Kubu hesitated, then agreed, guiltily thankful he could leave the depressing ward.

"I'll be there in half an hour," he said.

He returned to the ward and told Joy that he had to go, that a body had been found. He leaned over and kissed Nono again. "I have some work to do," he said. "I'll see you later today. I love you."

He turned to Joy. "If I'm not back, please get a ride home with Pleasant."

SAMANTHA MET KUBU at the rickety gate at the entrance to Rra Gampone's home. As they walked to the garage where she thought Ramala had been held prisoner, she brought him up to date with what they'd found.

"There's blood at the bottom of the grave?" Kubu exclaimed. "I hope Zanele is checking if it's human. It would be very embarrassing to find a dog had been buried there. But if it is human, she should get a DNA sample from Ramala's house and have it checked for a match."

"She is. She'll have a preliminary answer tomorrow morning."

Then they reached the garage, and Samantha showed Kubu around, describing in detail what Zanele's people had found. Then she asked whether he wanted to see the grave where they thought Ramala had been buried.

"Yes," Kubu said. "Let's take a look."

AFTER KUBU HAD taken a look at the grave and surrounding area, he and Samantha walked back to his Land Rover.

"So, what are you planning to do now?" Kubu asked.

"First, I'm going to find out as much as I can about this Jonah Gampone," Samantha replied. "Where he's been, who his friends and associates are, what's his business, and so on. And check whether he has any criminal record."

Kubu nodded.

"And when he returns to the country, I'll meet him at the airport and bring him in for questioning. I'd like you to be there too."

"What about searching the main house?" Kubu asked.

"I did that last night," she replied. "There was nothing of interest, but I couldn't check a safe that I found."

"If we need to, we can do that when he returns. Anything else?"

"Yes," Samantha said. "I'll get hold of everyone who works at

Gampone's business and find out who knew he was going away. It's possible his garage was just used by someone who knew they wouldn't be disturbed."

"Good idea."

"Should I do that today?" Samantha asked.

"Definitely. And get back to me tomorrow with what you've found."

Samantha took out her notebook and made a to-do list.

"Have I missed anything?" she asked.

"Yes. Go through Ramala's appointment book and check whether Gampone was a client of his. If he was, that would raise a lot of issues."

Kubu opened the door to his Land Rover, but Samantha stopped him.

"I don't know what to do about Mma Ramala. I should take the shoes we found and ask her if they're her husband's. If they are his, she'll know he's dead. But if they aren't, what's she going to think?"

Kubu hesitated. "I wouldn't do anything at this point. But if Zanele gets a positive match on the blood, you'll have to tell her that we think he's been murdered. Then you can have her ID the shoes."

"I've never had to tell anyone a loved one is dead—has been murdered."

"It's never easy, and unfortunately it doesn't get easier with practice. It's one of the most difficult things we have to do."

"Won't you come with me?" Samantha asked. "I'll do the talking, but it would help to have you there."

"Let's see what Zanele comes up with. Meanwhile, I'm going to try to find that Collins guy who was associated with our dead Bushman—the other body that's disappeared."

KUBU HEADED OUT on the Molepolole road to the big casino complex that housed The Grand Palm hotel. He had no interest in gambling, but he liked the restaurants and hoped he could fit in a hamburger and a steelworks after interviewing the staff.

The woman at check-in was helpful once Kubu showed her his police identification, and they soon established that Collins had been at the hotel on the seventh and eighth of that month but had left no forwarding address or any other details that might suggest where he was headed next.

"Who was on duty when he checked out?" Kubu asked.

After examining her computer, the woman told him. "Zanzi."

"Is she here?"

"I'll see."

The girl disappeared into a back room and returned with an older woman and a smartly dressed man.

"I'm Joseph Nimako," the man informed Kubu. "I'm the manager here. Is there a problem?"

"I'm trying to trace one of your previous guests," he replied. "A Dr. Collins. He stayed here on the seventh and eighth and then left. I was hoping he might have said something about where he was headed."

The manager examined the register as though some secret might be revealed if he looked hard enough. "I have his passport number written down here," he said at last. "We kept all the required information."

"He was going camping," Zanzi offered.

"How do you know that?" Kubu asked. "Did he tell you?" It seemed unlikely that Collins would chat up Zanzi, but anything was possible.

She shook her head. "He had one of those camping vehicles. They're all set up with tents and everything. He had one of those."

"How do you know that?" the manager asked, frowning.

"He drove it up to the front door to collect his suitcase. A lot of guests do that. The parking is quite far, so they fetch the car and then load up." She glanced at the manager.

"I see," he said.

Now Kubu was interested. "He must have rented it. There can't be too many companies that do that here."

Zanzi shook her head. "It was 4x4 4U."

"And how do you know that?" the manager snapped.

"My husband is a tour guide. He knows these things. Their vehicles are yellow. He had one for a client once, and I saw it."

The manager turned to Kubu.

"We really can't help you any further."

Kubu nodded. "That's more help than I expected to get." He turned to Zanzi. "Thank you, mma." His stomach rumbled. "I'll have something to eat before I go. The food's good here."

The manager didn't smile. "Of course," he said coldly. "Order anything you like. On the house."

Kubu frowned. "Thank you, but I'll pay for my own lunch."

He turned on his heel and walked away, insulted and upset. Nevertheless, he ordered a hamburger and a steelworks and, by the time he'd consumed both, his mood had improved.

Just as he was finishing his coffee, he saw Zanzi coming toward his table and wondered if she had remembered some other tidbit. However, she just handed him a slip of paper with an address and phone number on it. He thanked her, and she smiled and left.

What luck! he thought, reading the note. The 4x4 4U agency is just down the road at Game City.

THE MAN BEHIND the counter glanced up from his computer when Kubu walked in. "Can I help you?" he drawled.

Kubu pulled out his police identification and showed it to the man, who immediately stood up.

"How can I help you?" This time he sounded eager to please.

"You rented a four-by-four to a Christopher Collins on the seventh or eighth of this month. I need as much information as you have. Where did he say he was going? For how long? Does the vehicle have a tracking system on it? If so, where is the vehicle right now?"

"What's he done?" the man asked. "You're the second person to ask for him."

"Who was that, and when was he here?"

"I can only remember his first name—Festus. And he was here a few days ago. On Wednesday, I think."

"And what did you tell him?"

The man looked down and mumbled something.

"I asked what you told him." Kubu's patience was wearing thin.

"I told him he went to the Ghanzi area."

"Did you give him the vehicle's coordinates?"

The man squirmed.

"Did you?" Kubu raised his voice a notch.

"He said he was a colleague, and they were worried about Collins. They hadn't heard from him."

"So you gave him Collins's location."

The man nodded.

"You'd better pray that this Festus person didn't kill Collins. If he harmed him in any way, I'll be back."

"I didn't mean any harm," the man whined. "I was just trying to help."

For a price, no doubt, Kubu thought.

"I need those coordinates now," Kubu said. "And if this Festus comes back in, you call me immediately." He handed the man his card.

"The coordinates, please. *Now!*"

CHAPTER 18

When Kubu returned home, he was glad to see Pleasant's car parked in the driveway. At least Joy had had her sister's support while he'd been out. He pulled up, finessed Ilia's usual overenthusiastic greeting, and headed into the house. He found Joy and Pleasant in the living room, drinking tea. Neither looked particularly cheerful. After he'd kissed Joy and greeted Pleasant, he asked, "How's Nono?"

Joy shook her head. "We saw her again this afternoon. When we got there, she was asleep, but she woke up when the doctor came. She seemed a bit better, but the doctor wasn't happy, because she's running a bit of a temperature now. They want to keep her for a few more days."

Kubu didn't like the news of the temperature. Wasn't that what happened to HIV-positive people when they developed AIDS? Didn't they start picking up every infection going around? "Where's Tumi?" he asked.

"She's playing in her room." The way Joy said it suggested that this might not have been exclusively Tumi's decision. "She kept asking about Nono coming home, and it was getting on my nerves. I told her to draw a picture or something."

Kubu walked across to the children's room and found Tumi lying on the bed with a coloring book. She was working on a picture with trees, a cottage, and a boy with a dog. She was finishing the edges of the boy in dark brown, being careful that the brown color didn't spill into the green of the lawn.

She looked up and said, "Hello, Daddy."

Kubu reached down for her, and she dropped the book, stretched her arms as far around him as she could manage, and hung on as tightly as she could.

"What's wrong, darling?"

She dropped back onto the bed. "Nothing."

Kubu could see that tears were close, so he sat on the bed and waited. At last she said, "I'm trying to finish this picture. But it's not very good."

"It looks fine to me."

There was another silence, and then she asked, "Daddy, when can Nono come home?"

"Soon, darling. The doctor wants to be sure she's all right. She mustn't get sick."

Tumi nodded, but her eyes were still moist.

"I hope she comes home soon. Maybe tomorrow?"

Kubu nodded. "I'm going to make us all steelworks. Would you like one?"

"Can I have a Coke instead?"

Kubu smiled. "Yes, you can have a Coke."

THE WOMEN TURNED down the offer of steelworks in favor of wine, so Kubu opened a bottle of sauvignon blanc. After he'd spent a little time serving drinks and unsuccessfully trying to cheer Joy up, he excused himself to make the promised call to Mabaku.

The director had already heard about the probable death of *Kgosi* Ramala from Samantha, and he wasn't happy.

"So much for your theory about him being involved with the break-in at the mortuary."

Kubu had to admit that now seemed unlikely.

"What's happened about Collins?"

Kubu told him what he'd discovered at the hotel and the car rental agency.

"So someone else is looking for Collins. Interesting. Any idea who this Festus could be?"

"No idea. But I'd like to find out." He paused. "I'm going to phone Segodi after we hang up and ask him to go out tomorrow to the coordinates I was given. It's too late today. I checked the location on my GPS, and it's off the road. It'll be dark by the time he gets there, and he'll never find the vehicle."

"I hope we don't find another unpleasant surprise there," Mabaku commented. Then he wished Kubu a good night and rang off abruptly.

Why, Kubu wondered, did it always feel as though the director was dissatisfied with the progress on a case? As though something more could, and should, have been done. And that Kubu could, and should, have done it.

DETECTIVE SERGEANT SEGODI had a tradition of watching soccer with a few friends on a Saturday afternoon. He wasn't an extravagant man, but he'd invested in a large-screen TV and supplied salty snacks to go with the beers his friends brought with them. That always ensured that he had company for the afternoon. His wife usually took herself off for tea and gossip with her friends. She had no great interest in sports, and the men usually got rowdy as the beer empties built up.

Today's match hadn't been great, and the Botswana Zebras were two goals behind, so Segodi was not as upset as he might have been when his cell phone started demanding his attention.

"Yes?" he answered gruffly.

"Detective Sergeant Segodi? This is Assistant Superintendent Bengu from the CID in Gaborone."

"Oh yes. Good evening, Assistant Superintendent." There was not much enthusiasm in Segodi's voice. He knew the CID director was unhappy with his report on the dead Bushman.

He listened to what Kubu wanted him to do, then bristled.

"Tomorrow is Sunday," he said flatly. "I take my wife to church on Sunday."

"You can go after church."

"I have other arrangements tomorrow. I'll go on Monday."

"Detective Sergeant Segodi, I don't think you understand the situation. Let me explain it to you again. This Dr. Collins may be involved in the murder case of the Bushman, Heiseb, that you investigated. And even if he isn't, he may be missing in the Kalahari. He should've been in touch with his wife in the United States last week, but wasn't. He may have broken down somewhere in the desert. I know what that's like! This does not wait until Monday."

Segodi heard a commotion from the TV and cheering from his friends. Apparently, against all the odds, the Zebras had scored a goal. And he'd missed it because this man was bullying him.

"Look, Assistant Superintendent," he said angrily, "you're not my superior officer. I report to the station commander in Ghanzi. And I don't believe that this Dr. Collins came out from America to murder a Bushman. And I don't believe he's broken down in the desert. Maybe his satellite phone battery is dead. That happens. I will find out on Monday. I . . ." His voice trailed off as he realized that Kubu had hung up. He snorted and went back to the TV, but the match was over. Despite the late goal, the Zebras had lost.

A minute later his phone rang again. He was tempted not to answer, but he saw it was a different number. This time it was Director Mabaku.

Segodi's ears were burning when the call was over, but he was stubborn. He had no intention of spending his Sunday driving to New Xade and then *bundu*-bashing to try to find some lost vehicle. But he had an idea.

He hunted through the contacts on his phone until he found

the number for Constable Ixau, and called it. Rather to his surprise, the constable answered almost at once. Segodi explained what he wanted, and Ixau agreed to go out the next morning and try to find the vehicle. Segodi smiled, thanked him, and hung up, happy to have put one over on the brass in the CID, who sat on their backsides dishing out work to the people in the country. He returned to the TV room, only to discover that his friends were getting ready to leave.

"Hey, I've finished my business," he told them. "We can't celebrate a win, but at least we can have another beer."

One shook his head. "Sorry, my friend, we all had another one after that goal. They're finished."

Segodi silently cursed Kubu, Mabaku, and Collins, each in turn.

CHAPTER 19

As soon as Kubu left the Gampone house, Samantha phoned Edison to find out whom he'd contacted at Rra Gampone's business.

"There was no reply when I phoned the business," Edison said. "So I went to the warehouse—it's on Nyamambisi Street. Luckily there was a guard on duty, who had an emergency number to call. An Adam Mere answered. He said he was the warehouse manager. He told me that Rra Gampone was overseas and had been for about a week. When I asked where he'd gone and when he'd be back, he said he didn't know. He also claimed he didn't have a contact number for Gampone. I'm sure he's lying."

Samantha wrote down Mere's number and the address of the warehouse.

"Was there anything else he said that could be useful?"

"No. He said that he'd be at work on Monday at seven thirty in the morning if I wanted to talk to him."

"We'll see about that," snorted Samantha. "I'm about to spoil his weekend."

• • •

"RRA MERE? THIS is Detective Khama from the CID. I'd like to come over and ask you some questions."

"I told the other detective that he could speak to me on Monday morning when I get to work."

"Unfortunately, the questions can't wait until then. I'll give you a choice. I can come to your house. We can meet at your company's warehouse. Or you can come down to CID headquarters at Millennium Park."

"I'm busy for the rest of the day today and most of tomorrow, so the soonest I can meet you is about six o'clock tomorrow evening."

"Rra Mere, let me put this simply. I'm investigating a possible homicide. I think you can help me move the case forward. If you continue to put me off, a police cruiser will arrive at your home and arrest you for obstruction of justice."

"A homicide? Who?"

"All I want is for you to answer some simple questions. You are not a suspect, but if you continue to push back, you may well become one. Understand?"

"I have my family here, and neighbors. What'll they think?"

"Say something has come up at work and you have to go. You should be back in less than an hour."

"Okay. I'll meet you at the warehouse."

"Thank you," said Samantha. "I'll see you in half an hour."

WHEN SHE ARRIVED at the warehouse, two men were standing at the gate. One had a security uniform on, so she surmised the other was Mere.

"Detective Khama, what's this all about?" Mere asked as Samantha parked and stepped out of her car.

She looked at his enormous frame and wondered whether she should have brought someone with her. She wouldn't stand a chance if he wanted to hurt her.

"Rra Mere, please can we go somewhere we can sit?"

"Follow me," he said, and turned toward the building.

"Just a moment." She pulled out her cell phone and speed-dialed the CID.

"This is Detective Khama," she told the receptionist who answered. "I'm about to meet with a Rra Adam Mere of Gampone Import/Export. I'm at their warehouse."

She listened to the response, then replied, "No, I don't need backup at the moment. I'll call you back when I'm finished."

"WHO'S BEEN KILLED?" Mere asked, as soon as they sat down.

"I can't tell you that at the moment. But I can say that there appears to have been a break-in at your boss's home near the reservoir. We found signs that someone had been held prisoner there, and we also found blood on the floor. Human blood."

"Someone killed someone in Rra Gampone's house?"

Samantha decided not to say that all this had taken place in the garage, not the main house.

She nodded.

"The first thing I need to know is how to contact Rra Gampone. Second, I want to know when he left the country—you did tell my colleague that he was overseas, not so?"

Mere nodded.

"Third, please give me a list of everyone who knew that Gampone was going to be out of the country—everyone here, customers, suppliers, travel agents, and so on. Whoever broke in must have known he was away."

Mere scribbled notes on a piece of paper he'd pulled out of a nearby printer.

"And fourth, I want his itinerary—his travel agent will have a copy, I'm sure."

"When do you need all this by?"

"Tomorrow, lunchtime."

"Lunchtime tomorrow?" Mere's voice rose. "I've got church, then I coach my boy's soccer team."

"Do whatever you want, but meet me at my office at one o'clock. Here's my card."

"But . . ."

"And one other thing. You're not to tell anyone about this. Not your wife. Not Rra Gampone. Not the travel agent. No one. Understood?"

Mere's shoulders slumped. "I don't have a choice, do I?"

Samantha smiled and shook her head.

CHAPTER 20

Ixau was up early the next morning. There wasn't much to do in New Xade on a Sunday, and he thought he might as well see if he could find this Collins in his rented 4x4 before the man packed up camp and moved on. The sun was just creeping above the horizon as he fed the coordinates into his GPS and studied the display. The vehicle was well off the road, and that didn't make much sense. Why would Collins choose to crash through the desert scrub? He zoomed out and studied the location relative to the road and, after a moment, nodded. There was a firebreak in that area, and he'd bet that was where Collins was to be found. Satisfied, he headed onto the road toward the Central Kalahari Game Reserve, with the windows open to enjoy the cool of the early morning.

HE DROVE QUICKLY to where the firebreak intersected the road and pulled his truck over to the shoulder. He jumped out and looked around. The firebreak was quite broad, and the edges were very sandy, with stumps of hacked-down shrubs sticking out. Only the middle section had been bulldozed, leaving a reasonably level region where vehicles could drive. And there were plenty of tracks showing that some had done just that.

Ixau walked slowly along the edge of the firebreak, noting which tracks crossed which and checking the treads whenever a harder patch preserved a decent imprint. Then he would stop and examine whether the sand had started refilling the impression and how sharp the outline was. When he was satisfied, he returned to his truck, fetched his camera, and took a number of shots.

He was sure that there were four different tire tracks, three older and one quite recent. He was also fairly sure that two of the old tracks were of the same age and tread, probably from a vehicle that had driven up the firebreak and then returned. It would be easy to assume that the other tracks belonged to Collins's vehicle—that he'd driven up the firebreak some time ago and then returned yesterday. But Ixau didn't think so. He didn't think the tracks came from the same vehicle, and he thought the fresh track was more than a day old. It was hardly likely that the CID in Gaborone had sat on the information for a couple of days and then decided to send him out on a Sunday.

Ixau stood in thought for a few minutes, then clambered back into his truck and set off up the firebreak. He wanted to avoid obliterating the tracks, but the edge of the firebreak was too sandy, and he battled. After a minute or two, he shrugged and drove in the center, where the other vehicles had been. He doubted the other detectives would have much interest in the tracks anyway.

When he came upon the yellow Land Cruiser pulled off under a tree, his analysis of the tracks was confirmed. One of the old tracks led to it, and, of course, stopped there. He checked the Land Cruiser's registration number and confirmed that it was indeed Collins's. He saw where the other vehicle had turned, so he'd been right about it driving up and then back on the firebreak.

As for the third vehicle, its tracks disappeared into the bush. From the direction in which the shrubs were bent and snapped, it was obvious to Ixau that the vehicle had driven through the bush and then headed back to the road along the firebreak. Perhaps that vehicle had also been searching for Collins, probably also following GPS coordinates, and after it had found him—or at least his vehicle—it had taken the easy route back to the road.

Where had it gone after that? he wondered.

Ixau had had little training in detective work but, as a Bushman, he was used to reading the past from its traces in the sand. The state of its tracks told him that Collins's vehicle had been abandoned for some time.

Why had it been left there? he wondered.

He spotted the single set of footprints leading from the abandoned vehicle to the second one. If Collins had been the driver, he'd willingly joined the other vehicle. But if someone else had been the driver, where was Collins?

Another set of footprints approached the vehicle from the bush. It only took Ixau a few minutes to follow them back to the tire tracks from the third vehicle. Obviously the searcher had parked a little way away and then proceeded cautiously to Collins's vehicle. Had he taken Collins by surprise then? Ixau didn't think so, because these footprints seemed newer than the ones from Collins's vehicle to the other one.

He didn't know what had happened, but he had a strong hunch that something wasn't right.

He tried his radio, which was patched through to the Ghanzi police station, and eventually made contact, although it was poor quality.

"Hello, this is Constable Ixau at New Xade. I need to speak to Detective Sergeant Segodi, please."

"Detective Sergeant Segodi? Yes, I'll try his cell phone."

There was a long pause before the crackly voice returned.

"There's no reply. Is it an emergency?"

"No, it's not an emergency. Thank you. I'll try to contact him later."

Ixau switched off the radio. It was clearly not an emergency, and

Collins's vehicle wasn't going anywhere. There was nothing else but to return to New Xade. He could ask around. Perhaps someone there knew something about Collins or who had met him under a lonely tree in the Kalahari.

THE CID HEADQUARTERS was very quiet on a late Sunday morning. Even the baboons from Kgale Hill weren't visible.

Samantha made herself a cup of instant coffee, retrieved Ramala's appointment book from the evidence room, and sat down to see whether Gampone had been one of Ramala's clients.

As she skimmed through, she recognized the names of a number people who were seeking immortality—a lot of politicians, several sports personalities, a TV news anchor, and even an assistant commissioner of police.

I hope the *muti* doesn't work, she thought. He's such a pompous ass.

Then—bingo—Rra Gampone. On Tuesday, October 13, at 5:30 in the afternoon.

Samantha's skin prickled. Was this the break they'd been hoping for?

Just as she stood up to gaze at Kgale Hill, the phone rang. It was the man at reception.

"A man has just dropped off some papers for you."

Samantha looked at her watch: 12:55. She smiled.

"Thank you. I'll be right down."

WHEN SHE RETURNED to her office, Samantha looked over Gampone's itinerary. The first part of the trip was in Ho Chi Minh City, Vietnam. Then the rest was in several cities in China. She noticed that he'd left on the day after visiting Ramala. She wondered whether that was significant. She shrugged. There was no way of telling.

Then she checked for the hotel he was scheduled to be at.

Saturday, October 24—Hyatt Regency Chongming, China
Sunday, October 25—Hyatt Regency Chongming, China

A quick online search told her that Chongming was six hours ahead of Gaborone. Seven thirty in the evening there, she thought. Perfect.

She picked up her phone and dialed.

"Hyatt Regency Chongming. How can I help you?" The English was very good, but with a strong accent.

"I'd like to speak to Mr. Jonah Gampone, please," Samantha said.

"Please spell the name."

Samantha spelled Gampone's last name.

"Let me check." There was a long delay, then the voice returned. "Mr. Gampone checked out this morning. Sorry."

"Do you know where he was going?"

"Sorry, he left no information."

Samantha thanked the woman and hung up. Then she tried the hotel that Gampone was scheduled to stay at on Monday.

"Hyatt Regency Hong Kong, Sha Tin. How can I help you?" Again the English was very good, but with a strong accent.

"I'd like to speak to Mr. Jonah Gampone, please," Samantha said.

"Please spell the name."

Samantha spelled Gampone's last name.

"Let me check."

While she waited, Samantha wondered whether she was speaking to the same woman as before. They sounded identical.

After a short delay, the woman came back on the line. "Sorry. Mr. Gampone hasn't checked in yet."

"Do you know when he is expected?"

"His reservation is only for Tuesday. Would you like to leave a message?"

"No, thank you. I'll call back then," Samantha said. If he's involved, there's no need to alert him of what's going on at home, she thought. And if he's not, it doesn't make any difference.

She checked that she'd read the itinerary correctly. She had.

Why had he changed his itinerary? She shrugged. Businessmen do that all the time. There's no use in speculating.

Samantha picked up the other piece of paper Rra Mere had left for her. In addition to the travel agent, there were five people listed whom Mere thought knew that Gampone was away.

I'll go and talk to each of them in person, she thought. Better not to give them any warning, then I can see how they react to my questions.

She slipped the piece of paper into her notebook and headed for the door.

CHAPTER 21

It was after five on Sunday afternoon by the time Kubu, Joy, and Tumi returned home after spending the afternoon with Nono, who was no better than the day before. Kubu was irritated that he hadn't heard back from Segodi. He'd tried to call a couple of times, but it'd just gone to voice mail. Irritated, he punched in the number and waited for the phone to ring, half-expecting it to cut to voice mail again, but Segodi answered almost at once.

"Ah, Assistant Superintendent. I expected you to call earlier."

"I tried, but didn't reach you. Why didn't you call me?"

"I thought you might be busy. It is Sunday, after all."

Kubu let that go. "What did you find?"

"The vehicle *was* at the location given by those GPS coordinates. It seems to have been abandoned at least a week ago. There was no sign of Collins. He must've left in another vehicle, because Constable Ixau checked and there were no footprints leading away from the Land Cruiser into the bush."

"You took Ixau?"

"He's a Bushman and knows that area like the lines on his

hand. He's the best policeman to find anything out in the desert. He went straight to Collins's vehicle even though it was off the road, but it was on a firebreak he knew about."

Kubu was suspicious. "He was with you?"

Segodi hesitated. "Actually, he was on his own. I spoke to him last night, and he agreed to go out early. Since Director Mabaku said it was so urgent, he left at dawn. I was going to join him later in the morning, but by then he'd found the Land Cruiser, so I decided to go tomorrow with forensics people and then drive the vehicle back to Ghanzi."

Kubu fumed. "So you didn't go out at all?"

"I've just explained that." Segodi couldn't keep the smug tone out of his voice. He knew he'd cut a corner and come out ahead.

Kubu knew it too. Segodi had shoved the job off on the poor constable on the excuse of making an earlier start to the search. And he'd gotten away with it. Just like a cockroach slipping through a crack in the floor, Kubu thought. However, Mabaku might have something to say about it.

It took Kubu a few moments to react.

"Give me Constable Ixau's number," he said through clenched teeth.

"Why do you want to talk to him . . . ?" Segodi began to object, but thought better of it. "Hold on." After a few moments, he gave Kubu the number, and then once more found he was speaking to a dead line. Kubu didn't want to waste his time. There was no point talking to Segodi, who only knew what Ixau had told him. He wanted to talk to the man who had been at the scene.

He called Ixau, and again the phone was answered quickly.

"Hello. Constable Ixau here."

"Hello, Constable. This is Assistant Superintendent Bengu from the CID in Gaborone."

There was a moment's pause before Ixau responded politely, "Good evening, Assistant Superintendent."

"I'm investigating two cases at the moment, Constable—maybe linked. The one is the death of the man Heiseb, and the other is the disappearance of Dr. Collins. You went out this morning to look for Collins. I'd like to hear what you found."

"Of course." For the next ten minutes Ixau went through the story of the vehicles and the various sets of tracks he'd found. Kubu asked several questions and was impressed by the constable's thorough approach and careful observation at the scene.

Almost certainly, he'd done a better job than the wretched Segodi would have done, Kubu thought, and he complimented the constable on his good work.

Ixau didn't respond for a few seconds, then he said, "Assistant Superintendent, I know I'm not a detective, but I'm the only policeman out here. I know the people. I know what's going on in New Xade. So I asked a few questions this morning when I got back from the bush. I couldn't reach Detective Sergeant Segodi, so I just went ahead." He paused as if waiting for a rebuke.

"Very good. Did you find out anything?"

"You remember that I described the one track as quite recent, but not from yesterday? Well, I asked around, and I found a lady who'd seen a stranger on Thursday. Her name is Mma Kang. She remembers him quite well, because we don't get a lot of visitors out this way and because he was quite rough with one of the older residents here. He was also looking for Collins. I'm sure it was the man who found Collins's Land Cruiser out in the bush. Mma Kang sells Bushman art, and he drove his vehicle to her place and pulled it off the road. So I could see the tire marks. It's definitely the same tread as the recent one on the firebreak."

"Did she get the man's name or the registration number of his vehicle?"

"He said his first name was Festus. She didn't have the registration number of the vehicle, but she described it. It was a silver Nissan double cab."

Kubu recognized the name at once and was delighted. With a

bit of luck this Festus was the owner of the vehicle. How many silver Nissan double cabs could there be in Gaborone?

"That's very good work, Constable. It'll really help me. Thank you."

Once more Ixau hesitated. Then he said, "Assistant Superintendent, I know who you are. Many Bushmen know of you and the bad thing that happened to you in the Kalahari. Something bad happened to Heiseb, too. I want to know who did that. I'm happy to help you any way I can."

Kubu digested that. After a moment he said, "Constable, did you mention anything about this Festus to Detective Sergeant Segodi?"

"No, I wasn't sure . . ."

"Fine. Please report anything you discover directly to me."

"Thank you, Assistant Superintendent. I'll do that," Ixau said, sounding pleased.

Not much love lost between him and Segodi, Kubu decided. He wished the constable a good night, and then went to see how far along Joy was with dinner.

CHAPTER 22

Mabaku had called a meeting for eight o'clock on Monday morning—a time that Kubu did not appreciate. He preferred a slower start to the morning, enjoying a cup of coffee with Joy before facing the week's trials and tribulations. He tried hard but was still ten minutes late.

"Oversleep again, Kubu?" Mabaku growled. "We've been twiddling our thumbs for ten minutes. Why can't you ever be on time?"

"Sorry, Director," Kubu said as he sat down between Ian MacGregor and Edison Banda. "I'll be on time next Monday."

"I'll believe that when I see it," Mabaku said.

To Kubu's irritation, Edison stifled a snicker.

"All right," Mabaku continued. "Let's get started. Tell me if I'm missing something."

He walked over to the whiteboard and wrote "Bushman Heiseb" at the top left.

"First, we have the murder of this Bushman out in the Kalahari. When Ian autopsied him, he found his internal organs looking as though they were from a much younger man, and a bullet lodged in an abdominal muscle with no entry wound. Then the Bushman's body was stolen from the morgue." He shook his head in disbelief, then wrote "Ramala" on the board.

"Second, we have a traditional healer called *Kgosi* Ramala, whose claim to fame was that he provided *muti* that supposedly prolonged life. He disappeared ten days ago. Ian and Samantha found blood and a pair of shoes in a grave near the reservoir, but no body. It also appears to have been stolen. Zanele told me this morning that she'd heard back from the DNA people that the shoes and blood were Ramala's. She also told me that it appeared Ramala had been held nearby, in the garage of a Rra Gampone, who is currently out of the country."

He glanced at Zanele. "Did I get that right?" he asked.

She nodded.

"So we have what appears to be two separate cases where someone has been murdered and then later their bodies have been stolen. If that's not bizarre enough, one of the victims promised everlasting life, and Ian thinks the other was a hundred and fifty years old." He paused, then shook his head. "I'm getting too old for this job," he muttered.

He turned back to the board and wrote "Collins." "Kubu tells me that an American—a Christopher Collins—who befriended the dead Bushman has now gone missing, and that his rented four-by-four was found near New Xade, abandoned in the desert. He also tells me that someone asked the rental company for the coordinates of Collins's vehicle and may also be looking for Collins."

"Director, Director. There's a Christopher Collins in Ramala's appointment book." Samantha could hardly contain her excitement. "It has to be the same person."

"When was that?" Kubu asked.

"I don't remember the exact date—I'll check later—but I think it was about a month ago."

"It seems everyone in this town wants to live forever. They're all mad!" Mabaku looked around the room. "Anything else?"

"Director," Kubu said, "I have the first name of the person who is looking for Collins—a Festus someone or other. And I know what he's driving. Constable Ixau in New Xade confirmed that this Festus guy had been there looking for Collins."

Mabaku frowned. "Constable Ixau? I thought Detective Sergeant Segodi was doing that?"

"I'd like to talk to you about that afterwards," Kubu said. "Anyway, Edison's been searching the vehicle registration records for a match—but he doesn't have anything yet. Hopefully we'll have that information today."

Edison nodded.

"And what do you know about this Collins character?" Mabaku asked.

"Not much more than I've already told you," Kubu replied. "He's an anthropologist from Minneapolis in the States. He's interested in how Bushmen keep their history alive through storytelling."

"Please don't tell me he's a hundred and fifty years old too!"

Kubu smiled. "Not that I know of."

"Anything else?" Mabaku asked.

"Director," Samantha said, "I've been following up on Rra Gampone."

"I suppose he's also a hundred and fifty years old?"

Samantha shook her head. "No, Director. He's fifty-seven and the owner of a small import/export business."

"Thank God for that!"

"He's been out of the country for nearly two weeks," Samantha continued, "and is due back on Wednesday. Air Botswana will confirm when he boards their flight in Johannesburg so I can meet him when he lands. I've also spoken to everyone who we think knew he was overseas. Of course, I can't be one hundred percent sure that those are the only people who knew. However, my assessment is that none of them is involved." She paused. "But . . ."

"But what?" Mabaku snapped.

"But I think you need to put his name on the board too—he was also one of Ramala's clients."

CHAPTER 23

When the meeting had finished, Samantha set off on the mission she was dreading—to tell Mma Ramala that her husband had been murdered. She'd already called ahead, telling her that she needed to follow up on several items. Mma Ramala had assured her that she would be home.

As she drove, Samantha played through different opening lines in her head.

Dumela, Mma Ramala. How are you? What a nice day it is. I have some news for you . . .

or

Dumela, Mma Ramala. Let's go inside and sit down. I've something to tell you.

or

Mma Ramala, I have some bad news . . .

None of them sounded right, so Samantha tried to imagine how she would like such bad news broken to her. Eventually she decided on a direct approach, without preamble, without sugarcoating.

As hard as it would be, I'd like it straight, without beating around the bush, she decided.

However, as she pulled up in front of the house, her resolve started to weaken.

Perhaps I need to establish some rapport first, she thought. Maybe it's better if she's sitting down.

She walked up to the front door and knocked, and it was opened almost immediately. Mma Ramala looked exhausted; her face was drawn and there were bags under her eyes.

"He's dead, isn't he?" she said.

Taken aback, Samantha could only nod. Then, instinctively, she leaned forward and put her arms around the woman, softly patting her back.

"I'm so sorry," she said. "We think he was murdered."

Mma Ramala sobbed. "Where can I get his body?" she asked. "I need to prepare for the funeral."

Samantha took a deep breath. "We don't have the body, mma. We don't know where it is."

Mma Ramala let out a loud wail. "How do you know he's dead, then?"

"Mma, we found a shallow grave. Our blood tests show your husband's body was in it at some stage, then later removed."

"How can I put him to rest if I don't have his body?" Mma Ramala cried. "What will I do for his funeral?" She buried her face against Samantha's chest.

Samantha didn't know how to answer this, so she hugged the woman tighter.

Eventually, Mma Ramala pulled herself free and invited Samantha in.

"You'll have some tea, won't you?" she asked.

Samantha nodded and sat down in the living room and waited for Mma Ramala to return.

• • •

When the tea had been poured, Samantha gave Mma Ramala an edited version of what the police had discovered.

"Why would anyone want to kill Botlele?" Mma Ramala asked, preempting Samantha's first question. "He was kind and helped so many people."

"We think it has something to do with the *muti* he gave people to make them live longer. Perhaps someone wanted to do the same thing, to be the best-known healer himself."

Mma Ramala shook her head. "But why kill him? He would have shared his remedy."

I doubt that, Samantha thought. Why give away something that was making you rich?

"Did anyone else know what was in his *muti*?" she asked. "Did people know where he got his ingredients?"

"I don't think so."

"Did your husband mention if anyone had contacted him about such things?"

Mma Ramala shook her head. "He didn't say anything."

"Did he seem worried before he disappeared? How was he on the day he went missing?"

"I've told you before—he was fine, eager to go to work."

"I'm sorry to ask these questions, mma, but we need to get as much information as possible so we can catch the people who did it."

Mma Ramala nodded.

"Did your husband ever mention a person by the name of Gampone? A Rra Jonah Gampone?"

Mma Ramala shook her head. "I've never heard the name. Who is he? Do you think he killed Botlele?"

"He was overseas when your husband died, but his name was in your husband's appointment book." She paused. "And how about an American—Mr. Christopher Collins?"

"No. I don't think Botlele had any white customers. He's white, isn't he?"

"Yes."

"Is his name in my husband's appointment book?"

Samantha nodded. "Yes. We're interested in him because he's also disappeared."

Mma Ramala put her hands to her face. "*Aaii*. His wife must be very worried."

"I'm sure she is. And just a couple more questions: Who was the person your husband bought plants from for his *muti*?"

"I think he's called Ou Man. He's from the Shakawe area."

Samantha wrote that down in her notebook.

"And have you ever heard of a Bushman by the name of Heiseb?"

Mma Ramala shook her head. "Never."

"Mma Ramala, I've asked you this before, but I need to ask you again: Did your husband ever use human body parts in any of the *muti* he prepared?"

Mma Ramala shook her head. "Never. He thought some witch doctors did it to make lots of money. He said their *muti* would never work—that anyone who bought such *muti* was stupid."

As SHE DROVE back to the office, Samantha tried to figure out the conflicting emotions she was experiencing. She felt sorry for Mma Ramala—losing a husband and not knowing where his body was. She had mixed emotions about Ramala himself. He was a witch doctor—something she despised—but he appeared to be honest and aboveboard, even if there was no evidence that what he was selling worked.

As she turned into the parking lot behind the CID offices, she realized that she wanted to speak to Kubu.

SAMANTHA WENT STRAIGHT to Kubu's office, knocked, and opened the door. Kubu was at his desk, leaning back in his office chair.

"Yes, Samantha? What is it?

"I want to thank you, Kubu."

He frowned. "What for?"

"For persuading me to investigate Rra Ramala's disappearance. I've just come back from telling his wife that he's dead, and I realize that they deserve as much of our time and effort as anyone else. I still hate witch doctors who harm people, but now I realize not all witch doctors are like that."

Kubu smiled. "Well done, Samantha. You've come a long way in a very short time."

 **PART 3**

CHAPTER 24

Festus checked the monitors in the arrivals terminal at Gaborone International Airport. Air Botswana flights could be unpredictable, but fortunately Brian Ross's flight was on time for an eight p.m. arrival.

He wondered what sort of person his client was. He'd seemed rather abrupt on the phone, but perhaps it was just the worry of Collins's disappearance. Well, he'd soon find out.

When the passengers started coming through from customs, Festus held up a card on which he'd written Ross's name. A few minutes later, a tall man pulling a suitcase approached him.

"Festus Moeng? I'm Brian Ross." They shook hands, and Ross took in Festus's bulk. "Well, you look like you can take care of yourself," he commented. "Let's get out of here." He headed for the exit, leaving Festus to deal with the bag.

Ross was sweating by the time they reached Festus's truck. As they drove out of the airport, he said, "Does this thing have air-conditioning?"

It was on, but Festus turned up the fan. "How was your flight?"

"Tiring," Ross replied. He was concentrating on his cell phone. "Can't get this damn thing to work."

"It takes time to find a new network."

Ross glanced up. "Things move slowly here, do they?"

Festus shrugged and didn't reply.

"I need to talk to a Professor Thabo at the university. Can you set that up?"

Festus was tempted to point out that he was a private detective, not a personal assistant, but he shrugged it off. At the rate he was charging Ross, why should he complain about another hour or two? "Shouldn't be a problem. Does he know you?"

"He knows Collins. It's about the only connection I've got left, now that you've lost him."

Festus frowned. He'd hardly "lost" Collins, since he'd never found him in the first place. "Well, there might be some other leads I can follow up. Can you give me some more details about all this? I'd be more help if I knew what it's all about."

Ross was quiet for a few moments, then said, "I run a pharmaceutical company in the States. Collins is a consultant for my company, but he's also an old friend. We go back to college days, and naturally I'm worried about him."

Festus digested that. He was pretty sure that however far back they went together, Ross hadn't rushed to Botswana to rescue an old friend. "What was he doing out here?"

"He was studying the oral history traditions of the Bushmen."

"Yes, you told me that before. What I want to know is, what was he doing for you?"

Ross spent a bit more time fiddling with his phone, until he gave up and rebooted it. "He was keeping an eye out for wild plants that could lead to new food crops or drugs or whatever."

That made sense to Festus. Collins had spent a lot of time with the Bushmen, and they knew things. Collins had probably learned a lot from them.

"Did he find anything?" he asked casually. "Some desert plant that the Bushmen know about, perhaps?"

Ross gave him a hard look. "Look, Festus, I need your help to find Collins, and there'll be a big bonus for you if this works out for me. It doesn't matter what Collins did or didn't find."

Festus thought for a moment and then responded, "I think it matters a lot. If Collins found nothing, then why has he disappeared? Why has he gone to Namibia?"

Ross frowned and said, "I don't know."

Festus waited, but Ross didn't elaborate. "So what did Collins find?" he persisted.

At first it seemed Ross wasn't going to answer, but finally he said, "It's a plant that helps the healing process for cuts and scratches and the like. Apparently the Bushmen have used it forever. Could be very profitable if it works out, but there's lots of testing and development work ahead. Might be worth nothing at all. Just keep your mouth shut about it."

Is that the whole story? Festus wondered. Still, he's opening up a bit. Maybe, if I play my cards right, this could be worth a lot more to me than a few-thousand-pula fee. We'll see.

Then another thought struck him. "Does anyone else know about this?" he asked. "Another drug company?"

Ross shook his head. "Not as far as I know. Why?"

"Well, the way I see it, either Collins has taken off with this plant—maybe trying to sell it to someone else—or maybe he didn't run off but someone got to him in the desert." Festus hesitated. "Seems a lot of effort for something that's good for scratches."

"So it's not the cure for cancer, but you know how many people use aspirin and how much money there is in it?"

Festus nodded and let it drop, but he still thought Ross was holding back.

Ross changed the subject. "What's the story with the police?"

"I told you what I know. I think they want to question Collins about the death of some Bushman he knew."

"You didn't talk to them, did you?"

"You told me not to, so I didn't. But, of course, if they ask me about it, I'll have to tell them everything I know."

"Well, just keep me out of it."

"Look, Mr. Ross, I'm working for you, but I'm not your lawyer. There's no client privilege. When you've done your business here, you'll go back to your company and your nice home in America. I have to go on working with the police here. I can't afford to piss them off."

They slowed down as they entered a traffic circle, and Ross watched the cars building up around it. "Don't you have traffic lights?" he asked.

"Yes, but these work pretty well. We don't have the sort of traffic you have."

Ross said nothing more until they reached The Grand Palm hotel. "Looks decent," he commented.

"Yes. It's a nice hotel."

"Okay, bring my bag, and I'll check in. I need a drink and something to eat and a proper night's sleep. Come over tomorrow at nine. Then we can decide what the next steps are."

He climbed out of the truck, slammed the door, and headed for the hotel entrance. Festus jumped out, grabbed the suitcase, and followed him. He decided he didn't like Ross, but he was being well paid, and his meter was running.

CHAPTER 25

Festus phoned the university first thing in the morning, but Professor Thabo hadn't come in yet. So he made an appointment for midday, after the professor's postgraduate seminar. With some time to kill, he started Googling "plants and traditional medicines." After a bit of surfing, he came upon a Wikipedia article about the Bushman appetite suppressant *hoodia* and a big company's efforts to leverage local knowledge into something marketable. However, the article said that the company had never brought *hoodia* to market, despite a lot of expensive research, and the Bushmen, who'd been promised a share of the profits, had missed out—in the end there were no profits to share. It seemed that Ross was right when he said these things were very uncertain. Festus didn't think it likely that another drug company would kidnap Collins for the chance to develop a healing lotion. He guessed that Collins had found something much more exciting than that.

Festus needed information, and there were some contacts he could lean on, either because they owed him favors or because he had something on them. He made a few calls, but no one had heard of Collins. The last person he tried was nicknamed Legotlo, a nasty little character who would give a tip to the police and then tip off the target that the police were onto him, picking up a few pula each way.

"*Dumela,* Legotlo. It's Festus."

There was a brief silence before Legotlo reluctantly returned the greeting. "*Dumela,* Festus."

"Legotlo, I think you can help me with something. There could be a few pula in it for you."

"I'm listening."

"There's a white guy from the US who's missing. I'm trying to trace him."

"This guy have a name?"

"Collins. Dr. Christopher Collins."

"Can't help you. Never heard of him."

"Hang on, let me tell you a bit about this—maybe something will jog your memory. He disappeared about three weeks ago in the Kalahari—in the New Xade area."

"Where the Bushmen live? Why don't you ask them?"

"I have. I'm beginning to think someone grabbed Collins."

"You mean like kidnapped? For ransom or something?"

"Maybe."

"I don't get mixed up in that sort of stuff!" Legotlo squealed. "You think I'm a moron?"

"I think maybe you heard something through the grapevine. I know you're discreet, but we're old friends."

Legotlo took his time before he replied. "Look, I've heard nothing about a snatch. Not of a white guy. Now will you give me a break? I've got things to do."

"Okay. But keep your ears open, all right? We can do each other favors. You know what I mean?"

"Sure, sure. I'll keep my ears open. I'll let you know, okay? Now will you get off my back?"

"Sure, Legotlo. Thanks. You're a good guy."

Festus hung up, disappointed. He checked his watch and realized it was time to get going. But as he picked up his car keys, something from the conversation struck him. Why did Legotlo say "Not of a white guy"? Why not just that he'd heard nothing about a snatch? Festus made a mental note to follow up with Legotlo when he had a chance.

FESTUS PICKED UP Ross on time, and they reached Professor Thabo's office just before noon. He was still busy running his seminar, and the secretary told them to wait in the professor's office until he arrived.

"What can I do for you, gentlemen?" Thabo asked, when he walked through the door a few minutes later.

Ross started off. "We're looking for a Dr. Christopher Collins. I believe you know him?"

Thabo nodded. "I've met him a couple of times."

"I was in communication with him by satellite phone," said Ross. "At least I was until about three weeks ago. Then we lost connection. So I asked Mr. Moeng here to check up on him. To make sure he was okay. But Collins seems to have disappeared. We can't find any trace of him since he went off with his Bushmen friends into the Kalahari. I thought you might have a few ideas."

"Me? I only met him a few times. I understood that he was going back to the US."

"Yes, he did. And then came back here."

Thabo shook his head. "I'm afraid I can't help you. But I can suggest who might be able to." He scratched around on his desk and came up with a business card, which he passed to Ross. The card was from Assistant Superintendent Bengu of the Botswana CID and, at the bottom, was a handwritten cell phone number. Ross recognized the name at once, but didn't react. He passed the card to Festus.

"The police are involved? Are they also looking for Dr. Collins?" Ross asked.

Thabo nodded. "They're investigating the death of a Bushman named Heiseb. They think he was the man helping Collins with his work, and it seems that Collins may've been the last person to see him alive."

Ross's eyebrows rose. "They think Collins may have been involved in his death? That's very hard to believe."

Thabo shrugged. "I have no idea what they think. I suggest you ask them."

Something about the conversation didn't ring true to Festus. Thabo was supposed to know Collins—maybe not very well—but he seemed to have no real interest in what had happened to the man or whether he had, indeed, been involved in the Bushman's death.

Is he just a cold fish, Festus wondered, or does he have no interest because he knows this is all a bullshit story?

He decided to take a long shot.

"Professor, I'm concerned that Dr. Collins may be in danger, that Heiseb was targeted and Collins may be next. Perhaps Collins is already dead." He said it in a matter-of-fact voice, but his eyes never left Thabo's face. For a moment he saw shock there, then the bland expression returned.

"Why would you think that?" the professor asked.

"I'm afraid I can't go into the details of my sources, Professor," Festus replied. "But they are usually reliable." Which you are not, he added to himself.

"Well, perhaps you should raise that with the police also," Thabo suggested.

Festus nodded. "Oh, we certainly will, Professor. You can be sure of that."

Ross had taken no trouble to hide his surprise at Festus's question, and now he took back control of the conversation. "I don't think we need to pursue this aspect further. Professor, I have a couple of technical questions related to your area of expertise. Do you have a few more minutes?"

Thabo nodded without enthusiasm.

Ross turned to Festus. "Festus, I'd like to speak to the professor in private."

It took Festus a couple of seconds to realize that he was being dismissed. He was furious. He was pretty sure that Ross was going to talk to the professor about the real issues behind Collins's disappearance, and he very much wanted to be in on that.

"I'll meet you in the secretary's office in a few minutes," Ross persisted.

"Okay." Festus nodded curtly to the professor and left, closing the door behind him.

Ross turned back to Thabo.

"Professor Thabo, my business is finding new drugs. I'm not a philanthropist—I'm not rich enough to have that luxury. Collins has discovered a plant in the Kalahari that shows promise with healing skin lesions. Did he discuss that with you? After all, I believe you have a professional interest in herbal medicines from the Kalahari."

"As a matter of fact, I do, but Collins never discussed anything like that with me. Our discussions were all around Bushman oral traditions and his theory about a Bushman who narrated these events as if he'd been present himself. We never discussed anything to do with Bushman remedies or healing properties of plants."

Ross nodded, then continued. "Do you have a moment to tell me about your research, Professor? I'd be interested, and perhaps Ross Pharmaceuticals might be able to work with you on something."

That was enough to set Professor Thabo off on a description of his projects and what his students were doing. Ross listened carefully but soon came to the conclusion that it was the anthropology rather than the medicinal properties of plants that interested Thabo. After ten minutes he said, "Professor, that's been fascinating. Thank you. I mustn't take any more of your time, but perhaps we could meet again while I'm here, to discuss this further? And, of course, if you can think of anything more concerning Dr. Collins, I'd be very grateful. Here's my card. I'll be staying at The Grand Palm."

The professor took it. "By the way, Mr. Ross," he said, "I'm sure you've heard of biopiracy? What Collins was doing—or appears to have been doing—could infringe the rights of the Bushman people who discovered this plant, so you should be very careful about the exploitation of anything found in the Kalahari. If you need advice, I can be of help."

Ross thanked him, took his leave, and headed off to link up with Festus.

It's exactly the same here as it is in the States, Ross thought. The way to an academic's heart is through his wallet.

IN THE SECRETARY'S office, Festus sat and fumed. The secretary was quite good-looking and tried to be chatty, but he was in no mood to flirt. He grabbed the *Daily News* and started skimming the headlines. On page two he spotted an article that seemed interesting, although at first he wasn't sure why. He read it through.

TRADITIONAL HEALER FEARED MURDERED!

The police fear that a well-known traditional healer, Botlele Ramala, has been murdered. Ramala, often called *Kgosi* by his clients, has been missing for nearly two weeks, and the police have evidence that makes them believe he was abducted and later murdered.

The police have called on anyone who has seen Ramala, or knows anything about his whereabouts over the last two weeks, to contact them immediately.

Mma Ramala was too distraught to speak to this reporter. She . . .

There was more stuff about Ramala's background and reputation. Festus read the article a second time, thinking about Ramala's abduction. His mind returned to the conversation with Legotlo. *I've heard nothing about a snatch. Not of a white guy.*

Of course, there was nothing to connect Ramala's abduction to Collins's disappearance, but Festus had a feeling that there just might be a link. Legotlo would be getting another call very soon.

CHAPTER 26

Kubu was frustrated by his lack of progress on the Collins case. His one lead was the mysterious Festus with his silver truck, but a search of the vehicle registry had turned up nothing. Perhaps Festus was a middle name or a nickname. Perhaps the vehicle was owned by someone else. It seemed to be a dead end.

Collins's 4x4 had been towed to Ghanzi, and forensics had been through it. There was no sign of blood or anything else that might point to a struggle in the vehicle. And although the vehicle was covered in fingerprints, Zanele was not optimistic. Apparently, cleaning between rentals didn't include polishing off fingerprints. She said there were at least half a dozen different people who had been in the vehicle at some point. And even Collins's prints couldn't be positively identified. Kubu had asked the police in Minneapolis for a copy of his prints, only to discover that they weren't on record.

He'd also asked Detective Sergeant Segodi to check the hotels in Ghanzi to see if Collins had stayed over in the area, but he doubted anything would turn up.

Kubu's gloomy mood was interrupted by his office telephone.

"Assistant Superintendent Bengu."

"Good afternoon, Assistant Superintendent. This is Professor Thabo. You spoke to me last week about Dr. Collins and the dead Bushman."

Kubu perked up. "Yes, Professor. I remember. Did you come up with some more information?"

"No, not really. But this morning two men came to see me, and it turned out they're also looking for Collins. I gave them your number and suggested that they contact you, but I thought I should let you know about it. It's probably nothing, but . . ."

"You did the right thing, Professor. Some people aren't keen on contacting the police. Who were they? Do you know what they were after?"

"One of them is an American called Ross, who's just come out from the States. He's the head of a pharmaceutical company there. He asked about Collins, as you did, but he was also interested in knowing about plants that the Bushmen might use for medicinal purposes. I warned him to be careful not to fall foul of biopiracy laws."

Kubu was more interested in how Ross linked with Collins. "So what was Ross's connection with Collins?"

"Apparently they are old friends. But there's more to it than that. Collins had come up with something potentially valuable, and I think Ross was worried about missing out on that."

"I thought Collins was an anthropologist?"

"He is, but apparently he has some sort of deal with Ross to look out for plants that could be useful to the pharmaceuticals industry."

"What sort of plants? How would he know about them?"

"He'd be asking his Bushman contacts which ones they used for their traditional remedies."

"Something that might extend life?"

"Very unlikely! More something like *hoodia,* which the Bushmen use as an appetite suppressant."

"Speaking of herbal remedies, did Collins ever mention a *Kgosi* Ramala to you?"

"Ramala? The witch doctor? No, why would he?"

"Because it seems he had a meeting with Ramala. I wonder if that was connected to these plants he was looking for."

"Well, he said nothing to me about it. I doubt a Western scientist would take someone like Ramala seriously, but I really can't help you with that."

Kubu decided he would get better information on what Collins had been up to directly from Ross. "Did Ross say where he was staying?"

"Yes, at The Grand Palm. He asked me to contact him there if I had any suggestions about medicinal plants."

"And the other man?"

"I think he was hired to drive Ross around and so on. Rather a rude man. His name was Moeng. Festus Moeng."

Suddenly, Kubu's mood greatly improved. He was sure that Festus was doing more for Ross than driving him around, and he wanted to know what he *was* doing, and why.

"Professor, this has been very useful. Thank you very much for taking the time to contact me."

"I would've spoken to you earlier, but I've been busy all day."

"No problem. Thanks again, and have a good evening."

Kubu hung up, wondering why the professor was suddenly going out of his way to help. He hadn't seemed particularly cooperative before. Nevertheless, he was grateful for that change of heart, whatever had caused it.

He pulled out a telephone directory and looked up the name Moeng. There were many, but he skimmed through them quickly. And there it was. Festus Moeng—Private Investigator. So that's what brings Festus to this party, he thought. He's been hired by Ross.

Kubu picked up the phone again and called Zanele.

"Hello, Zanele. I think I may have something for you on the

fingerprints in that vehicle. Would you check the prints they sent you from Ghanzi against those of a Festus Moeng? He's a PI, so they'll be on record. I think he's the one who was looking for Collins before me, and I'm looking forward to asking him why."

FESTUS CALLED LEGOTLO and told him there'd been further developments and that they needed to talk face-to-face. Legotlo was reluctant, but agreed when Festus promised him a beer. He nominated a bar at the Africa Mall.

After taking a first gulp of the beer and wiping the froth off his lip with the back of his hand, Legotlo asked, "What's so urgent?"

Festus took his time. "Nice place," he said, taking in the dilapidated, smoke-filled room.

"The drinks are cheap," Legotlo responded. "So what's up?"

Festus waited until Legotlo was taking another mouthful, then asked, "What do you know about the snatch of *Kgosi* Ramala?"

Legotlo finished the mouthful without reacting. "What makes you think I know anything about that?"

Festus sighed. "Look, Legotlo, let's not waste time. Why don't you just fill me in? I'm willing to add a few pula to the beers."

Legotlo hesitated. "This goes no further, understand? And, anyway, it didn't come from me. These are nasty people. I don't want to get involved. You know what I mean?"

Festus nodded.

"Five hundred pula."

Festus nearly choked on his beer. "Ridiculous! A hundred."

Legotlo drained his glass. "Two fifty. And I'll have a whiskey first."

Festus felt he was being cheated, but he called the waitress over and ordered the whiskey. "So what have you got?"

"What I've got," said Legotlo thoughtfully, "is a friend who hangs around Riverwalk Mall. He makes a few *thebe,* you know, from the tourists. Sells stuff." He shrugged.

"Go on."

"He keeps his eyes open for customers and for cops and security. He's not always welcome there, you know?"

"This friend have a name?"

Legotlo shook his head.

Festus frowned, realizing he wasn't even going to get a name for his two hundred and fifty pula.

"Anyway," Legotlo continued, "he knows Ramala."

"Ramala's expensive, I hear."

Legotlo nodded. "That's only after he came up with his eternal-life scam. He used to sell potions for luck and sex, like the other *muti* pushers."

"Okay, so what did this friend see?"

"Well, he sees Ramala walking round the front of the mall towards the Mugg and Bean, so he goes over to see if he can interest him in a little *dagga* or something. But then he sees where Ramala's heading—towards this group of tough-looking guys sitting at a table at the back. One of them gets up to greet Ramala. My friend gets lost fast, but keeps an eye on what's happening because he's the curious type, you know? They start talking to Ramala. At first, it's all very friendly, but then there seems to be an argument. One of the men gets really close to Ramala, and a few moments later Ramala goes off with them, no more argument. My friend sees them get into a car together. Except one of the men is left behind, so I guess he goes and drives Ramala's car off."

"You think the man pulled a gun or a knife or something?"

Legotlo nodded.

"What did these guys look like?"

"That's the interesting part. They were Chinese." Legotlo nodded again, as if that explained everything.

"Chinese?"

"Don't you get it? It's the Chinese mafia! They've got their paws in the casinos, whatever. I bet Ramala owes them big bucks. He's in trouble." Legotlo finished his whiskey.

"Ramala gambled?"

"Sure he did. He owed them money. Why else would they be after him?"

"Your friend should tell his story to the police."

"You crazy? These are not nice people. If he does that, he'll be joining Ramala in some hole in the ground somewhere. Or maybe thrown out for the hyenas."

"So how come he told you?"

Legotlo shrugged. "People tell me things. I'm a good listener. And like you said, discreet."

Festus summed it up in his head. Ramala meets these Chinese people at Riverwalk. They talk, argue, maybe one pulls a weapon and hustles him into their car while the other drives his car. That's what I've got for two hundred and fifty pula of my client's money. All the rest is just Legotlo's speculation.

"But what's this got to do with Collins?" he wondered aloud.

Legotlo gave him a quizzical look. "Who said it had anything to do with Collins?"

He's got me there, Festus thought, as he forked out the money.

WHEN FESTUS DROVE up to his house, he noticed a car parked in front. He pulled up at his gate and, as he climbed out to open it, a man he didn't recognize approached him.

"Festus Moeng?"

"Yes, that's right. Who are you?"

"I'm Detective Sergeant Banda of the CID. Is that your twin cab?"

Festus nodded. "What's this about?"

"We need to ask you a few questions."

"Okay. I'll park and we can go inside."

"At our offices, rra."

"Now?"

"Yes. It's quite urgent. I'll drive you there."

Festus was irritated, but there seemed to be no point in making a fuss.

"Okay, I'll be out in a minute."

"No, just park and come with me."

Reluctantly, Festus drove in, parked his car, and rejoined the detective. They drove in silence. Festus knew enough about police procedure to realize there was no point in asking what this was about again—he wouldn't be told. Then his cell phone rang, and he answered.

"Festus? This is Ross. I've been picked up by the police! I've no idea what it's about, but I'm at the Criminal Investigation Department. Get out here right now. Bring a lawyer."

"I'm on my way," Festus said wryly, and hung up.

CHAPTER 27

Kubu introduced himself to Brian Ross and sat down opposite him in the interview room. He noticed that the American looked upset, but at least he wasn't making a fuss.

"Thank you for coming in to answer our questions, Mr. Ross," Kubu said.

"I wasn't aware I had a choice," Ross replied.

Kubu chose to ignore that. "I understand you're a friend of Dr. Christopher Collins. Is that correct?"

"That's right. I'm an old friend of Chris and his wife. Understandably, she was very upset after the call from the police here, and I hadn't heard from Chris for a while either. So I felt I should come out and see for myself what's going on."

"Were you in contact with him before?"

"He'd call me from time to time on his satellite phone, but I hadn't heard from him for a week or so. I wasn't too concerned, because he was traveling around. But when Petra told me about your call to her, I got really worried."

"Were these calls about the work he was doing for you?"

"Yes, that's right."

"And just what was it that he was doing for you?"

"He'd been given some ointment by a Bushman friend that seemed to accelerate the healing of wounds. He was trying to find the source. Of course, we'd have followed all the proper channels if he *had* found it. My company follows strictly ethical procedures." He paused, but Kubu didn't comment. "He was also looking at other desert plants that might have useful properties."

"I see. Who was Collins's Bushman friend?"

Ross hesitated. "I don't know. He had his academic studies, and he interviewed many Bushmen about a variety of topics, I suppose."

"Did he mention a man called Heiseb?"

"He may have. I don't recall."

"And when was the last time you heard from Dr. Collins?"

Ross thought about it for a moment. "I think it was on October tenth."

Kubu made a note of that. The date correlated quite well with Heiseb's death.

He changed the subject. "What's your connection with Festus Moeng?"

Ross looked surprised. "I hired him to help me trace Chris."

"And when was that?"

Ross shifted in his seat. "It was a few days after the last call from Chris," he said at last.

"So before my phone call to Mrs. Collins?"

"Yes."

"But you said you weren't worried about Dr. Collins at that time?"

"Well, we'd lost contact. I just thought it would be good to have someone here . . ."

"Keep an eye on him?"

Ross nodded.

"You didn't trust him, did you? You thought he might've discovered something and was keeping it to himself."

"No, no. Nothing like that," Ross replied.

"Mr. Ross, as I told you before, I'm engaged in a murder investigation here. If you have any information, anything that might be relevant, that you're not telling me, the consequences for you will be very serious. Is that clear?"

Ross nodded.

"Do you have anything more to tell me?"

Ross hesitated. "Apparently he sent a message to his wife saying he was going to Namibia. He hadn't told me he was going there, so I—"

"Namibia? When did he send this message?"

"I think it was a day or so before you called Petra."

Kubu digested that. "So when I asked Mrs. Collins if she'd heard from her husband, she knew this and didn't tell me?"

"I don't know what she said, but her husband said not to tell anyone, so—"

"Why did she tell you, then?"

"I'm an old friend! Of course she trusts me. But she knows nothing about you."

Kubu decided he needed another talk with Mrs. Collins. Perhaps she would be honest this time. And perhaps she'd received more messages since Ross left the US.

"Do you have any idea why Collins might have gone to Namibia?"

Ross shook his head. "It makes no sense."

Kubu changed the subject. "Do you know anything about a man named Ramala? He was also interested in Bushman traditional remedies, I believe."

Ross looked puzzled and shook his head. "I've never heard the name, but I'd be interested to meet him."

Kubu shook his head. "That would be hard, Mr. Ross. He's dead."

Kubu noted Ross's expression and decided that the American was telling the truth.

At that point Edison came into the room and passed Kubu a note. He glanced at it and said to Ross, "I'll be back shortly. Please think about what I said." Then he headed for the door, with Edison following.

As HE WAS walking, his phone rang, and he saw it was Joy.

"Hello, my darling, how are things?" he asked.

"I've got good news, Kubu. I can fetch Nono from the hospital tomorrow morning and bring her home."

Kubu's face broke into a broad smile. "That's wonderful news!"

"Yes, isn't it?" Joy said, after a moment.

Kubu realized something was not right. "What's the matter, Joy?"

Again there was a pause. "Well, they say she's stabilized. That she's much better, but . . ."

"Darling, they can't cure HIV," Kubu said gently.

"The doctor said we'd have to watch her. See how she reacted to the new drug regimen. Kubu, I'm still worried."

"Darling, she's going to be fine. I'm sure of it. Listen, I'm in the middle of a case here, but I should be home in half an hour or so. Will you be all right?"

"Yes, of course. We'll talk later."

"Love to Tumi."

Kubu disconnected, but paused for a moment in the corridor. He knew Joy. If she was worried, the chances were that there was something to worry about.

Edison glanced at Kubu's face. "Is everything okay?"

Kubu frowned. "I hope so . . . Well, let's get to Festus. I'm looking forward to meeting him."

CHAPTER 28

Festus was waiting in another interview room. Kubu introduced himself and started straight into his questions.

"Rra Moeng, what is your connection with Dr. Christopher Collins?"

"I was hired by his boss in the US to find him. A Brian Ross. Is Mr. Ross here?"

"Why did he hire you?"

"Ross thought Collins might be lost in the Kalahari."

"I've been in that position, rra. You don't hire a private detective. You alert the police immediately."

Festus shrugged, but Kubu waited him out. At last Festus said, "I'm paid to investigate for people. As long as what they're doing isn't illegal, I don't ask their motives."

"So how did you go about trying to find Collins?"

"I persuaded the car rental agency to give me the coordinates of the four-by-four he'd rented, and then I went to look for it."

"And did you find it?"

"Eventually I did. Between Ghanzi and New Xade. But it was

abandoned, and I couldn't find any trace of Collins. So I reported to Mr. Ross, and he decided to come out here himself."

"And you spoke to people at New Xade."

Festus looked surprised. "Yes, I did. But no one there knew anything either."

"And it didn't occur to you to report any of this to the police?"

Festus shrugged. "I had no idea the police were interested, and I was waiting for Ross to decide what to do."

Kubu leaned back in his chair. "And what is your connection to *Kgosi* Ramala?"

Kubu noted the momentary surprise on Festus's face, and the hesitation. "Nothing. Why would I have a connection with a witch doctor?"

"Rra Moeng, you got an official of the rental car company to give you information that you had no right to obtain. Probably bribed him. Then you found Collins's vehicle and illegally searched it—"

"You've got it wrong, Assistant Superintendent. I was looking for a missing person. The vehicle wasn't locked, and I didn't take anything. I was just looking inside, in case—"

"There was evidence in there of where Collins had gone." Kubu leaned forward. "You contaminated what may well be a crime scene."

"I knew nothing about a crime! I was looking for someone in the desert."

"The vehicle had been abandoned for some time, hadn't it? Yet you didn't think it was worth reporting to the police."

"I was going to, but I needed to inform my client first."

"That's a good excuse. And then you roughed up an old man at New Xade, who reported it to the police there."

"I just grabbed his arm! Look, Assistant Superintendent, I was doing my job. I didn't know anything about an investigation. I suggested to Mr. Ross that I should talk to the police in Ghanzi, but he wanted to come out here himself first."

Kubu leaned forward and stared at him. "Rra Moeng, you're a

private investigator. That means you're licensed. If I don't think you're cooperating, I can make renewing your license very difficult."

"I've done nothing wrong," Festus said. "If I can be of help, I will."

"Let me ask one last time. What do you know about *Kgosi* Ramala?"

Festus shifted in his chair. "I don't *know* anything." He paused. "But I heard a rumor." He held up his hands. "Through the grapevine. I can't tell you who told me, and I can't vouch for it at all. It may all have been made up to get a few pula out of me."

Kubu leaned back and folded his arms. "Tell me the whole story. Then I'll decide what to do with you."

HALF AN HOUR later, Kubu led Festus into the interview room where Ross was scowling.

"About time," Ross exclaimed when he saw Festus.

"You're both free to go," Kubu said, "but I'll need to talk to you both again." He turned to Ross. "How long are you planning to stay in Botswana, Mr. Ross?"

"Perhaps another week."

"And what are you planning to do now?"

"I was considering going to New Xade and seeing what I could find out. About medicinal plants, of course."

"Indeed. Well, you're allowed to go anywhere you like in Botswana, but be warned: If you go to the Kalahari, base yourself in Ghanzi and get a proper guide and translator. And if you go to New Xade, check in with Constable Ixau there. I'll let him know, and he can help you."

And keep an eye on you, he added to himself.

"Also, please let me know if you're planning to leave the country."

Kubu turned his attention to Festus and glared at him. "And if you learn anything more about Collins or Ramala, you let me know. And leave the following up to us. That's our job. Remember, at least two people have been murdered already."

Festus looked as if he wanted to object, but in the end he said nothing.

"Is that absolutely clear?" Kubu waited until both Ross and Festus had acknowledged that it was. "Detective Banda will take you back now."

Kubu watched them leave with Edison.

I can't see Ross being behind a murder, he thought. But I'm sure he's hiding something. And as for Festus, although he's a thug, I doubt he's a murderer. Still, at least we have a possible lead on what happened to Ramala. Chinese mafia? Then there's the professor. Suddenly he's helpful, but he was pretty offhand the first time I interviewed him. Kubu shook his head. And we've no idea if Collins is really out of the country.

He wanted to sit down with Samantha and brainstorm the whole situation. He tried to phone her, but it was after six o'clock and she'd already left.

I'll talk to her first thing in the morning, he decided. Maybe we can come up with some new ideas.

He did a quick calculation: it wasn't even midday in Minneapolis. He could call Petra Collins.

He let Joy know that he was going to be late, then picked up the phone.

"HELLO, SUPERINTENDENT BENGU. Have you made contact with Chris?"

"No, Mrs. Collins, but it seems I was looking in the wrong place. You told me he was in Botswana, but you knew he was actually planning to go to Namibia."

There was a long silence. "Chris made it very clear that I was to tell no one about that," she replied at last.

"But you told Mr. Ross."

"Yes, he's an old friend, and I was worried because Chris had suddenly left Botswana and the police were looking for him."

"This is a murder investigation, Mrs. Collins. Withholding

information from the police here is as bad as doing so from your police in Minneapolis."

"I . . . I didn't know it was a murder investigation. You didn't tell me that."

"It makes no difference what sort of case it is. You've wasted our time and delayed our investigation."

There was no reply. Kubu breathed deeply a couple of times to calm down.

"Mrs. Collins, I want to explain to you what's been happening here. It will take a few minutes."

He told her about the two murders and how he believed they were somehow connected through Bushman herbal medicines. "You can see why I'm so eager to find your husband. Not only can he help us with what actually happened to the Bushman, but he could be in real danger himself. Whoever is behind this doesn't care what happens to anyone who gets in their way."

"But he's not even in Botswana!"

"We don't know that for sure. All we know is that you received an email saying so. We have no record that he left the country. Was there anything about the email that struck you as unusual? Something that your husband wouldn't normally say?"

She hesitated. "Just when he signed off . . . but I'm sure it's nothing."

"Would you read it to me, please?"

"Okay, wait a minute while I find it."

Kubu could hear menu tones as she worked on the phone. "Ah, here it is. He said, 'Hi darling, I'm going to Namibia and don't want anyone to know. Please don't tell ANYONE. I'll be out of touch for some time but don't worry. All's well. I love you, Chris.' It's just that he usually just says 'Love,' not 'I love you.'"

Kubu thought for a moment before he responded. He was sure Petra Collins had been shaken by the story he'd told her and that she was ready to cooperate.

"Mrs. Collins, this is what we're going to do. We can trace where the email message came from. Once we know that, we can at least look for your husband in the right place."

There was another long silence. At last she said, "All right. What must I do?"

"I'll speak to one of our IT people. Her name is Helenka Koslov. She'll know what to do. She may call you directly or she may call the Minneapolis police. Worst case is that they may need to take your computer for a few hours. It shouldn't take long."

"Oh, God, I hope he's all right. I had no idea . . . Please do what you can as quickly as possible."

"We're working on it. I'll phone you back as soon as I have any information."

After he hung up, Kubu scratched through his internal directory until he found Helenka's number. He'd worked with her before and liked the skill and enthusiasm of the young Russian IT whiz, who'd emigrated to Africa for its wildness and its warmth and had joined the Botswana police.

"No problem," she said, after he'd explained what he wanted. "Have answer tonight. Email in your Inbox in the morning."

As he hung up, he decided to call it a day. *I wonder what state my dinner will be in when I get home,* he thought. *Dried out in the oven or chilled in the fridge?*

CHAPTER 29

The next morning Kubu brought Samantha up to date on developments, finishing with the rumor about the abduction of Ramala.

"Please check Riverwalk Mall," Kubu suggested. "Maybe they have video cameras facing the parking lot. Security may still have the data."

"Can I send Edison? That Gampone guy is arriving this morning. How do you want me to handle that?"

"You should meet him at the airport and bring him here," Kubu replied. "We can both talk to him."

"Do you think he's involved?"

"I doubt it, but let's assume he is. He'll be very tired, so it won't be too difficult to upset him. Maybe something will slip."

"What about his safe?"

Kubu thought a moment. "When we've finished here, go with him to his house and make sure you've got the search warrant with you. Let's see whether he shows you the safe."

"And if he doesn't?"

"Don't say anything until you're leaving. Then ask if he has a safe. If he says he does, take a look at it. If he says he doesn't, arrest him for obstructing an investigation and bring him in. Then I'll really look forward to talking to him."

While Samantha was making notes, Kubu checked his email.

"What is it?" Samantha asked, seeing the expression on his face.

"Helenka in IT says that the message Mrs. Collins received was sent from an IP address here in Gaborone. She's following that up."

"So Collins was here in Gaborone, not in the Kalahari!" As soon as she said it, Samantha shook her head. "No, we don't know that. Anyone who had his email details and his wife's address could have sent the message."

Kubu nodded. "My guess is that Collins is still in Botswana, and probably in Gaborone—or at least he was last week. When Helenka traces the IP address, that could be the breakthrough!"

JONAH GAMPONE WAS not pleased when Samantha met him at the airport and told him that he had to accompany her to CID headquarters.

"Goddammit," he spluttered. "I've been flying for sixteen hours. I'm tired. I'm jet-lagged. I want to go home, take a shower, then get some sleep. What's this all about?"

"Rra," Samantha replied, "there was a break-in at your house. We need some information from you."

"A break-in? When? What did they take?"

"We think it was this past weekend and, of course, we don't know what they took. That's why we need to speak to you."

Once they had retrieved Gampone's suitcase, they walked out to her car, conveniently parked in front of the terminal.

"What about my car? It's parked over there. How will I get it home?"

"If you give me your keys, my colleague will drive it to the CID."

Reluctantly, he handed her the keys.

"I apologize for the inconvenience, rra," Samantha said, as they reached her car. "But time is important in these cases. I'm sure you'll be home in an hour or two."

"Rra Gampone? I'm Assistant Superintendent Bengu. I'm sorry we have to meet in these circumstances, but we need information urgently with respect to the break-in at your home. Would you like some tea or coffee?"

"Coffee, please."

"Samantha?"

"Tea, please."

Kubu picked up the phone and asked the man at reception to bring two teas, a coffee, and a plate of cookies to the conference room.

"Now, rra," Kubu said, turning to Gampone, "while you were away, someone broke into your home . . ."

"I know. She told me," Gampone said, nodding at Samantha. "How can I help you if I'm sitting here? I need to go home and see what's been taken."

"I realize that," Kubu responded, "but we need some other information first. Please bear with us." He opened his notebook. "First, you've been overseas for two weeks. Please tell us where you've been and what you've been doing."

"What's that got to do with the break-in? You're wasting my time," Gampone snapped.

"Just answer our questions, please, rra. The sooner you do, the sooner you'll get home."

There was a knock on the door, and the receptionist came in with a tray.

"Thank you, Joshua. Just put it on the table."

Kubu handed Gampone a cup of coffee, then offered him milk and cookies. He gave Samantha her tea and slid the plate of cookies to her. Finally, he put three cookies on his own saucer and took a bite of a fourth.

"So, rra, please tell us about your trip."

For the next few minutes, Gampone told the two detectives where he'd been—Vietnam, Hong Kong, mainland China.

"What business are you in?" Kubu asked.

"I import different types of merchandise and materials from those countries, and I'm trying to establish an export business, too."

"What's in Botswana that you can export?" Samantha asked.

Gampone paused before he answered. "Cowhides, small soapstone sculptures from Zimbabwe, indigenous artifacts, and beadwork ornaments."

Samantha frowned. "What are indigenous artifacts?" she asked.

"Mainly replicas of old Bushman hunting kits. You know, bow and arrows, spears, containers for holding poison, and so on."

"Cowhides and ornaments? That's a strange combination."

"Not so strange if you know the Eastern markets," Gampone responded. "Distributors handle a wide array of products. I've found two who want that combination."

"Do you export any plants that are found in Botswana?"

Gampone jumped to his feet. "Something's going on that you're not telling me about! Why are you asking me about things that have nothing to do with the break-in?"

"Rra Gampone, please sit down. We'll tell you what's going on." Kubu pointed to the seat Gampone had left. "Please sit down."

Reluctantly, Gampone slumped back in his chair.

"Samantha, tell him."

FOR THE NEXT few minutes, Samantha related the story of Ramala's disappearance, the break-in at Gampone's garage, and the discovery of the shallow grave. She didn't include the fact that the grave was empty.

"Ramala?" exclaimed Gampone. "*Kgosi* Ramala, the witch doctor?"

Samantha nodded.

Gampone shook his head. "I know the man."

"We know that," Kubu said. "Your name was in his appointment book."

"You think I'm involved in his murder?" Gampone fumed. "That's why I'm here, isn't it? It's nothing to do with the break-in."

"We don't think you're involved," Kubu said. "All we're doing is trying to find out what happened at your home." He took a sip of his tea. "I'm curious," he continued. "What were you seeing Ramala about?"

"Every healthy man wants to live longer, Assistant Superintendent. The earth is such an interesting place; I'd like to live forever, if my body and brain held out. Wouldn't you?"

"Not really," Kubu replied. "But what makes you think that Ramala's *muti* works?"

"I've no idea whether it works, but as long as it doesn't kill me, why not try it? And if it does work . . ." His voice trailed off.

Kubu stared at Gampone for a few moments.

"We recently received some information," Kubu continued, "that leads us to believe that people outside the country are trying to get their hands on some plants . . ."

Gampone straightened up in his chair. "Some plants? What sort of plants?"

"As I'm sure you know, Botswana is home to many plants, such as *hoodia*, that have been used by Bushmen for hundreds of years for a variety of purposes."

"But the Bushmen get royalties when it's used overseas."

"True, but some people could make a lot of money using it illegally."

"Come on, Assistant Superintendent. It's not really that valuable. What other plants are you interested in?"

Kubu hesitated, then changed tack. "Rra Gampone, please let us know if anything is missing from your home." He handed over his card. "Also, if anything else occurs to you, please let us know."

He stood up. "Thank you for coming in. Detective Khama will accompany you home."

"I'm quite capable of finding my own way home. Thank you."

"I'm sure that's true, but I'd like Detective Khama to be with you when you check whether anything is missing."

Gampone didn't look pleased. "I suppose I have no option, then." He turned to Samantha. "Let's go. The sooner this is over with, the better."

CHAPTER 30

Samantha drove Gampone home, with the constable following in Gampone's car. When they reached his house, Samantha first took him to the garage.

"It looks as though someone broke in here," she said. "One of the back windows is broken. Please take a look and see if anything is missing."

Gampone took a few minutes looking around, then turned to Samantha. "As far as I can remember, everything is here."

"Why would anyone break in and not take anything?" she asked.

He shrugged. "Maybe kids being kids. How did you know something had happened?"

Samantha responded without hesitation. "We received an anonymous tip-off."

"What did they say?"

"I don't know the exact words because it went through to reception. We sent a car out right away, and they found this. If you're sure nothing's missing, let's go inside the house."

. . .

FOR THE NEXT half hour or so, Gampone walked through each room in the house, carefully checking whether anything was missing. Eventually, he stopped. "That's it," he said. "I don't think anything is missing. How did they get in?"

"We don't know they did get in, but we have to assume they did."

"You mean we've been wasting our time?"

"No. Knowing that nothing is missing is important. You're sure now?"

He nodded.

They walked to the front door and shook hands.

"Thank you for your time, Rra Gampone. I'm sure you're ready for a shower and a long sleep."

"I can't wait."

She turned to leave, then turned back.

"Do you have a safe?"

He stared at her without saying anything.

"Rra Gampone, I asked if you have a safe."

"Um, yes. It's in my bedroom upstairs. I checked it when I looked through the cupboard. It was locked. They couldn't have found it. And even if they did, they couldn't open it. It's a very good one."

"Let's go and check, just in case." She walked back into the house.

"It's a waste of time, Detective. They couldn't have opened it."

"There are some very sophisticated thieves these days, rra, with electronic apparatus to help them break into safes. It'll only take a minute."

"Detective, believe me. There's nothing missing."

"Rra, we have to check. This is my job."

"No, Detective. It is a private safe. I know nothing is missing, so there's no need to open it. Thank you and good-bye." He walked outside.

Samantha followed him, pulling the search warrant from her pocket. She handed it to him.

"Rra, this is a valid search warrant. You are required to open the safe for me."

She turned to the constable, who was waiting patiently outside. "Constable, please come here. I want you to be with me when the rra opens his safe." The constable walked inside.

"Detective Khama," Gampone said, "I want to talk to my attorney before I open the safe."

Samantha wasn't sure what to do, so she told Gampone to stay where he was while she moved away to phone Kubu.

Kubu listened carefully, then said, "Arrest Gampone for obstructing the search warrant, and handcuff him. Then lock up the house and bring him back here. And bring the constable as well, just in case Gampone thinks of causing any trouble. I'll organize another constable to watch the house tonight." He paused. "I'm looking forward to another conversation with our Rra Gampone."

"WHY DO YOU want to look in my safe?" Gampone said as he walked into the interrogation room.

"For two reasons, Rra Gampone," Kubu replied. "First, to make sure nothing was taken when your home was broken into. And second, we're investigating the possible homicide of *Kgosi* Ramala on your property. We have to check everything. I believe you want to talk to your attorney?"

Gampone nodded. "I'd like to call him. If he's free, he can come here."

Kubu thought for a moment. "Okay," he said. "Samantha, please get Rra Gampone an outside line. Then tell reception to expect a visitor."

He turned to Gampone. "Who's your lawyer?"

"Jeffrey Davidson."

"Jeffrey Davidson?" Kubu repeated in surprise. "Nothing but the best for you, I see. Samantha, tell reception that a Jeffrey Davidson will be coming to see Rra Gampone. No one else is to see him without my permission."

Samantha nodded as Kubu left. Then she picked up the handset, put in her code for an outside line, and walked out.

ABOUT AN HOUR and a half later, Kubu's phone rang. It was reception.

"Assistant Superintendent, Mr. Davidson and the other man want to speak to you and Director Mabaku. They say it's very important."

Kubu frowned. He had no idea what was going on.

"I'll see if the director is available," he said. "I'll let them know myself."

He hung up, then dialed the director's assistant. "Miriam, is the director free?"

"Do you want to see him or talk to him on the phone?" she asked.

"The phone is fine."

She told him to hold on while she checked. Half a minute later Mabaku came on the line.

"Yes?" he asked.

"I hate to interrupt your afternoon, Director, but something most unusual has come up. Is there any chance you could come to the conference room?"

"Now?"

"Yes, Director. If possible."

"What's it about?"

"That's it, Director. I'm not sure. We brought in that Rra Gampone for questioning when he arrived from overseas this morning—he owns the house where we think *Kgosi* Ramala was murdered. Samantha took him back to his home, but he refused to open his safe for her, even though we have a search warrant. He said he wanted to see his lawyer. Here, at CID headquarters. Now he wants to see you and me."

There was a silence. Then Mabaku spoke. "What do you think?"

"I think so, Director. You can always leave if it's a waste of time. But I doubt it is."

"Why do you say that?"

"You know Jeffrey Davidson, the defense attorney, don't you? Well, he's the one with Gampone."

"GOOD AFTERNOON, DAVIDSON," Mabaku growled as he walked into the conference room with Kubu and Samantha. "Good afternoon." He nodded at Gampone. "This had better be good. I'm a busy man."

"Good afternoon, Director," Davidson responded. "Thank you for coming. I know it's on short notice. We ask that you treat what you hear now with the greatest circumspection. Of course, we understand your responsibilities and chain of command, but I think you'll find what Jonah has to say quite intriguing." He nodded at Gampone, who cleared his throat, then spoke.

"First, I apologize for my behavior when you brought me here this morning and for what happened at my home. I was trying to prevent myself being in the situation I now find myself in. To put it bluntly, my import/export business is a cover for my real job, which is working for CITES, in Geneva. CITES stands for the Convention on International Trade in Endangered Species of Wild Fauna and Flora. It's the international oversight agency for endangered species."

"So, what you're really doing here in Botswana is tracking the movement of illegal substances, such as elephant tusk? And you haven't alerted the proper Botswana authorities what you're up to?" Kubu could see Mabaku's temper rising. Of all the people he knew, Mabaku was the greatest stickler for protocol.

Gampone nodded. "We—my colleagues and I—felt that it was a risk to do so, because we believe that some of your high-up officials—politicians of the highest rank—may be involved. And maybe even some of your superiors in the police." He paused. "If they got wind of what we were doing, they'd close down all their operations here in Gaborone and move them elsewhere. And we'd have nothing."

Kubu glanced at Mabaku, whose fists were clenched. Kubu wondered how he was going to react.

After what seemed a very long silence, Mabaku stood up and walked to the window and gazed out on Kgale Hill. Eventually he took a deep breath and returned to his seat.

"I take it you have illegal substances in your safe and want to preempt being arrested?"

Gampone nodded. "I have five hundred grams of powdered rhino horn."

Nobody said a word.

After a moment, Gampone continued. "My trip to the Far East was to find buyers for it, and elephant ivory. I was hoping to find out who in Botswana was currently doing the supplying. We know it's happening, but we don't know who it is."

"Rra Gampone." Kubu injected himself into the conversation. "There are two separate issues here. You say you're working for an international agency trying to stop illegal trafficking. *We* are investigating two murders and a possible third. There is a good chance that our three cases are linked through plants that supposedly extend life or cause the human body to heal perfectly. Is it possible that the people you're trying to find would be interested in plants, too?"

"Yes, it's possible. Biopiracy is a relatively new activity, but the potential profits are enormous."

"Do you know anything about two Americans, Brian Ross and Christopher Collins? We think they may also be mixed up in this."

Gampone shook his head. "Never heard of them."

"And what about a Bushman who lived in the New Xade area, called Heiseb?"

Gampone shook his head again.

Another silence fell over the room. Eventually Samantha spoke.

"Rra Gampone, I'm investigating the murder of *Kgosi* Ramala, who we believe was murdered on your property. What do you know about that?"

"All I know is what you told me. I can only assume that they chose my house as a message to me of some sort. A threat. Telling me not to meddle."

"Are they—whoever *they* are—suspicious of you?"

"They're suspicious of everyone. The fact I've started an export business to the Far East would worry them—that I could be competition. They wouldn't like that one bit." He shrugged. "The trip I just made was the first time I've made contact with buyers in both Vietnam and China. They've probably already heard about it and are warning me to keep off their turf."

Again there was a silence. Eventually Mabaku stood up. "Rra Davidson, Rra Gampone, please wait here. You have posed a nasty dilemma. I need to check with CITES that you're for real, Rra Gampone. If you are, I'll confer with my colleagues to see if we can untangle the dilemma. If you're not . . ." He shook his head. "Samantha, please ask reception to bring some more tea or coffee." With that he turned and stalked out.

It was nearly an hour before Mabaku, Kubu, and Samantha returned to the conference room. After they'd settled down, Mabaku spoke.

"This is how we are going to proceed. First, you must give us the names of your contacts in Vietnam and China. Second—"

"But—" Gampone interrupted.

"No buts. Just listen. If you get killed, we want that information. Second, you will leave here with Detective Khama and open the safe for her. She will take any contents that she thinks pertain to our cases. Understand?"

There was no reaction from Gampone, but Kubu could see he was angry.

"Understand?" Mabaku snapped.

Gampone nodded.

"Third, if there is rhino horn in the safe, she will confiscate it and make you sign a statement that you were in possession of it."

"Director Mabaku—" Davidson started to say.

"I've not finished." Mabaku's tone left no room for negotiation. "This is the only way we can both have a chance of accomplishing what we want." He turned to Gampone. "If the people you want to find have the sort of connections you suspect, they almost certainly know that you've been brought in here. They also know that Davidson arrived not long after. If they think we're collaborating, they're going to disappear. I want them to see you go back to your home with Detective Khama and see her leave. Hopefully, that will allay any suspicions that you're involved with us. I'll also release a press statement about our concerns that your garage was used in Ramala's abduction and that you're not a person under suspicion. That should leave you free to continue your work." He paused. "But there's a condition."

"Which is?" Davidson asked.

"Gampone will share with me any evidence of wrongdoing by any of our government officials. You can trust me to be discreet. I won't leave you for the hyenas. But you must understand that the very fabric of the success that is Botswana is threatened by corruption. I won't let that happen."

No one said anything for a few moments. Then Mabaku continued. "I also make this promise, Rra Gampone. If I find you withholding any useful information from me, I'll treat you like one of them and do all I can to have you rot in prison."

CHAPTER 31

When Kubu returned to his office after the meeting, he digested what he'd learned over the last couple of days. He was still suspicious of Gampone: Even if he was working for CITES, there was nothing to stop him doing some smuggling on the side. If he was caught, he could always say he was laying a trap, which is exactly what he *had* said. Still, for the moment Kubu was willing to take him at face value, and that meant he might have people from the Far East to worry about. And although there still seemed to be no connection between the Heiseb and Ramala cases, it was too much of a coincidence that both were apparently connected to longevity. So there could be an Asian link there, too.

He settled himself at his desk and scrounged in the drawer for a snack. He was delighted to discover a health bar.

He munched slowly, savoring the honey and nuts, thinking that a cup of tea afterward would be good to take the sweetness away. Perhaps it was the energy reaching his brain, or perhaps he'd given his subconscious the chance it needed, but suddenly he had a thought: *the Chinese body*. He stopped midchew.

He dug out his notes and checked the name and number of the person he'd spoken to at customs. He grabbed the phone and dialed the number.

"Rra Tole? This is Assistant Superintendent Bengu. We spoke on the phone last week about a body being transported out of Botswana."

"Yes, *dumela*, Assistant Superintendent. I do remember. I promised to phone you back if there was another request to transport a body. Is that why you're calling? There haven't been any other requests."

"No, actually I wanted some further information about the Chinese girl."

There was a pause before Tole replied. "I think I told you everything I know."

"Would you look up the records? I have a few more questions."

"Of course. Please hold on; I'll need to fetch the file." There was the sound of the receiver being dropped on the desk. After almost five minutes, the man returned.

"Assistant Superintendent? Sorry to keep you waiting. I have the file here, but there's not much in it."

"What've you got?"

"Mmm . . . Here's the original request for Ho Lan's body to leave the country by air. Minor, aged thirteen, from the People's Republic of China. Died of cerebral malaria at Kasane, where she was visiting relatives. It's signed by Ho Fang, father. That's funny—the name's the wrong way around."

"They do that in China. Go on."

"Here's the airline manifest. Gaborone to Johannesburg, change to Air China to PEK—that's Beijing—and then TAO. Hang on, I need to look that up." There was a moment's pause. "It's Qingdao. That's another city in China."

"Anything else?" Kubu asked.

"I also have a copy of the death certificate." He paused again. "Yes, it confirms cerebral malaria. Date of death, October nineteenth.

There's a separate note from the doctor. Apparently she hadn't taken the pills to prevent malaria and came down with a fever. It progressed very quickly, and by the time they got her to hospital in Kasane, it was too late. Tragic."

"You said you saw the father?"

"Just briefly. I was signing off the documents at the plane, and he was boarding. I didn't speak to him."

"Can you describe him?"

Tole hesitated. "Well, he was Chinese, of course. He looked about forty, I think. But I don't really know Chinese people."

Kubu thought for a moment. "Who was the doctor? Is there a report from the hospital?"

"It's a Dr. Wang. No, there's no report from the hospital. That's not required if we have the death certificate."

"How did the body reach you? Was it flown down from Kasane?"

Tole thought about it. "I suppose it must've been, but a man from the Chinese embassy brought it in a hearse. Probably they needed to keep it cool while they did the documentation and so on."

"Would there be a record of the transport from Kasane?"

"There should be." Tole sounded doubtful. "But look, Assistant Superintendent, the embassy authorized the paperwork, so it's all aboveboard."

Perhaps, Kubu thought.

He thanked the man for his help and asked him to fax copies of the manifest and other documents to the CID right away. Then he hung up and sat thinking about the conversation. He looked in the drawer for another health bar, but he was out of luck. He needed to buy some more.

It took some time to find someone at the hospital in Kasane who was able to help him, but eventually he reached a harried administrator.

"Mma, I'm investigating a murder. I'm sorry to bother you, but I need your help."

"Yes, rra, I understand. What do you want?"

"I need the records of a Chinese girl, Ho Lan, who was admitted with malaria. She died on Monday, October nineteenth."

"Wait, please." There was the sound of typing on a computer keyboard. "Would you spell the name?"

Kubu did so—hoping he had it right—and reminded her that the names might be in the reverse order. There was more typing, spaced by short pauses.

"No," the woman said at last.

"What do you mean?"

"There's no such record. No patient was admitted with that name."

"But . . ." Kubu hesitated. "Perhaps the name is wrong. Is it possible—"

"Detective, I checked the name and some different spellings. No such person. I checked deaths also. No one's died of malaria here this month. It's not such a common occurrence, you know, and we haven't had much rain up here yet this year."

"Is there another hospital in Kasane where she might have been taken?"

"No. Kasane isn't a big place. Now, is there anything else?"

Kubu admitted that there wasn't. The woman said good-bye, and the line went dead.

Perhaps what the doctor wrote was that it was too late to take her to the hospital, he thought.

He realized he'd have to wait until he received copies of the documents from customs to be sure. Meanwhile he'd try to locate Dr. Wang. The medical council would have a list of all practicing doctors, and immigration would be able to give him the details about the Ho visitors, and possibly about Wang also. He would check it all, but he was already sure what he'd find. He no longer believed that Ho Lan had died of malaria. In fact, he no longer believed that she'd ever existed.

CHAPTER 32

The next morning Kubu started to follow up on the journey of the coffin. He started with the fax from Tole at customs. The sender was listed as Ho Fang, as Tole had said, and the coffin was to be picked up in Qingdao by Wei Cheng Funeral Service, presumably an undertaker. There was an address and phone number on the manifest, which had been prepared by Botswana Logistics in the industrial area of Gaborone. Kubu picked up the phone and dialed the number on the letterhead.

When it was answered, he introduced himself and explained that he needed information about a shipment they'd been responsible for.

"What is the manifest number, Assistant Superintendent?" the man asked.

Kubu read off the number.

"Hold on."

A few minutes later, the man returned. "Please repeat the number."

Kubu did so.

"I'm afraid we don't have any manifest with that number. Are you sure it's a Botswana Logistics manifest?"

"Yes," Kubu replied. "The manifest is for a coffin containing the body of a girl, a Ho Lan, to be sent to Qingdao via Beijing. Please check if you can find any record of that and call me back."

Next he tried immigration and the medical council, but had no more luck than he'd had with Botswana Logistics.

It's not only Ho Lan who doesn't exist, Kubu thought. It seems everyone involved is also fictitious!

Kubu spent several minutes assessing his options. He decided that he'd ask Interpol's assistance in tracking down the Chinese undertaker—if it existed—and he made an appointment to speak to someone at the Chinese embassy to find out who'd authorized repatriation of the body.

He thought about Ho Fang and what the customs officer Tole had seen when the coffin was delivered to the airport. A Chinese man had been with the coffin, and Tole thought he'd traveled with it. Assuming that, the man would have been compelled to show the immigration officer his passport and fill in the departure form with his real name. There couldn't have been that many Chinese people on the flight to Johannesburg. He called Edison and explained what he wanted.

Next he checked with Orange to see if they'd traced the cell phone that had been used to send the message to Petra Collins.

"Yes, Assistant Superintendent, I was going to call you. We have identified the handset that was used to send that message. It's the same one you asked us about before."

"Which one was that?"

"The one that was found at the Game City Mall. We weren't able to trace the owner of that phone, but it's definitely the same phone that was used to send the email message. That's all I can tell you, I'm afraid."

Kubu thanked the man, and then digested the implications. It was too much to hope that the phone would conveniently point to a culprit. So this seems to be another dead end as far as finding Collins is concerned. But we were right all along. Now we know that there is a link between Collins and Ramala.

Then he checked to see if there had been any follow-up from Ghanzi. Detective Sergeant Segodi was supposed to check if Collins had stayed at one of the hotels, but there was nothing from him. Kubu frowned. Obviously Segodi had no interest in the case.

He wondered if Constable Ixau could discover something more. He was obviously interested and had initiative. Kubu dug out Segodi's original report on his visit to the village, added a note asking Ixau to see if he could discover anything further, and faxed it off to him.

AFTER LUNCH, KUBU made his way to the Chinese embassy to keep an appointment with the most senior consular official he'd been able to reach. The embassy was off Independence Avenue, hidden from the road by thick trees. The security guard checked Kubu's identification before returning to the guardhouse to announce his arrival. Eventually he returned and waved Kubu through.

After waiting in the reception area for a short while, Kubu was met by a man who introduced himself as Chan, who checked his identification and then took him through to his office.

"Now, Assistant Superintendent, how can I help you?"

Kubu opened the file of papers he'd brought with him and gave the manifest to Chan. "I want to talk to the official who handled this paperwork."

Chan read the document carefully. "Yes, I helped with this," he said. His English was accented but easy to follow. "I got a call from the doctor—Dr. Wang—after the child died. He asked me to help Mr. Ho. Mr. Ho came to see me the next day."

Kubu pulled out the note attached to the death certificate. "Dr. Wang wrote that 'Lan developed a powerful fever very quickly and it was too late to save her when we got her to the hospital in Kasane.' The strange thing is that the hospital has no record of her."

Chan glanced down at his desk. "Assistant Superintendent, in Botswana sometimes things are not done properly. Perhaps this is an example of that."

Kubu bristled, but kept his temper. "Did you get identification from Mr. Ho?"

Chan looked surprised. "He showed identification at the gate. He had just lost a daughter and was very upset. I did not ask for identification."

Odd behavior for a consular official, Kubu thought. Perhaps it's not only in Botswana that things aren't done properly.

He tried a different approach.

"Did you accompany the body to the airport?"

Again Chan looked surprised. "No. Why should I do that? I helped with the documents Mr. Ho needed. That is all. Maybe an undertaker dealt with the body."

"The official at the airport said that the body arrived by hearse and was accompanied by someone from the embassy."

Chan shrugged. "He also made a mistake. Perhaps because a Chinese person was with the body. Maybe Mr. Ho himself."

Kubu let that go and thought for a few moments before he continued. "Mr. Chan, you will certainly know that Chinese citizens need visas to come to Botswana. I discovered this morning that we have no record of a Ho Fang or a Ho Lan ever applying for a visa."

"They were here illegally?"

"Maybe. Can you trace Mr. Ho? In China?"

"I don't have any information about him, but there are contact details on the manifest for the undertaker who would have picked the body up. Assistant Superintendent, what is this about? Do you believe that Ho Lan was murdered?"

"I believe Ho Lan didn't exist. I believe someone else's body was flown out of Botswana."

Chan took a moment before replying. "Why? Why do that?"

"Do you know anything about this Dr. Wang?"

Chan shook his head. "He was in Kachikau when I spoke to him."

"How do you know the call was from Kachikau?"

"That is what he said."

"The Ministry of Health has no record of a Dr. Wang on its health professional registry, nor is there a record of a visa application from a Dr. Wang, either."

Chan shrugged. "I'm sure there is a simple explanation for all this, Assistant Superintendent. I'm afraid I cannot help you with these odd facts."

Clearly the interview was at an end as far as Chan was concerned, but Kubu wasn't satisfied. The man had been quite convincing, but Kubu had experienced embassy officials before and had discovered that they could be accomplished liars. Yet the only flaw in Chan's story was the matter of the identification.

Surely he should have checked Ho's bona fides, he thought. And how did Ho get into the embassy in the first place?

"Mr. Chan, I want you to know that these 'odd facts,' as you call them, are a very serious matter. Last week the body of a murdered man was stolen from the mortuary. We believe that may have been to hide the identity of the killer. In any case, the body vanished. Then, the next day, a coffin is flown out of the country, supposedly containing the body of Ho Lan, but there's no record that she ever existed. We now believe that coffin was used to smuggle the stolen body out of Botswana. You assisted with that, and by doing so you've become an accessory to a serious crime. I expect your full cooperation to understand these 'odd facts.' If I don't get it, the minister will be in touch with the ambassador."

Kubu wasn't at all sure he could make good on that threat, but it had the desired effect. Chan sat in silence for some time before he responded.

"Of course we will do whatever we can to help. Possibly an error of some sort was made. It will not be necessary to involve the ambassador."

"We'll see. Now, why didn't you ask for identification from Mr. Ho?"

"I have explained that. But it may have been a mistake. We will try to trace Mr. Ho. We will also interview the guard who let him through."

"Do you have security cameras?"

Chan frowned. "I don't think we would have the pictures from those."

Kubu smiled. "Mr. Chan, I'm sure the ambassador would have them."

Chan frowned again. "I will have to check if—"

"Please do so," said Kubu rising. "I want them this afternoon. We need to move quickly on this case."

"I will try," Chan said, as he took Kubu back to the reception area.

Kubu shook his hand. "I'll hear from you later on, then," he said.

As Kubu drove out of the embassy, he was feeling rather pleased with himself. By evening, he would have pictures of one of the men involved in the theft of Heiseb's body. Chan's mistake concerning the identification had bought his cooperation. Kubu's smile faded. That was, if indeed it had been a mistake, and if indeed he was now cooperating. If not, Kubu was going to receive pictures that had no relation to Ho whatsoever.

CHAPTER 33

For the third time, Constable Ixau read the faxed report on the Heiseb case that the assistant superintendent in Gaborone had sent to him. He was puzzled. It said that a young man had spoken to Detective Sergeant Segodi when he'd been in New Xade, and had suggested animosity between some New Xade men and Heiseb. Yet Ixau had been with the sergeant when he'd interviewed the men—and afterward—and no one had suggested such a thing. His mind went back over the meeting, and he recalled who'd been present. As usual, the one who'd done most of the talking was N'kaka, he thought. But he's certainly not a young man; he's one of the oldest men in the village. The youngest person there was Daniel. I remember how he grabbed for a cigarette, but he didn't say anything.

Ixau decided he'd have a chat with the boy. After all, he wasn't busy. He was hardly ever busy. There were some quarrels, some fights—usually with alcohol involved—and some petty theft. But really, very little happened in New Xade.

He stood up and went in search of Daniel.

He found the boy with a small herd of goats at the watering

point behind the school. The animals milled around and drank, and then headed back toward the bush. The area inside the village was barren—every blade of grass and green shoot had been eaten—but a little way outside the village, the goats would find plenty. This year, the gods had been generous with rain.

"Must you stay with the goats?" he asked Daniel.

The boy shook his head. "It doesn't matter. There's nowhere for them to go."

"Mma Doha said one of hers was stolen."

Daniel snorted. "Her? She knows nothing. Probably it became lost." He watched the goats making their way toward the outskirts of the village.

"Did you talk to the police detective from Ghanzi when he was here?" he asked.

Daniel swung round to face him. "Yes. I was with the others when he brought us cigarettes and asked about Heiseb."

"But you also spoke to him alone." Ixau deliberately made it a statement, not a question. Daniel's reaction had already answered the question.

"No, I—"

"You didn't do anything wrong. You were trying to help."

Daniel hesitated. "You won't tell the others?"

Ixau shook his head. "I'd just like to hear what you know. I'd also like to help."

Daniel started to follow the goats, and Ixau walked with him.

"What did you see?"

At first Daniel didn't reply, but after a moment he said, "Sometimes Heiseb was followed. To see what he was doing in the desert. He had powerful magic. Everyone knows that!"

"I have also heard so."

Daniel nodded. "So he was followed. Without him knowing. Until he was far from here, and they had to give up and come back."

"Did you follow him?"

"Never."

"Who did follow him, then?"

Daniel glanced at him again and shrugged. "I don't know. You know who to ask. He sent them."

Ixau sighed. He didn't know, but he could guess. Somehow, if there was conflict in New Xade, one man was always involved, using the status of his age to persuade the others to do things that were better not done.

"N'kaka?"

The boy nodded. "But I said nothing to you," he reminded Ixau. They'd reached the last road bordering the village, and the goats had spread out in the bush to forage. Daniel stopped and squatted at the side of the road. "I don't know anything else." He turned his back on Ixau and watched the goats.

IXAU FOUND N'KAKA outside his house, under his usual tree, with a scattering of St. Louis beer bottles around him. It was late afternoon, and the old man had already emptied several. Ixau greeted the old man respectfully.

"What do you want?" N'kaka responded.

"Just to talk to you for a few minutes."

N'kaka didn't reply.

"May I sit down?"

N'kaka shrugged, and Ixau took that as permission. He made himself comfortable in the sand and asked about N'kaka's family. The man spoke for a while, having nothing good to say about any of them, but at least he seemed less unfriendly after that.

"Do you have a cigarette?" he asked.

Ixau shook his head and apologized for not smoking. N'kaka grunted.

"Heiseb's body has disappeared," Ixau told him. "So there can be no proper funeral. It's very sad."

Still N'kaka said nothing, but it was hard for him to hide his interest in this news.

"You knew Heiseb well," Ixau continued. "What do you think happened to him?"

N'kaka sat for a few moments without answering. He took a swig of St. Louis. "Someone killed him," he said at last.

Ixau nodded. "Who would want to do that?"

"Who? People who wanted what he had."

"And what was that?"

"He had a secret. The way to long life."

"He was very old, but—"

N'kaka interrupted. "You know nothing. I am an old man now, but my mother knew him. Not as a boy but as a man." He took another swig.

Ixau digested that. Heiseb must have been well over a hundred if what N'kaka said was true, but he didn't pursue it. Instead he asked, "Who were these people? People from here?"

N'kaka shook his head. "Once or twice someone from here would follow him to see where he went and what he did. But he always gave them the slip. Once, when I was a boy, I went with him. He taught me things, but he never shared his secret. Not with me." He shook his head. "No, it was the others who killed him. The people out there." He waved his arm to encompass the world beyond New Xade.

Ixau's heart sank. N'kaka knew nothing. It was all speculation. But the old man hadn't finished.

"That white man who said he was studying our traditions. He used to talk to me, maybe bring me cigarettes. He said he wanted to know how we remembered our past, how we told stories of it." He shook his head. "That wasn't what he was interested in. He wanted to find someone *old*. Not to hear his stories but to find out the secret of long life. That was what he wanted. When he met Heiseb, he wasn't interested in me anymore."

"Dr. Collins?"

N'kaka shrugged. "I don't remember his name. He was a greedy man. Greedy. Like the others."

"Others? There were more white men?"

N'kaka shook his head. "A black man. Mrs. Kang brought him to me. He was after the secret too. He hurt my arm." He held up his arm to show Ixau. "But I cursed him," he added with satisfaction. "A powerful curse. He will be sorry for his greed."

Ixau was silent. A powerful curse was a serious matter.

"And that other man who came here. They are all the same. Filled with greed."

"Another man?"

"Yes, before the white man came back."

"A black man?"

N'kaka nodded. "He had Twi with him. The man who works in Ghanzi for the blacks. As you do. He gets money to spy on us here."

"He's a translator. He doesn't spy."

N'kaka spat on the ground. "He does what he's told, for money. Like you."

Ixau ignored the insult. "Who was this man? What did he want?"

"I don't know who he was. But he was looking for Heiseb—he wanted the secret, like the rest of them."

"Did you tell him where Heiseb was?"

N'kaka looked at him as if he were an imbecile. "How would I know that? Heiseb was here, or he was not here. That time he was not here. I told the man Heiseb was in the desert. Twi suggested he could track him, but Twi couldn't track a herd of goats! And if Heiseb didn't want you to find him, you didn't find him." He said it with the conviction of personal experience.

Ixau asked him to describe the man, and N'kaka did so. He claimed the man was fat, but there was nothing else special he re-membered about the visitor. Plenty of Batswana men would fit his description. Ixau thanked the old man and left him to his beer.

As Ixau walked back to his office, he decided he had learned something. They already knew about Heiseb's meetings with Collins, and the time that Festus had come, following him. But who was the black man who had come seeking Heiseb *before* Collins's last visit? It seemed he'd left empty-handed, but perhaps he'd come back when Collins had returned. Ixau walked more quickly. The assistant superintendent in Gaborone would be interested.

IT WAS QUITE late in the afternoon when Kubu received a package from the Chinese embassy, containing a memory stick. He went over to see Zanele and asked her what she could make of it.

It contained a video of what appeared to be a Chinese man arguing with the gate guard, but there was no sound. He was showing the guard a document and pointing at his watch. At several points, there were good images of his face. Zanele froze the picture at one of those.

"I think we'll get some good shots of him from this."

Kubu thanked her, asked her to send copies to him and to Edison, and headed back to his office. Perhaps the Chinese official had been true to his word.

He was just about to pack it in for the day and head home when his phone rang. It was Constable Ixau.

"Good afternoon, Assistant Superintendent. Are you busy, or can I talk to you?"

Kubu could hear Ixau's excitement. "Yes, of course. What've you found out?"

Over the next several minutes, Ixau explained that he'd identified the young man who'd spoken to Segodi, and that this had led him to N'kaka. "I suspect that he was having Heiseb followed, but I'm sure it was never successful. They say no one knows the desert like Heiseb did. But the interesting thing is that someone else was looking for Heiseb, *before* Collins came back the last time."

Kubu felt a hint of excitement. He's going to tell me it was a Chinese person, he thought, but he was wrong.

"It was a black man."

"Festus Moeng?"

"No. N'kaka knows him from their meeting last week."

"So any idea who it might have been?"

Ixau hesitated. "He gave me a description. It was a black man, and he said he was overweight. It could be almost anybody. He didn't notice anything special about the man."

Kubu thought about it. "This is very interesting news, Constable. Well done. What we'll do is this: Tomorrow morning I'll fax you some pictures of black men who might have some connection with this case. Ask N'kaka if he can pick out the man who visited him. Maybe we'll strike gold."

Ixau thought this an excellent idea and promised to find N'kaka as soon as he received the pictures.

After he'd disconnected, Kubu sat for a few minutes.

There aren't any obvious black male candidates for the photo lineup other than Festus, he thought, and he's been excluded. Well, I may as well try some long shots. Ramala, for one—after all, he was also interested in the long-life story, and his father was supposed to have some connection with the Bushmen. And Professor Thabo. He knows more than he's letting on. And I may as well put Gampone in as well. Why not? We don't know what he's really up to. And then another face or two.

He looked at his watch and realized that it was time to head home for dinner. He'd promised not to be late again, so that he could spend time with the girls. It was wonderful that Nono was home again.

CHAPTER 34

When he got to the CID on Friday morning, Kubu phoned Samantha to come to his office.

"Sit down," Kubu said when she walked in. "What's been happening with Gampone?"

"Well, the powdered material he gave me from the safe was rhino horn all right. We've had it analyzed. There was nothing else of interest in the safe. There was a lot of foreign cash—US dollars—but I suppose that makes sense with his business, and there's nothing illegal about that anyway."

Kubu nodded. "We'll need to keep him under surveillance. I'm not sure I trust him. But if he is on the level, and if he's right about the Ramala killing on his property being a warning, then he may need our help very quickly."

"I arranged that before I went out to his place." Samantha said.

"Excellent. Good thinking. Now, I've a lot to tell you, too." Kubu then related his conversations with the man at customs and with Chan at the Chinese embassy.

"You mean someone used the Chinese embassy as a front to ship Heiseb's body out of the country?"

"If it was his body. It certainly seems that it wasn't a young Chinese girl's, though. I got the CCTV tapes of the person who brought the paperwork to the embassy. The images are pretty good, and I think the tapes are genuine." He paused. "My gut feeling is that the Chinese official isn't involved but just on the take. Probably willing to help anybody for a fee."

"And the name of the person who sent the body was fictitious?"

"Yes. Same last name as the nonexistent girl. Name of Ho. There's no record of such a person at immigration."

Both sat quietly for a few moments.

"I've an idea," Samantha said. "Obviously, someone had to pick up the body at the airport in Qingdao, probably an undertaker of some sort. We should try to find out who that was. The information has to be on a manifest somewhere, most likely with whoever filled out the documentation here in Gabs."

"I thought of that, and called the shipping company listed on the manifest. They have no record of shipping a body or anything else on that day. Someone must have stolen a blank form and filled it out themselves. So I've asked Interpol to see if they can uncover any useful information. Chinese customs should have a record. There can't have been too many bodies arriving from Botswana on about the twenty-fourth of October."

"It could take a while before Interpol gets back to you."

Kubu nodded. "Yes, but you've given me an idea."

He opened his notebook, found the telephone number of his contact at customs, and dialed it.

"Rra Tole? This is Assistant Superintendent Bengu again. Sorry to keep worrying you. Do you happen to know which shipping agents are typically used for shipments to China, other than Botswana Logistics?"

He listened for a few moments.

"That's very helpful. Thank you."

He turned back to Samantha. "There are only three shipping agents who typically deal with China: Botswana Logistics—they're the outfit on the fake manifest—FedEx, and UPS. They're all in the industrial area. Go and ask them if they've ever sent packages to Qingdao. If they have, get the details of the sender and receiver. If we're lucky, they won't have used a fake name for routine shipments. If the companies don't want to give you the information, tell them you'll be back with a search warrant, and you'll take their computers away. That should persuade them."

He handed Samantha his notebook so she could copy the address to which the coffin was shipped. She wrote down the information, then stood up to go, when his phone rang.

"Wait, there's more," he said to her as he answered the phone. "It's Edison," he said. "I'll put him on speakerphone. This could be interesting." Samantha sat down again.

"Hello, Kubu." Edison's voice sounded tinny. "I checked the passenger list for the plane that was carrying the coffin. There were only two Chinese-sounding names, but I asked immigration to check the nationality of all the passengers. In fact, only those two came from China—one from the People's Republic and one from Taiwan. I've followed up on both of them. The Taiwanese was on an organized tour to the Okavango the whole time he was here. The other is working here on a project for a Chinese engineering company, and I got a picture of him from them. I'm not very good on Chinese faces, but he really doesn't look like the picture Zanele said you got from the Chinese embassy."

Kubu thanked him and hung up, disappointed. He then turned to the information from Ixau.

"I had a call from the constable in New Xade yesterday afternoon. I'd asked him to poke around to see if he could come up with anything else about Collins. It turns out that someone else was looking for the Bushman Heiseb, other than Collins and that Festus Moeng character. He asked one of the old men in the village if he knew where Heiseb was. So I faxed the constable some photos to see if the man could recognize the visitor. It's a long shot, but I sent him photos of Ramala, Gampone, Thabo—and Edison, as a ringer. It would certainly be interesting if Gampone had been there. That would change things."

"It would," Samantha said, "but it wouldn't help me on the Ramala case. I wonder what it would mean if it was *Ramala* who'd been there."

"Well, there's no point in speculating right now. I'll hear from the constable later this morning, I think, so let's meet again this afternoon."

Samantha stood up and left Kubu to his hated paperwork.

CHAPTER 35

Ixau carefully cut out the four pictures he'd received from Kubu. He didn't remove their names; he didn't want to get them confused, and N'kaka couldn't read anyway. He said their names aloud. "Professor Thabo." He was shocked. How could a professor be involved with a murder?

"Botlele Ramala." This was an older man whose face looked quite thin, but maybe N'kaka would think him fat. "Jonah Gampone." This man's face was round. Ixau thought he might be the man.

"Edison Banda." The man had a pleasant open face and was younger than the others. Ixau shook his head.

Taking the pictures, he went to N'kaka's house. There was no sign of the man, so he rapped on the door. After several repetitions, N'kaka appeared, looking half asleep and wearing only tattered shorts.

"Why do you bang on my door so early and wake me? Have you no respect?"

Ixau looked at his feet. "I'm very sorry to disturb you, but it's very urgent."

"So early?"

Ixau glanced at the sky. "The sun is high already."

N'kaka followed his gaze. "Well, what do you want?"

"I'd like you to look at some pictures and see if any of them came here looking for Heiseb."

"You wake me for that?" N'kaka shook his head. "Well, show me, then."

Ixau presented the pictures one by one, starting with Edison. N'kaka looked briefly at the images and made some unflattering comment about each man. When he'd looked at the first three, he said, "Show me that last one again."

Ixau handed it to him.

"It is that man," N'kaka said firmly. "He is fat. He is the man who came to see me. He is the man who wanted Heiseb." The photograph was of Professor Thabo.

"You haven't seen the last picture."

N'kaka shrugged. "It is that man."

Ixau took back the pictures. "Look once more," he said. This time he started with Ramala, followed by Gampone, and then Edison.

"I told you already," N'kaka said. "It is that one. There is no doubt." He pointed to the picture of Gampone.

Ixau held back his anger. Either the old man couldn't see or he wasn't trying. Although many black men did look similar, Gampone and the professor had quite different faces.

"Thank you. I'm sorry I disturbed you," he said stiffly, and turned to go.

"It is that man," N'kaka called after him. "I am quite sure."

DISAPPOINTED, IXAU WENT back to his office to phone the assistant superintendent. He'd hoped to identify the suspect and give the senior detective good news.

What would a real detective do next? he asked himself.

And as soon as he posed the question, he had the answer. He would find the guide, Twi.

He checked that his vehicle had enough fuel and loaded an empty drum to fill up at the police depot in Ghanzi. Then he headed off. An hour later, as he drove past the tourist ranches that surrounded the town, he started to worry about his plan.

What if I can't find Twi? he wondered. I don't know where he lives, and what if he's working and not in town?

He filled the drum and his truck with fuel and filled out the paperwork. He needed some provisions, also, but would wait to get those until he headed back. Fresh stuff might spoil in the heat if it took him a long time to find Twi.

He wondered where to start. Perhaps the tourist hotels would know? He headed toward the Kalahari Arms, but before he reached it he passed a shop selling Bushman artifacts. He pulled over and went in. The interior of the shop was filled with items—a much more extensive choice than the little gallery at New Xade. There were bracelets and necklaces made from ostrich shell, paintings by well-known Bushman artists, Bushman hunting kits made for tourists but including all the items you might find in one—arrows, empty poison containers, digging sticks, dry kindling to make a fire.

While he was taking it all in, he was approached by the manager. "Can I help you, Constable?"

Ixau focused on the job at hand. "Thank you, rra. I'm looking for a Bushman called Twi. He's a guide and—"

"I know him," the manager interrupted. "What do you want with him?"

"I want to ask him a few questions. To help me with my inquiries." When he noticed the man's suspicious look, he added, "He's done nothing wrong."

"I don't know where he is, but I can give you his cell phone number. Occasionally one of my clients wants to hire a guide, and I recommend him. He's a good man for a Bushman." The man hesitated, realizing the implications of what he'd said. "I mean, some of them are not as hardworking as Twi."

"I will be grateful for the cell number," Ixau said stiffly.

When the manager found it, Ixau copied it into his notebook, thanked the man, and left.

Outside, he dialed the number and waited. It rang several times, and Ixau was about to give up, when a voice said, "*Dumela*. This is Twi."

Ixau switched to Naro and greeted Twi in their language. They had grown up together in New Xade but, although Ixau studied and worked hard to be accepted by the police, in the end it was Twi who'd made it out of New Xade.

Ixau quickly discovered that Twi was in Ghanzi and that they could meet right away. Twi suggested a small place that sold coffee and cheap sandwiches.

As soon as they'd greeted one another and asked after each other's families, Ixau got down to business. Twi remembered the man who'd hired him but didn't remember his name. The man had been curt and expected to be called "rra" in every sentence. The manager of the curio store had arranged the job, and Ixau realized that he should have asked him more questions.

He took out the pictures and showed them to Twi, one by one. He kept Gampone for last, having decided that he was the likely candidate. When he saw the second picture, Twi reacted immediately. "Yes, that's him. Thabo—yes, I remember his name now."

Ixau was very excited. "You're absolutely sure? Why was he looking for Heiseb?"

Twi shook his head. "He wasn't exactly looking for Heiseb. He wanted to meet very old Bushmen with good stories to tell of the past. I thought of N'kaka, but Heiseb was far older, so that's who he said we must find. He's a professor? Why are you interested in him?"

Ixau had no idea. "He'll help with our inquiries," he replied. "I'm not allowed to discuss these things, you know. The coffee here is good. Shall we get a sandwich?"

• • •

As soon as they'd finished their snack and had said good-bye, Ixau phoned the assistant superintendent, excited to share his news. He first told Kubu about N'kaka and how he was an unreliable witness, and then how he'd tracked down Twi and obtained a positive identification of the professor.

There was a short silence before Kubu responded. "Well done, Constable! That is excellent work. I'm very interested to hear about the professor. I've had my suspicions . . ." But he didn't complete the sentence.

"Thank you, sir," Ixau replied. "I've very much enjoyed working for you. I hope, perhaps, it might be possible . . ." He hesitated and then rushed on. "Rra, I do nothing in New Xade all day, because there is nothing that needs to be done. I thought, perhaps, I could be trained to be a detective. Then I would be useful to the Police Service."

There was another pause, and Ixau feared he'd annoyed the senior officer. Then Kubu said, "I can't promise anything, Constable, but I'll see what I can do."

CHAPTER 36

By the time Kubu returned home on Friday evening, he was feeling positive about the various cases. He was reasonably confident that the CCTV tape that had been delivered by a courier from the Chinese embassy was authentic and, surprisingly, the pictures of the man who had asked Chan to help with the paperwork were clear enough to make a positive identification, should they ever find him.

In addition, newspaper reporters had eagerly listened to Mabaku's press announcement that Gampone had been arrested on suspicion of being in possession of banned substances—which Mabaku had declined to identify—and that the police were investigating whether there was any connection between him and the murder of *Kgosi* Ramala. Kubu was sure that this news would make the front page of the weekend newspapers. He also believed that the press briefing would be covered on the various TV news broadcasts. He'd noticed several camera crews there, all eager for information on the murder of such a well-known man.

Kubu's thoughts on how to proceed with the case were interrupted when he opened the gate to his house and Ilia bounded up, yapping excitedly. After pawing Kubu's leg, Ilia jumped into the Land Rover and sat on the passenger seat.

"I'll shut the gate, Daddy," Tumi shouted, as she ran from the house.

Kubu edged the car forward to the end of the short driveway, turned the engine off, and climbed out to give his daughter a hug.

"Where's Nono?" Kubu asked.

"She was sick and we took her to the hospital."

Dammit! Why didn't Joy call and tell me? Kubu wondered.

He took Tumi's hand and walked into the house. As soon as he was inside, Joy came running out of the kitchen and threw her arms around him.

"I'm so worried. Nono's back in hospital." Tears streamed down her face.

"What happened?" he asked, patting her on the back.

"Just after you left this morning, she complained of being uncomfortable under her arms. I checked, and her glands were swollen, there and on her neck. She was also hot and sweating, so I took her temperature. It was over a hundred and one." She stifled a sob. "Oh, darling, it was normal when she left hospital on Wednesday."

Kubu pulled Joy tighter. "It's probably just a reaction to the new medication," he said.

Joy shook her head. "These are all signs the HIV is becoming AIDS. And the doctor called this afternoon and said her CD4 count was approaching two hundred. Below two hundred *is* AIDS."

"Oh, my darling. What else did she say?"

"She thinks she must have an infection of some sort. They've been doing tests all afternoon. Oh, I'm so scared she's not going to make it."

Kubu was at a loss as to how to comfort Joy—and himself, for that matter. So he hugged her more tightly.

"Daddy, Daddy, hug me too," Tumi shouted. "I want to be hugged."

Kubu and Joy separated a little so Tumi could squeeze in between them.

"You don't want a hug," Kubu said with a smile. "You want a . . . big . . ." He paused dramatically. "Tumi sandwich." He and Joy joined arms and enveloped the little girl.

They stood like that for quite some time. "What are we going to do?" Joy asked.

"She's getting the best treatment available," Kubu replied. "We must have faith in our doctors."

"And look at how many kids have died in this country."

"She's not going to die. She's a fighter."

"I think we should take her to Johannesburg. They've got the best doctors in Africa, and some are the best in the world."

"Darling, our doctors are just as good, just as experienced at dealing with HIV and AIDS."

"So why aren't they making any progress with a cure?"

"My darling, just look how far they've come in a few years with antiretrovirals. A few years ago HIV was a death warrant; now, millions live normal lives."

"But Nono's getting worse. What good's that doing her?"

"Mommy, Mommy, is Nono going to die?" Kubu and Joy had both forgotten that Tumi was between them. "Will she meet Jesus?"

Kubu pulled Tumi close to him. "Darling, she's sick now, but she's not going to die. She'll be back with us any day now."

"Run off to your room," Joy said. "Daddy and I need to talk some grown-up talk. Go on. I'll call you when dinner is ready."

Tumi looked at both of them. "Okay," she said, and ran off.

"She's really worried," Joy said. "She keeps asking when Nono will be home."

"I know," Kubu said. "But I don't think you should be so negative around her. Try to be positive."

"How can I be positive when Nono's deteriorating, and you're your normal cheerful, optimistic self. Aren't you worried?"

Kubu reached out, but Joy backed away.

"Of course I'm worried. But I have faith in Nono, in the doctors, and in our family."

"The doctors are useless, and her being in the hospital is like signing a death warrant. It's unhygienic and full of bugs that could kill her. We've got to do something!"

"Darling, we're doing—"

Joy looked at Kubu. "We're not doing enough." She paused. "Do you know what that Bushman who was so old was taking? What plants he was eating?"

Kubu stared in amazement at his wife. She was ordinarily so sensible, depending on data for her decisions, depending on science.

"We don't know what he was eating, if he was eating anything special. I think he was just a freak of nature, an outlier. I think his condition was just luck."

"And what about *Kgosi* Ramala? Can you get some of his *muti*? I think we should give it to Nono. I'll try anything right now."

"Joy, darling. What are you saying? It's *muti*. Hocus-pocus. Make-believe. It's not real."

She pounded on his chest. *"I don't care,"* she shouted. *"I'll try anything! Get some for her!"*

"But, darling—"

"Go and get some!"

Kubu had never seen Joy like this. He didn't know what to say.

"Go, for fuck sake. Get some and take it to her" she shouted.

Kubu took a step back, shocked.

"Go! Get out!" she screamed. *"And don't come back until you've got it!"*

Kubu turned and hurried out to his Land Rover. He climbed in, not knowing what to do. He decided he'd better leave. He started the engine and backed out.

Crash.

"Shit." He'd forgotten to open the gate. He heaved himself out of the car, opened the gate, climbed back in, and reversed to the road. Once again, he jumped out to close the gate.

Where's Ilia?

He looked up and down the street. No dog to be seen.

She'd better be inside.

He pulled himself once more into the driver's seat and headed down the road.

Where am I going?

After a few minutes driving, he pulled over and took his cell phone from his pocket.

"Pleasant? It's Kubu. Your sister needs help. Please can you go to her? Nono's taken a turn for the worse and Joy's thrown me out of the house. She . . . well, quite frankly, she's having a meltdown."

He listened to her reply.

"Thank you. As quickly as you can!"

After hanging up, he decided he should go to his office. It would be quiet on a Friday night. He needed time to think.

 **PART 4**

CHAPTER 37

Kubu wanted to cry.

He'd never thought that Nono could die! She'd come so far in the year she'd been with the family. When she moved in, she wouldn't say boo to a mouse, but recently had become nearly like Tumi—playful, energetic, and self-confident. Until she got ill.

He blinked a few times to clear his vision.

He felt the depths of despair. Yesterday he and Joy had agreed on almost everything. Today she wanted *muti* to save Nono. She'd gone back to the beliefs of the past.

He took a deep breath.

And the worst thing was that she'd shouted at him. Screamed, actually. She'd never done that before.

He stood up and went to the window, hoping the pain would go away.

He replayed the traumatic scene in his head. And again. And again. No matter how he changed what he said, the result was the same—Joy screamed at him.

He wondered what he should do. Should he find some *muti* and give it to Nono? To appease Joy?

He shook his head.

That was against everything he believed. Believing in *muti* was a thing of the past. He couldn't go back there. He wanted to look to the future.

He went back to his chair and sat down.

Will Joy and I ever be the same? he wondered. Can we still love each other after what's happened?

He felt so alone.

He took another deep breath and put his head in his hands.

KUBU DIDN'T KNOW how long he sat like that. It seemed forever. He felt paralyzed, unable to make any decisions.

"Get hold of yourself," he eventually said out loud. "You're behaving like a child."

He stood up and started pacing.

He thought of making some of his own *muti*—totally harmless—and giving it to Nono. Joy would be happy. It wouldn't make any difference to Nono. That would solve the problem.

He stopped at the window.

But what if Nono recovered? Maybe Joy would forsake hospitals for witch doctors. And if he told her that the *muti* he gave Nono was a placebo, she'd be furious and never trust him again.

He put his hands in his pockets.

And he couldn't live with the lie, anyway. That wasn't going to work.

He thought of calling his mother, but decided not to because she would support Joy's decision to use traditional medicines.

"It's all bullshit!" he said out loud.

He wondered whom else he could call for advice. Pleasant was out because, hopefully, she was with Joy; he wasn't close enough to her husband, Bongani; and he didn't feel Mabaku, his boss, would be sympathetic. So who was left?

Ian, of course. He was a doctor. He knew how to listen, and they'd known each other for a long time.

Relieved, Kubu picked up the phone and dialed.

"COME IN, LADDIE," Ian said as Kubu walked in the door. "Here, take this." He handed Kubu a cut crystal glass with an inch of golden liquid. "Nothing like a wee dram to put problems into perspective. Sit down and tell me about it."

For the next ten minutes, Kubu tried to explain what had happened, how he'd been thrown out of the house in order to find *muti* for Nono, how Joy normally scoffed at the idea of *muti,* and how he didn't have any idea of what to do.

"I assume you've considered giving Nono a placebo—something that looks like *muti* but is harmless."

Kubu nodded.

"And you've rejected the idea because it would be a big lie."

Kubu nodded again.

Ian lifted his glass and savored the peaty Scotch he'd poured for both of them.

"I have a tough question for you. How important is your relationship with Joy?"

"It's more important than anything. But—"

"But not at the price of abandoning your principles," Ian interrupted.

Kubu looked down at his near-empty glass.

"Not at the price of lying, right?"

Kubu nodded.

Ian took another sip of his Scotch and rolled it around his mouth.

"Do you think Joy is a sensible woman?" he asked.

"Normally, yes. But in this case she's going against everything she believes in."

"And you think it's your duty to put her back on the straight and narrow? To bring her to her senses?"

Kubu didn't reply.

"What are the chances of you and Joy being happy together if Nono dies and you didn't find *muti* for her? In fact, how are *you* going to feel if Nono dies and you haven't tried everything? Even stuff you think is mumbo jumbo?"

Kubu didn't say anything.

"You know very well that spells by witch doctors often have bad consequences for those who've been cursed. Can you explain that? Of course you can, and do. It's all in the mind, you'd say. Same as *muti*. If it works, it's purely psychological, you'd say. Am I right?"

Kubu shrugged.

"You know I'm right, laddie."

They sat in silence for several minutes.

"You think I should fake it?" Kubu asked eventually.

"Think about it, my friend. What is the downside? Joy will think you've done everything in your power to help, and it's not going to affect Nono one way or the other. The only thing that will suffer is your ego—that you abandoned your principles to save your marriage."

"I have to live with myself, Ian. I don't want to live a lie—I'd be constantly mortified at what I had done. Principles mean a lot to me."

"That's codswallop!" Ian continued. "I've seen you having very malleable principles when it comes to solving a case. Stretching the truth here, embellishing the facts there, to get a confession. Get real, laddie. We'll concoct something here tonight. No one will be the wiser. And you'll call Joy and apologize for storming out. Tell her—"

"I didn't storm out," Kubu protested. "She told me to get out."

"Laddie, laddie. It doesn't matter what she told you. You phone her now and tell her that you love her but are going to stay here tonight, and that you'll get some of that witch doctor's *muti* in the morning from the evidence room at the CID. What's his name? Ramala? That you will give Nono some of *Kgosi* Ramala's potion as soon as you can."

He put his hand on Kubu's shoulder. "Go and phone her. Then come back and have another Scotch."

"I'll do it later," Kubu said. "I'm not up to it right now."

Ian shrugged and walked over to the table to top up his drink.

At Kubu's home, Pleasant was trying to console Joy.

"He loves you, Joy. He really does. More than I've known any man to love his wife. He worships you."

"Why doesn't he want to help Nono?"

Pleasant shook her head. "Joy, Joy. Of course he wants to help her. He loves her just as much as Tumi. He'd be devastated if she died."

"But he doesn't want to try the *muti* of that witch doctor, whatever his name is. She's dying, Pleasant. Doesn't he realize that?"

"He knows how sick she is, and he knows how worried you are. If he was here, he'd be holding you."

"But he's not here," Joy snapped. "He left, just when I need him."

"I thought he said you told him to leave."

Joy burst into tears again.

"I did, but he should've known I didn't mean it."

Pleasant took Joy in her arms. "He said you'd never shouted at him before. He sounded lost. Didn't know what to think. He wasn't sure you wanted him back."

"Of course I want him back."

"Why don't you call him and tell him."

"And if he doesn't want to come back? What'll I do then?"

"Of course he wants to come back. This is his home. You're his wife, and Tumi and Nono are his children."

"Then why hasn't he called? He should've called by now."

"He thinks you threw him out. He doesn't know that you want him back. Call him and tell him that you love him, that you need him, and he should come back home."

"Where will he be staying? Will he get a hotel room?"

"It doesn't matter where he's staying. He's got his cell phone."

Joy wiped her eyes. "I'm so scared he won't come back. I'll call him in the morning, after I've had some sleep. I'll feel better then."

Pleasant let Joy go. "I'm going to get a glass of wine. Do you want one?"

Joy shrugged, then nodded.

CHAPTER 38

Samantha was up early on Saturday morning. She had the day off and intended to spend it at the women's shelter where she volunteered. They were expecting her, so she wasn't pleased when her phone rang, showing "Work" as the caller.

"Detective Khama."

"*Dumela*, Samantha. Seleke here. I have a report from a Constable Kirwa. He's down on the Lobatse road—near the police college—and there's a body there."

Samantha bristled. Detective Sergeant Seleke was not one of her favorite people. She guessed that he'd chosen to phone her to spoil her day off.

"I'm not on duty, Detective Sergeant. Try Edison."

"The constable thinks the man may be the missing witch doctor, and that's your case. But, of course, if you're not interested, I'll see if Edison's around."

At once the women's shelter was gone from Samantha's mind. She was excited about the possibility of progress on the Ramala case at last. "Okay, give me the constable's number."

She jotted it down, grudgingly thanked Seleke, and called Kirwa.

"*Dumela*, mma. Yes, there's a body here. It's not in good shape, and the smell is really bad. It was buried, but not deep. A couple of students from the police college saw some dogs digging in the sand, so they went to take a look. Then they called us. I'm waiting near the body, in case the dogs come back."

"What makes you think it's Ramala?"

"Mma, I'm not sure. The body is wrapped in a sheet, but the dogs pulled it out enough so I can see the face. It's cracked and swollen and covered with dirt, but I studied his picture when you sent it out, and I think it could be him. But I'm not sure."

Samantha sighed. Maybe it wasn't Ramala after all, she thought. Still, if the body had been buried in the bush, it probably wasn't a death from natural causes. It would have to be investigated.

"Right, Constable. Please tell me where you are, and I'll come out. In the meantime, don't touch anything."

Next she dialed Kubu's number, but it went straight to voice mail. That was unusual. Kubu almost always answered his phone. She left a message telling him about the body and asking him to call her. Then she phoned Ian MacGregor and explained the situation to him.

"I'll meet you there," he told her.

THE STENCH WAS indeed awful. Samantha took statements from the two students who'd discovered the body, grateful that Ian was dealing with the corpse. However, after about ten minutes, he beckoned her over. She put on a mask, gloves, and shoe covers and carefully walked over, watching where she trod.

Ian had carefully brushed the dirt off the face, and she could see it quite clearly now. She'd brought a picture of the witch doctor with her, and they compared it against the remains of the face. Despite the marbling and a bad dog bite that had removed most of one cheek, the resemblance was clear.

"It's him," Ian said after a moment. Samantha nodded, keen to move away from the body, but Ian motioned her closer and lifted one of the arms.

"Take a look at the hand."

Samantha leaned forward and tried to focus through her rising nausea.

"The fingernails," Ian prompted.

"There aren't any," Samantha said. "Have they fallen off because of the rotting . . . ?" She swallowed hard.

Ian shook his head. "Much too soon. From the state of the body, I'd say he's been dead less than a week, but that can't be right. I think he was buried near the Gampone house after he was killed, and later moved and reburied here. Decomposition is much slowed if the body is buried."

Ian took a close look at the fingers and brushed them carefully with what looked like a paintbrush. "It's hard to see with all the dirt on the hands, but I'd guess these are premortem wounds."

Samantha swallowed again. "You mean someone tore them off?"

Ian nodded. "Could be. And there seem to be chest wounds too. Probably he was stabbed to death. We need to get him to the morgue for an autopsy. There's nothing more I can do here."

Samantha gratefully backed away.

"I need to phone Kubu," she said.

Ian said nothing, but watched as she dialed. Again the call went to voice mail.

"Dammit, he's not answering," Samantha said.

"He's rather busy this morning," Ian told her. "I'm sure he'll call you as soon as he can."

Samantha looked at him with surprise, but before she could question him, he walked off to supervise moving the body to the waiting ambulance.

Meanwhile, Zanele had arrived and was getting togged up. She waved Samantha over. "Hello, Samantha. Is it Ramala?"

Samantha nodded. "I'm pretty sure it is. And Ian thinks he was tortured. Fingernails pulled out. Who knows what else."

Zanele grimaced. "Did you find anything around the grave?"

Samantha shook her head. "I hope you can."

"We'll look, but I'm not optimistic we'll find anything here. I was talking to the constable. He said the students had to chase off dogs. And one of them admitted that he threw up by the body. I'm not sure he's cut out for the police."

Samantha thought that was a bit harsh, especially as she'd come close to doing the same thing.

"I'd say our best bet will be with his clothes and the sheet," Zanele continued. "There might be fibers or hairs from someone else. Something. And where did the sheet come from?"

"They probably took it from the house."

Zanele shook her head. "They didn't break into the house. Most people don't keep sheets in their garage."

"Of course. Stupid of me," Samantha said. "Probably they brought it when they came back to move him."

"You don't look so great, Samantha. Did you have anything to eat before you came out?"

Samantha shook her head. "I'm fine. I just want to look around a bit."

Zanele nodded and got to work.

CHAPTER 39

Kubu pulled into the parking lot at Princess Marina Hospital at about the same time Samantha arrived at the body. He felt terrible. He'd decided to follow Ian's advice and had brought with him a glass container the size of a spice jar, filled with a golden-brown liquid with some vegetable matter floating in it.

"It's harmless," Ian had told him. "Grape juice, chopped mint, and dried rosemary. It'll do the job."

As he walked to Nono's ward, Kubu was worried that a doctor would come in while Nono was drinking the *muti*.

I'd feel such a fool, he thought.

He could just imagine the gossip: Kubu, the modern man, has resorted to *muti*.

He pushed open the door and peered inside. Nono was lying with her eyes closed, her face very pale; the only other patient was in a bed at the other end of the room, reading.

Kubu sat down on the edge of the bed and held Nono's hand. "How are you feeling today, darling?" he asked quietly.

Nono's eyes flickered open. "Daddy?"

"Yes, my darling. How are you?"

"About the same as yesterday. I just want to sleep the whole time. Where's Mommy? And Tumi?"

"They're coming a little later."

"I want Tumi to be here."

"She'll be here soon. As soon as I leave, I'll call them and tell them to hurry up."

Nono closed her eyes.

Kubu looked around.

"Darling, I have some medicine for you to take. Can you sit up for a few minutes?" Kubu put his hand in his pocket and pulled out the small jar. "It tastes nice; I tried it. Just like fruit juice."

Nono didn't move.

"Please, Nono, darling. Please sit up."

Nono's eyes opened. "I'm tired, Daddy. I want to sleep."

"You can sleep as long as you like after you've taken the medicine. Please, darling, sit up."

Nono stirred and struggled to pull herself up the pillow.

"Here, let me help you." Kubu leaned over and put his arms under Nono. He gently lifted her so she could sit up.

He unscrewed the cap and passed the jar to her. "Please drink it up. It will help you get better."

Nono hesitated, then took a sip. She frowned.

"It tastes weird," she said, pulling a face. She took another sip. "Do I have to drink all of it?"

Kubu nodded. "Yes, my darling. But only this one time."

Just as Nono lifted the jar to her lips, the door opened. Kubu swung around, praying it wasn't the doctor.

It was Joy. And Tumi.

Joy and Kubu stared at each other, not knowing what to say.

"Daddy, Daddy!" Tumi cried as she rushed forward to hug her father. "I missed you. Where were you last night?"

Kubu lifted her off the floor and gave her a big kiss on her forehead. "I missed you too." He put her back on the floor.

"How are you Nono? I missed you, too," Tumi said as she ran to Nono's side and jumped on the bed. She gave her a big hug. "What's Nono drinking, Daddy?"

Kubu turned to Joy, still unable to say anything.

She moved to the other side of the bed, all the time staring at Kubu, eyes red, face stricken. After a few moments, she glanced at Nono.

"What's that?" she asked, pointing at the jar.

"You told me to give her the *muti*."

"That's *muti*?"

Kubu nodded.

"Can it harm her?"

"Darling—"

"What if it makes her worse?"

"But, you—"

"I don't think we can take the chance."

She took the jar from Nono and walked over to the basin at the end of the ward. Turning on the water, she poured the contents down the drain and washed out the jar.

"It smells of mint and something sweet." She turned up her nose and went back to Nono. "Darling, how are you feeling today?"

"I'm so tired, Mommy. When will I get better?"

"The doctor says you will start feeling better any day now."

"Can we go and get Nono an ice cream?" Tumi asked.

"Not today, dear. Maybe tomorrow."

Kubu stared at his family, an ache developing in his stomach as Joy ignored him. What have I done to deserve this? he wondered.

After a few more moments, he turned and walked out.

CHAPTER 40

Kubu walked out of the hospital and sat in his car, not noticing the heat. He didn't know what to do.

He could stay at Ian's for another night to make Joy realize she was in the wrong; in reality to punish her, he admitted to himself. But what if she thought *he* was to blame for the situation? Doing nothing could make things worse.

On the other hand, he could swallow his pride, go back home, and talk things through, hopefully clearing up the misunderstandings. The risk was that she'd send him away again. That would cut deep.

The pain in his stomach was much worse now.

Half an hour later, sweat dripping down his face, he came to a decision. He wasn't going to sit back and do nothing. That wasn't who he was. Whatever the risks, he was going to talk to Joy and hash out what had happened. There was no other way.

He was relieved that he now had a plan, but he was aware of the deep disquiet that lay on his heart. What if . . . ?

• • •

KUBU WAITED UNTIL after lunch to drive to his home. He was full of foreboding. How could two people who loved each other so much suddenly be so far apart? he wondered. Maybe he'd misjudged Joy. Maybe she hadn't felt as deeply about him as he did about her.

The short drive seemed to take forever.

When he drove up to the gate, he was pleased that Ilia hadn't also abandoned him. She came skidding off the veranda, yapping excitedly, and jumping up against the gate. Kubu climbed out of the Land Rover, leaving the door open, and opened the two halves of the gate. Ilia immediately jumped into the car and sat, panting, on the passenger seat.

Kubu returned to the car, drove in, and parked next to Joy's car. At least she and Tumi were home.

He took a deep breath.

But where was Tumi? She was normally like Ilia, rushing out to welcome him home.

He walked onto the veranda, Ilia tangled in his feet, and called out as he often did: "Joy, I'm home."

He stopped, hoping she would rush out and throw herself into his arms.

She didn't.

He walked inside.

"Joy?"

No response.

"Joy, are you here?"

The house was silent.

What if they've moved out?

He couldn't believe they'd do that, but he wandered around looking for a note. Then he went into the bedroom and opened a closet. Thank God, all her clothes were still there.

Where were they?

Suddenly, Ilia started yapping and raced out of the house, and Kubu heard the gate squeaking open. I'll have to oil that, he thought, as he hurried to the veranda.

"Daddy, Daddy, we're home."

Kubu's eyes moistened as he heard Tumi's voice.

"I love you, darling," he said, as Tumi threw herself into his arms.

"I love you too, Daddy."

Kubu looked up as Joy climbed the stairs to the veranda. He put Tumi down and took a deep breath.

"Hello, darling," he said quietly. "I love you, too."

Joy hesitated, then looked at Kubu.

"And I love you too," she said. Then she walked inside.

CHAPTER 41

Mabaku called a meeting for Monday midmorning, to allow Ian time to complete the autopsy of the body. The mood was somber. Mabaku saw everything becoming more complicated after the discovery of Ramala's body; Kubu was brooding that things were still not right between him and Joy and that Nono hadn't improved; Samantha was thinking about having to break the news to Ramala's wife; and Ian was sickened by the treatment the man had suffered before he was killed.

Mabaku opened the meeting and thanked Ian for working over the weekend. The Scotsman shrugged.

"I wish I could say it's been a pleasure," he said. "Pretty grim actually, I'm afraid. Everything I suspected was true. The man was beaten and viciously tortured before he was killed. He had his fingernails pulled out one by one, and there was plenty of premortem bruising. And three of his fingers were broken."

No one said anything for a few moments, then Mabaku asked, "How was he killed?"

"Multiple stab wounds. One went into the heart."

"When did he die?" Samantha asked.

Ian shook his head. "It's hard to say, after all this time. If we assume that he was buried, the first time, shortly after he was killed, then a window from Saturday to Tuesday works, but it could have been even earlier. Then again, we don't know how long it was before he was dug up and moved. Being buried—"

"Why?" Kubu interjected.

Ian frowned. "Why what?"

"Why was he moved?"

"I can't answer that," Ian replied.

Kubu backtracked to let the others catch up with his thoughts. "We've talked about the Bushman case and the witch doctor case being connected through the longevity thing. My guess is that Heiseb's body was stolen not for *muti* but for further investigation. Maybe in China. We know that a body—or something—was flown to China with false documentation just after the break-in at the mortuary. I wonder if they wanted Ramala's body for the same reason. Was there any similarity between Ramala's and Heiseb's organs?"

"You mean any parts of him apparently younger than one would expect?" Ian shook his head. "No. I can go into detail if you like, but basically everything was consistent with a man in his midfifties in reasonable shape. If you're going to tell me he was midseventies or something, I'd have to think again."

"Do you know how old he was?" Kubu asked Samantha.

"I'm not sure. His wife looks midfifties, but that doesn't prove anything, of course. I'll find out."

"I've never bought this long-life story," Mabaku said, "and it doesn't apply to Ramala anyway, from what Ian's telling us. Still, it's a good question. Why was the body moved?"

"Is it possible they left something with the body that pointed to them?" Samantha asked. "Or something they realized they wanted, after they'd buried him?"

Kubu shook his head. "Why would they move the body? They'd

just dig it up, take what they wanted, and rebury it. Moving it wasn't only a very unpleasant job, it was dangerous. They had to carry it up that footpath, probably at night, load it into a car, and drive it somewhere else. And they didn't plan it well. They chose a spot where it was hard to dig, and the body came to light sooner than they would've wanted."

"What about the cell phone?" Mabaku asked. "The phone we found in Ramala's car. Once they realized it was missing, they would also realize that we'd be able to trace them to Gampone's house."

"And from the way they hid the grave there, they obviously didn't want the body to be discovered," Samantha added. "So they got there ahead of us and moved it."

"But does the timing work?" Kubu asked. "The obvious thing to do when they missed the phone was to go and retrieve it. They abandoned the car at Game City on Monday morning, and we didn't find it until Wednesday."

"Maybe they didn't discover it was missing right away," Samantha offered. "Then they would've returned to the car and, as soon as they realized we had it, they would've moved the body. It could even have been on Friday night." She frowned, thinking how close they might have been to catching the culprits.

"It's possible," Kubu admitted. "But if they didn't want the body found, why not take it out into the desert for the hyenas or whatever? Why bury it only ten miles away—and make a bad job of it, at that?"

"Perhaps they didn't want us to find it near the house," Mabaku suggested.

Kubu thought about that. "But why not?" There was silence for a few moments.

Mabaku frowned. "Do you have any better ideas?"

Kubu shook his head. "Not really. All I know is that it doesn't add up." He turned back to Ian. "Nothing had been removed from the body, had it? Organs, bones, anything?"

Ian shook his head. "Not as far as I could tell. I wouldn't have picked up a blood sample or something like that, but anything significant I would've noticed."

"We'll trace these murderers the way we always do," Mabaku said. "Routine and hard work. These people moved the body. They had to carry it in a sheet. They had to drive it some distance. They had to dig a new grave and dump it there. They can't have done all that without leaving any traces. Where's Zanele? What does she have?"

"I spoke to her before the meeting," Samantha replied. "The sheet isn't anything special—common material—and she hasn't come up with anything else useful so far either, I'm afraid. But she's working on it."

"Check out the houses around Gampone's," Mabaku said. "Someone may have seen something. And ask at the police college. Sometimes the students sneak in late at night."

Samantha nodded and jotted down notes.

"Did you get anything on those companies shipping stuff to China and Vietnam?" Kubu asked her.

Samantha shook her head. "I haven't had a chance. I've been focused on Ramala."

"Well, fit it in," Mabaku told her. "Now what else do we have, Kubu?"

"First, we've made no progress on locating Collins. There's no record of him leaving Botswana, and none of him entering Namibia. Second, we've got Gampone under surveillance, both to keep an eye on him and for his own safety. It's very discreet. He'd have to be very good to notice. And we've a tap on his phones—at least the ones we know about. But he'll anticipate that."

Mabaku nodded.

Then Kubu filled them in on his meetings with Ross and Festus.

Mabaku frowned when he heard about the supposed Chinese abductors. "Find out who that informant is and grill him."

Kubu nodded, wondering how he was going to do that. Next he reported on his conversation with Ixau.

Samantha perked up when Kubu mentioned Professor Thabo and his search for Heiseb in New Xade. "Do you know his first name?" she asked him.

"No. Why?"

"The name Thabo is familiar. I think . . ." She hesitated. "I'll check after the meeting."

"Check now," Mabaku said. "We need some progress here. This is going to be a media circus when they hear about Ramala's body being found. He's become a celebrity since he went missing." Samantha nodded and hurried out. By the time Kubu had finished the rest of Ixau's story, she was back, carrying a well-used notebook.

"This is Ramala's appointment book," she explained. "I've only followed up the appointments from a few days before he disappeared, but I did look through the whole lot. About six weeks ago there's an appointment with an S. Thabo. I thought I remembered the name. It's not that common." She paused. "I just checked the professor online. His first name is Sichle."

"Good work, Samantha," Kubu said. "So our professor not only went searching for Heiseb, but he had links with Ramala also. I've always suspected that he knows more than he's telling."

"Right!" Mabaku said. "Ian, let us have your report as soon as possible, and give us your opinions on Kubu's queries as well. Samantha, follow up on the door-to-door around Gampone's house and the police college and find out about those shipping companies. Get some help. Kubu, you need to talk to this professor, and also find out who the witness was to the abduction." He checked his watch. "I have to see the press liaison officer. We'd better have some progress by tomorrow. We're going to have to let the press in on this pretty soon." He rose and gathered his notes.

"By the way," Samantha said, "I also checked Ramala's file while I was out. He was fifty-three years old. Pretty well what Ian thought, so no surprise there."

Mabaku glanced at her, nodded, and headed for the door. A few moments later, Ian followed him, leaving Samantha and Kubu sitting at the large conference table.

"I'm really frustrated, Kubu," Samantha said. "I'm not making any progress on any of the murders."

"I know what you mean," Kubu responded. "But we need to keep plodding along, step by step, concentrating on the details, following up on everything." He winced as he realized he was beginning to sound like Director Mabaku. "You never know when something will turn up, but you have to have your eyes open to be able to see it. Go back over everything. See if we've missed anything."

"I know that's what I have to do, but I want things to move faster."

"Don't we all," said Kubu.

CHAPTER 42

After his meeting with the press liaison officer, Director Mabaku was not in a good mood. The media were hounding them about the Ramala murder. And he was far from happy about the situation with Gampone, who was also under pressure from the press. So far, he'd had the sense not to comment.

Mabaku was also worried about his upcoming meeting with the commissioner. He wondered how he could keep his promise that the CITES story would go no further. He hoped that he hadn't misjudged the situation, so he had mixed feelings when Miriam phoned and told him Gampone was on the line.

"The devil himself," he muttered. "Put him through."

"Director Mabaku, Gampone here. I've been trying to reach you."

"What have you found out?"

"Yes, I do have news. I may have information about the local source for rhino horn and ivory."

Mabaku grunted, waiting for him to go on.

"As I told you, I got a lot of useful information in China and

Vietnam when I was there, but there were missing pieces. The trail led back to Gaborone, all right, but I didn't know how. I think I have that missing link."

"And what is it?"

"I had a call last night from China. They're interested in what they call a 'trial shipment.' And they've told me how to do it. I'm to speak to a woman at a shipping company called Botswana Logistics and give her a package of statues, with the rhino horn powder concealed in one of them. Apparently she has a way of shipping it without customs problems either side."

"How?"

"They won't tell me that! There's no reason for me to know. But that's how they get the goods out of Botswana. Now we have the company and the contact there, it should be easy for you to break the whole gang—provided they're not protected from above."

Maybe *too* easy, Mabaku thought.

"Give me the details," he said.

Kubu wondered what was up as he made his way to Mabaku's office, following the urgent summons from Miriam. He didn't have long to wait. Mabaku waved him to a chair and said, "Gampone says he had a call last night from someone in China—he gave me the name—who told him to send them a package as a test. He's to talk to a Mma Tomale at a company called . . ." He checked his notes. "Botswana Logistics. Apparently they arrange the transport."

"Botswana Logistics? That's interesting. That's the company that shipped what we think was the body of the Bushman to China. If they handle the contraband, then maybe the same group is involved in the murders. But how do they deal with customs and so on?"

Mabaku shook his head. "Gampone didn't know, but it's pretty obvious, isn't it? Some grease is applied at the sticking points."

Kubu frowned, sure that Mabaku was right. "But there's a problem," he said.

"There certainly is. Maybe the whole thing is a test for Gampone. His Chinese friends will be watching and, if we go after this company, they'll know. I wouldn't want to be in Gampone's shoes in that case. And we'll be left with nothing."

"Even if it isn't a trap, if we go after these people, they'll know Gampone's tipped us off, and they'll be alerted. But I have an idea. I'll do the follow-up with Botswana Logistics about the address the coffin was shipped to, instead of Samantha. Maybe I can tease out something about this Tomale woman. If she's involved in smuggling, the chances are she helped ship the coffin as well."

"That makes sense," Mabaku said. "But there's a third possibility, you know."

Kubu nodded. "Yes. That the whole thing has been dreamed up by Gampone, and it's a red herring. Well, we'll have to live with that until we can check his phone records."

"That's easy for you to say. You don't have to deal with the commissioner and all these hyenas from the press. Anyway, what else have you got?"

"I spoke to Thabo, but he's slippery. I think he was concerned by my questions, but he had a good story. He researches the practitioners of traditional medicine, so he interviewed Ramala. That was the only time Thabo saw him, and he summed him up as a charlatan. For the same reason, he was interested in the traditional remedies from around New Xade. He claimed he wasn't looking for Heiseb, specifically, until that was suggested by the guide he hired. I'll ask Constable Ixau to check if that's true."

"No slipups?"

Kubu shook his head. "It was almost too consistent."

There was a pause, and then Kubu said, "By the way, I've been planning that mentoring project you and the commissioner gave me, and it made me think of Constable Ixau. He's a lot of initiative and did a great job discovering that Thabo was snooping around New Xade. What about putting him up for detective training? He's really keen."

Mabaku thought for a moment. "A Bushman? Well, Samantha was our first woman, and she's worked out pretty well. Okay, I'll put his name forward. Now let's get back to the case. Have you traced the informant who saw Ramala abducted?"

Kubu shook his head again. "We questioned Festus's contact. His nickname's Legotlo—'the Rat'—and he gave us the name of the man who saw the abduction. But he's disappeared. I think he's been tipped off. This Legotlo loves to play both sides against the middle."

"Find him and lean on him," Mabaku said. "I bet he knows more than he's telling."

"There's something else, too. The American, Ross, called me. He said that Mrs. Collins got another email on Sunday from her husband—at least it claimed to be from him. It says he's fine, and she mustn't worry. Helenka from IT checked it out. It was sent from here in Gaborone, like the previous one. She traced it through an ISP here in Gabs to the Orange cell network and to a phone, but the phone was unregistered, like the one we found in Ramala's car."

"So, no help there. Do you think these messages can be genuine?"

Kubu shook his head. "I very much doubt it. I think whoever had Ramala had Collins too. My guess is they're after whatever Heiseb was using, supposedly, to keep young, and they wouldn't want anyone else knowing about it."

Mabaku digested that. "You think Collins is dead?"

"That seems the only thing that makes sense. There's no record of him leaving the country. If he knows we're looking for him, he's hardly likely to be hiding under our noses, and if he doesn't, why not catch a flight home?"

"So where's his body?"

Kubu shrugged. "Maybe they killed him in the Kalahari when they grabbed Heiseb. They had Heiseb, and Collins was an inconvenient witness."

"And the emails are just misdirection? Trying to make us think that Collins is still alive and behind all this?"

Kubu nodded.

"But then why kill Heiseb?" Mabaku asked.

"My guess is that Heiseb's death was an accident. They would want him alive to study and question. No one would've missed him. He was probably lucky they were rough enough with him to break his neck right when they grabbed him."

Mabaku pondered. "It does all add up that way. Three people dead for some hocus-pocus that no one with any sense would believe."

Kubu said nothing for several moments, thinking back to Ian's reaction and to his experience with Joy about Nono.

"That's not the point," he said at last. "What matters is what these people believe."

"But who are 'these people'?"

Kubu shrugged.

Mabaku shook his head. "Go after that shipping company. Their name is on the manifest for shipping the coffin, and now Gampone has linked them to smuggling to China. I don't believe in coincidences any more than you do."

Kubu nodded, already thinking how best to handle the delicate job of investigating Botswana Logistics.

CHAPTER 43

When Kubu arrived at Botswana Logistics the next morning, a receptionist greeted him at the main entrance and escorted him to the manager's office. The man introduced himself as Rra Mendepe and seemed completely cooperative and at ease.

"I can assure you that we keep very strict records; we have to, in our business. You said this matter is about a delivery that you're investigating?"

"We're investigating a particular shipment that this paper-work indicates was handled by your company. Please take a look."

Kubu passed him the manifest and sat back. Mendepe spent a few moments going through it. At one point, Mendepe glanced at Kubu, looking puzzled, and then returned to his reading.

At last he said, "The papers look okay, but I can't remember this matter at all. I don't think we've ever handled the shipping of a dead body, and it would certainly have been referred to me. Also, I don't recognize the signature. Frankly, I think it's a fake. Someone stole one of our blank forms and filled it in. Let's go and check with shipping."

Mendepe took Kubu on a rapid tour of the facilities, checking with each person they met, but no one could add anything. Eventually they came to Mma Tomale's small cubicle, which was so stacked with papers and printouts that she hardly had room for herself and her computer. Mendepe introduced her as his bookkeeper and explained the problem to her.

She frowned as she scanned the waybill. Kubu watched her carefully for any reaction. At first he thought she looked a little nervous, but she hid it well.

"I've never seen it before," she said. "We should check the manifest number."

"That's not going to work," Kubu responded. "I phoned last week and was told that there's no record of that number."

"No record? That's impossible!" she said. "Then it must be a fake. There's no other explanation." She handed the document back.

"How difficult would it be to copy your documents? Or to get a blank form?" Kubu asked.

She shrugged. "They're just preprinted forms. There're stacks of them all over the place. They're not like checks, Assistant Superintendent."

She's a cool customer, Kubu thought. If she's up to her neck in this—and if Gampone is to be believed, she is—then she's a good actress.

"Let me fill you in," Kubu said. "We think this document was faked to ship something out of Botswana, and it wasn't the body of a Chinese girl, as the papers claim."

Mendepe was looking uncomfortable. "Assistant Superintendent, this issue has nothing to do with our company. We operate strictly within the law. No shortcuts."

"I think the people behind this simply wanted to get their goods shipped safely through customs. What interests us is whether this is the first time or if it's an ongoing situation."

Before Mendepe could answer, Tomale said, "Impossible. We'd

have a stack of invoices not matching our system. We'd have picked it up long ago."

Kubu tried another approach. "Can you check if other parcels have been sent to the same address—even the same city—over the past six months? Maybe smaller parcels were just sent through the usual channels with genuine documents. Then we might get a link to the sender."

"I can check," Tomale said. "If Rra Mendepe says it's okay, of course."

Mendepe nodded. "The police can obtain that information from customs anyway. We want to help in any way we can."

"Thank you, rra, mma," Kubu said. "You've been very helpful. I want to ask you to do two things. First, keep this to yourselves; don't discuss it with your colleagues here."

Mendepe nodded at once. Kubu wasn't surprised he was pleased to keep the matter private.

"Yes, of course," Tomale said, looking relieved.

"Second, please come to the CID today and make a statement about what you've told me, and let us have the details of any other shipments to Qingdao, and their manifests, if possible. If anything else occurs to you, you let me know."

Again they agreed.

Kubu left his card and took his leave. He didn't really care about the statements, but he wanted a sample of Tomale's handwriting to compare with the signatures on the waybill for the coffin. It was worth checking, but probably it wouldn't lead anywhere. Tomale wasn't stupid. His hunch was that if they were going to catch her, it would have to be red-handed, and in that case they were going to have to take a risk. Gampone was going to have to ship that package of rhino horn to China.

As SOON AS he got back to his office, Kubu phoned Gampone.

"Rra Gampone, this is Assistant Superintendent Bengu. We need to talk about your shipment to China."

"What about it?"

"Director Mabaku wants to use it to see if we can smoke out some snakes. It's a chance not to be missed."

There was no response.

"We checked out the logistics company you were told to use."

"And?"

"We think the company is legitimate," Kubu continued. "We think that the manager doesn't know what's going on. That makes it much easier for us."

"How so?"

"This is what we want you to do. You told the director that your contact in China told you to conceal the rhino horn powder in one of four similar wooden statues. Correct?"

"Yes."

"Can you find appropriate statues?"

"No problem. That's part of my export business. I have thousands. I'll drill a hole in each of them from underneath the base up towards the head. I'll put the powder in one and plug it with a bolt that's flush with the bottom. For the other three, I'll stuff the hole with sawdust and then seal it with an identical bolt. All four will look the same. As an added precaution, I'll glue green baize on the bottom."

"What if they x-ray the parcel?"

"Unless they've a very sophisticated machine, nothing will show up. Even with the best, it'll be difficult to detect."

"Thank you, Rra Gampone. Please bring the statues here as soon as possible so we can fill one with powder."

"No way! I can't arrive there with a big box, stay awhile, then leave with it. And then take it to the shipping company. You're crazy! I'll be dead meat."

Gampone had a point.

Kubu thought for a moment. "Here's what we'll do. Go and have dinner at the Wimpy at Game City about six o'clock. We'll arrange to get the powder to you without being noticed. Just try to behave normally. If you aren't contacted, go home, and we'll try again. That'll only happen if we don't think we can make the drop safely."

"And then?"

"Then you'll deliver your parcel to Botswana Logistics tomorrow morning. That's it."

"And then what happens?"

"Then it's in our court. You don't have to worry about that."

After he hung up, Kubu wondered whether what they were doing was wise. It would cause an international ruckus if something went wrong and the Botswana police were reported as dealing in rhino horn.

GAMPONE ARRIVED AT Game City just after six o'clock and found a parking spot reasonably close to the Wimpy. He walked through the mall, went to the Wimpy, and waited to be given a table.

"Inside or out, sir?"

"Inside is fine," he replied.

He sat down, perused the menu, and ordered a hamburger and a large coffee.

How is this going to happen? he wondered, looking around.

He signaled the waitress, who walked over.

"Do you have a newspaper?" he asked.

"I'll get one for you," she replied.

Gampone browsed through the paper, not paying attention to anything until his meal arrived.

He ate slowly to give the person making the drop some time. But nothing happened. When he finished the hamburger, he ordered a waffle for dessert and another cup of coffee.

When he drained the last of the coffee, still no contact had been made, so he decided to leave. He paid and walked outside, wondering what would happen next.

As he approached his car, the inevitable parking attendant trotted over. "I watch your car," he said. "Car safe with me."

Gampone put his hand in his pocket to find a two-pula coin—anything more was tantamount to paying a blackmailer's ransom. To his irritation, all he had was a five-pula coin, which he reluctantly gave to the attendant.

"Thank you," he mumbled.

He unlocked his car and climbed in. Just as he was about to put the key in the ignition, he noticed a parcel on the passenger seat. It hadn't been there before.

He looked around, but there was no one to be seen. Even the parking attendant had disappeared.

"Fuck," he said.

CHAPTER 44

Kubu's mood was much improved the next morning. He and Joy were closing the gap between them and had held each other in bed as they tried to explain what had happened. They didn't make love, but the renewed intimacy filled him with hope.

There was a glimmer of good news, too, about Nono. The doctor had reported that her signs had made a small, but significant, improvement with the new cocktail she was now taking.

"Give it a few more days," the doctor had said. "Then we'll have a much better prognosis."

So there was a spring in Kubu's step when he arrived at work early to keep track of the parcel Gampone was sending to China. Since Gampone had indicated that government officials could be involved in the rhino horn smuggling, Kubu was hesitant to include anyone else in his plans. However, whatever way he looked at it, he couldn't accomplish what he wanted alone. He was going to have to trust someone else.

He'd decided that Tole, his contact at customs, was the obvious person, even though his position could allow him to be on the take.

He'd ask Tole to track parcels going to China over the next few days and report back.

I have to take the risk, Kubu thought.

First, he called Gampone to find out the status of the parcel.

"I have it packed and ready to go," Gampone told him.

"Please take a few photos and email them to me, together with the dimensions." He gave Gampone his email address. "When are you going to drop it off?"

"I spoke to this Tomale woman, and she said to come in at half past twelve. Probably there won't be many other people there then. They'll be out to lunch."

"Good," said Kubu. "We'll take it from there."

"What'll you do?" Gampone asked.

Kubu decided that Gampone didn't need to know. "We won't do anything this time. We'll let it go through. We hope that you'll get another request for more sometime soon. Then we can take action."

There was silence on the line.

"You don't think you should strike now?" Gampone asked.

"No. It's not like someone's about to be murdered. We need to play this very carefully so we have a chance of getting the big boys in China."

"You know how much that rhino horn powder is worth?" Gampone asked. "You can't just let it go."

"If we lose it, we lose it," Kubu responded. "It's more important to catch who's responsible, don't you think? Anyway, it's not yours; it belongs to CITES, doesn't it?"

"Yes."

"So, what are you worrying about?"

"If I lose it, I'll lose all the contacts in China. I'll be back to square one."

"No. We're going to do it my way."

There was silence on the line for a few seconds. "Well, it's your call," Gampone said, and hung up.

After he'd finished talking to Gampone, Kubu called Tole at customs and made an appointment to see him.

Then Kubu sat for a few minutes, thinking through his plan. He hoped he'd convinced Gampone that the parcel was going to China unimpeded. He still didn't completely trust the man, so it was prudent to be careful. Now he was going to see if he could trust Tole.

It would be so much easier if people were honest, he thought. But then I would be out of a job!

AT LUNCHTIME, KUBU decided to stop in and see Nono. When he saw her, he was encouraged. She was sitting up, although her eyes were closed. He sat on the edge of the bed and took her hand.

"Hello, darling."

She opened her eyes. "Hello, Daddy. I'm not so tired today. I've even watched a little TV." She pointed to a set that was positioned on the wall opposite her. She lifted the remote and turned it off.

This is a little progress, he thought, unconsciously touching the wooden bedside table. She'll be back at home soon.

"I want Mommy and Tumi to come and see me today."

"They're coming later. Would you like them to bring you an ice cream? Maybe an Eskimo Pie?"

Nono didn't reply. Her eyes were closed again.

Kubu sat for a few more minutes, then leaned over and kissed her gently on the cheek.

"I love you," he said, then left.

WHEN KUBU RETURNED to his office after lunch, there was a voice mail from Gampone saying that the parcel had been delivered safely to Mma Tomale. She hadn't said anything, other than thanking him for dropping it off, and when he'd tried to ask a few questions, she'd ignored him and gone into a back room. The message ended with Gampone asking Kubu to call him.

Kubu decided that could wait and settled down to fill out some expense sheets.

A short while later, Samantha came into his office and sat down.

"A dead end," she said. "I went to FedEx and UPS. They do ship to China, of course, but neither of them had any manifests with delivery addresses or shipper addresses anything like the one on the coffin. I asked them if they had ever shipped coffins. They said they hadn't. I think they're both in the clear."

"I expected that," Kubu said. "I only hope that Botswana Logistics comes through with something useful. If they have anything, they'll drop it off just after five this afternoon. You can stop by, if you like, and we can go through whatever they have together."

IT WAS HALF past four when reception called Kubu. "A Rra Mendepe from Botswana Logistics is here to see you."

"Bring him up, please."

A few minutes later, when Mendepe had settled in a chair across from Kubu, he handed Kubu an envelope.

"My statement is in there. Also Mma Tomale's. They've both been witnessed. If you need anything more, please let us know."

"What about the addresses?"

"Surprisingly, we found three other shipments in the past seven months to the same address in Qingdao as the coffin was shipped— two from the same sender and one different. I've enclosed the manifests in the envelope too." He hesitated. "What are you going to do?" he asked. "If something like this coffin thing happens again, it's going to cause us a lot of problems."

"I don't know what we'll do just yet," Kubu replied. "But if we find out anything, we'll let you know. Thank you for your cooperation."

He stood up and escorted Mendepe to the front door.

"Make sure you keep this confidential," Kubu said. "It'll be much more difficult to resolve if it gets out."

Mendepe nodded and left.

Kubu stopped by Samantha's office on his way back. "They've dropped off the information. Come and let's take a look."

A few minutes later, Samantha and Kubu were excited. Two of the parcels had been sent from a shop in Africa Mall and the third by a Ben Dan with a Gaborone street address. The only disappointment was that all fees had been paid in cash, so there was no credit-card or bank trail.

"Look," Kubu said. "The one shipment from the shop was sent just before the Bushman was killed, and the other just after. The one from the other address was sent just after we think Ramala was kidnapped." He gave a little fist pump.

"This may be the breakthrough we've been looking for," Samantha said.

"Tomorrow will tell," Kubu responded. "Get on it first thing in the morning."

CHAPTER 45

Samantha didn't wait until the next day to follow up the addresses from Botswana Logistics. After she left Kubu's office, she immediately went online to check them. The first turned out not to exist; there wasn't even a street with the name given on the manifest. She wasn't surprised. It would be more surprising if someone engaged in illegal activities used their real address.

Then she Googled the shop in Africa Mall. It did exist, and specialized in herbal remedies, potions, and lotions.

She picked up the phone and dialed Kubu's office. There was no answer.

"Damn!" she said out loud. She'd have to wait until the next day to share her news.

Samantha arrived at Africa Mall at eight o'clock the next morning and found a woman taking down the shutters at the address she'd written in her notebook. The banner above the window read "Dr. Nyoka," and below it, "Herbalist—Penis enlargement—Pregnancy." And below that, "Satisfaction Gauranteed! Mony back."

Obviously didn't use a professional sign writer, she thought.

"*Dumela,* mma," she greeted the wizened woman.

The woman looked at her and nodded. "Wait inside," she said, and continued taking down the shutters.

"I'm not here for an appointment or medicine," Samantha said.

"Wait inside."

"My name is Detective Khama, from the police." Samantha showed the woman her badge. "I need to speak to you."

"Wait inside."

Samantha gave up and walked into the dark shop and was assailed by a variety of smells, both sweet and bitter. She gazed at the rows of jars containing who knew what. She shuddered. She certainly wouldn't trust her life or her sex life to this woman.

Eventually the woman came into the shop.

"Why are you here? I pay my taxes. Everything is proper. Do you want to see my certificate?"

"No, mma. Do you remember anything about these parcels you sent to China?" She handed the woman the two manifests.

"Yes. I sent these to the sick mother of Dr. Hairong."

"Dr. Hairong?" Samantha asked. Somehow the name seemed familiar, but she couldn't place it.

"Yes. He comes here often to ask about medicine to help his old mother. Sometimes he sends some to her."

"What sort of medicine?"

"Medicines I make from plants I get from the Kalahari."

"What plants were they? Where did you get them?"

"They are very powerful and secret. Where I get them is secret."

Samantha decided it wasn't going to help at the moment to push for those details.

"Do you know where Dr. Hairong lives or how I can contact him?"

The woman shook her head. "I don't know. He pays cash for everything."

"Does he come in often?"

"No. Every now and again. Why do you want to see him?"

"We need some information about one of the parcels. Please let me know if he comes in again. Here's my card."

The woman took it and studied it carefully.

"One other thing," Samantha continued. "Please take a look at this photo. Do you recognize the man?"

The woman looked at the photo. "Yes, that's Dr. Hairong, all right. Not a very good picture though."

Samantha could barely contain her excitement. The photo she'd shown the woman was from the Chinese embassy's CCTV video of the Mr. Ho who'd arranged the shipping of the coffin.

KUBU WAS SITTING in his office when Samantha came bursting in. "Ho isn't his real name!" she exclaimed. "Actually it's Hairong." Then she paused. "Or maybe that's not his real name either."

"Slow down, Samantha, and sit down. Tell me what you've found out."

Samantha sat down, took a deep breath, and explained what had happened at the herbalist shop of Dr. Nyoka. "The person who sent those parcels to Qingdao calls himself Hairong. It's the same person as the Mr. Ho in the CCTV, who got the embassy to authorize the shipment of the body back to China. It's probably the same person who signed the girl's death certificate."

"That's very interesting." Kubu leaned back in his chair. "What about the address on the third parcel? Does this Hairong live there?"

"The address doesn't exist. But, Kubu, I thought of something else. The afternoon that Ramala disappeared he had a meeting with a 'Hair On.' I could never find what that meant. But perhaps that's how Ramala wrote 'Hairong' in his appointment book." She paused. "We've made a good connection, but haven't got much closer to finding him."

"Well, I'm hoping we'll hear back from Interpol in the next few days about the rhino horn Gampone sent. It should go out today.

Then we'll arrest Mma Tomale at Botswana Logistics and squeeze her. I'm sure she must know our Dr. Hairong or our Mr. Ho or whatever his real name is. This is all related. I think it's safe to say we've made some progress at last. Well done."

Samantha smiled.

"To come back down to earth, Samantha, did you speak to Mma Ramala?"

"I did. It was awful, Kubu—telling her . . ."

"As I said, it won't get any easier. Now I have to do pretty much the same thing and phone Collins's wife and tell her we're beginning to believe he's dead too."

KUBU HAD JUST returned from lunch when reception alerted him that Rra Tole was there to see him.

"Bring him up," Kubu said, eager to find out where Gampone's parcel had been shipped to.

A few minutes later Tole had given Kubu a large envelope.

"There were seven shipments to China today. I took photos of each, as you asked. I thought it easier for you if I printed them. The dimensions of the parcels are on the back of each photo, and a copy of the manifest is stapled to it. There were a few odd-shaped parcels, so I took more than one photo."

"Excellent. Thank you," Kubu said, as he slid the photos out of the envelope. "This is just what I wanted."

"What are you going to do now?" Tole asked.

Even though he'd trusted Tole so far, Kubu wasn't going to trust him any further—at least not at this stage. "Nothing," he answered.

"Nothing?" Tole looked perplexed. "You mean I've done all this for nothing?"

"Not at all," Kubu said. "We're going to build a watertight case, but that takes time. I'll be asking you to do this several more times before we can take action. That's the nature of our work. Slow and methodical."

"I understand," Tole responded, even though he clearly didn't.

"Thank you for all you've done. I appreciate it," Kubu said, standing up.

"It's a pleasure. Let me know when I can help again."

As soon as Tole had left, Kubu shuffled through the photos and identified the parcel Gampone had sent. He was relieved—he'd thought it likely that Tomale would have repackaged the shipment to make it difficult to trace.

"Let's see who sent it," he said out loud.

The sender was listed as Ben Dan at a Gaborone address. Kubu Googled the address, but it didn't exist. He also Googled the sender's name. There was no such person in Botswana, as far as he could see, but the word *bèndàn* apparently meant "idiot" in Chinese.

"Very funny," Kubu muttered. Then the name struck him, and he checked his notes. Ben Dan was also the sender of one of the packages from the traditional medicine shop. That was interesting.

Next he Googled the address the parcel was going to in Shanghai. It existed, but there were no hits on the company name. Finally, Kubu opened Google Maps and typed in the address. The building that showed up was a high-rise.

Not very helpful, he thought.

Kubu decided it was time to update the director, so he walked over to his office.

"What've you got?" Mabaku asked as Kubu opened the door.

Kubu gave him all the details he'd just found out.

Mabaku thought for a moment. "Alert Interpol and let them run with it there. Perhaps they'll be able to track the parcel once it gets to China. Probably there's someone in customs or with a courier company who'll intercept it before delivery. It would be too risky for the address to be the real destination."

"Thank you, Director. I think things are about to break."

It was around four o'clock that afternoon that Kubu picked up his phone and dialed the Collins' number in Minneapolis.

"Mrs. Collins? Assistant Superintendent Bengu here."

"Do you have any news about Chris?"

Kubu took a deep breath. "No, I haven't. Mrs. Collins, you have to prepare yourself that he's not coming back. Sadly, we think it's very likely that he's dead."

She started to sob.

"Nothing's been heard from him for a month now, and the last two emails you received were from unregistered cell phones here in Gaborone. The last place we believe he was, was where the Bushman Heiseb was murdered, because we found his abandoned vehicle near there."

"Have you searched the whole area?"

"As much as we can. Unfortunately, the Kalahari is a big place, and we may never find his body. I'm so sorry."

There was silence on the line for a few moments. "I'm going to come to Botswana, Assistant Superintendent. Brian Ross and I will hire some people to help us. And a helicopter. Whatever it takes to find him—or his body."

"Mrs. Collins, obviously you must do whatever you need to do, but I must urge you not to get your hopes up. We know the country and haven't been able to find your husband. It's not likely you'll find him alive."

"But I have to try . . ."

"I understand that. If you do come, please phone me as soon as you arrive. I'll do whatever I can to help."

"Thank you. I will."

Kubu sat for a few moments, thinking about love. Petra Collins was willing to do anything to find her husband, and Joy was willing to do anything to save Nono.

But me—my head gets in the way of my heart.

CHAPTER 46

When Kubu arrived at work on Monday morning, he was keen to move forward on the cases. The weekend had been relaxed, but not without anxiety. On Saturday, the family had visited Nono twice. The good news was that she was holding her own—her CD4 count hadn't deteriorated, and she felt less tired than before. The bad news was that she wasn't improving. In the evening, Joy decided they all needed a change, so they had dinner at Riverwalk Mall and went to an animated children's movie, the name of which Kubu had already forgotten.

On Sunday, he'd wanted his mother to visit them in Gaborone, but she'd refused to allow him to drive up to fetch her in Mochudi and then make the return trip to bring her home.

"My son," she'd said, "when my Wilmon was alive, you used to visit us here. It is time you come here again. Now, do as I tell you."

Kubu had acquiesced. On the way, they'd visited an unchanged Nono, and although Joy had packed a lovely cold lunch, as in the old days, the mood had been restrained.

Just after ten o'clock, Kubu received the call he'd been anxiously awaiting—from Interpol in China. A Chief Superintendent Lu in Beijing told Kubu that the police in Shanghai had watched the parcel being picked up at the Shanghai airport, then followed it to an address that they'd had under surveillance for some time. It was not the one on the parcel. As soon as the parcel was inside, the police raided the house and arrested seven men and three women for possession of illegal substances. They'd recovered the parcel and verified that the contents were rhino horn powder.

"We thank you for the information, Assistant Superintendent," Chief Superintendent Lu continued. "Four of the men and one of the women are wanted for other offenses, so we will deal with them harshly. We think two of the other men are high up in the chain that is responsible for the smuggling. We are confident that they will tell us who is higher up."

Kubu shuddered as he thought about what would make them talk.

"Please email me the names of all the people you arrested and note which are the two most important ones. I may need them here for my follow-up."

Kubu gave Lu his email address.

"One last thing, Chief Superintendent. We would appreciate the return of the rhino horn powder. When can we expect it?"

"It may be a few years, because it will take time to bring all of these people to trial. Obviously we need the powder as evidence."

"I understand. But please send me a letter stating that you have the powder and confirming that it is the property of the Botswana police. We, too, will need it as evidence."

Chief Superintendent Lu agreed to do that and hung up.

I wonder if we'll ever see that powder again, Kubu thought. At least we can now move forward.

A CROWD GATHERED as soon as two police cars stopped in front of Botswana Logistics and a third raced around behind the building. There was a buzz when a handcuffed Mma Tomale was led out and pushed into the backseat of one of the cars. She was followed out of the front door by the manager, Mendepe, who was arguing with Kubu that he must have arrested the wrong person.

"What has she done?" he kept asking. "You can't take her away. She's my best employee."

When he reached the police car, Kubu turned to him. "Rra Mendepe, after I have questioned her, I'll tell you what this is all about. In the meantime, carry on as usual."

Mendepe opened his mouth to protest once again, but Kubu climbed into the car and shut the door.

"If he keeps on like this, I'll arrest him too," he muttered to the driver. "Let's go."

KUBU AND SAMANTHA kept Tomale waiting in the interrogation room for several hours while they had a leisurely lunch, spending most of the time planning their approach to extracting the information they needed—mainly the names of the people she worked with and the names of those involved in the two murders.

When they eventually opened the door to the interrogation room, she sat looking sullenly at them.

After he'd completed the formalities for taping the session, Kubu pulled out his notebook and turned to Tomale.

"Mma Tomale, you have been arrested for smuggling an illegal substance out of the country, namely rhino horn."

"That is not true! I—"

"Mma Tomale, let's not waste time here. Let me explain the evidence we have already."

Kubu then laid out the whole scenario: that the police had received information that a Jonah Gampone had been told to deliver a parcel to her, that he was already facing charges of smuggling, that she had prepared the manifest, and finally, that the parcel had been intercepted in China and was found to contain rhino horn.

"All your friends in China have been arrested. Just like you."

"Mma Tomale." It was now Samantha's turn. "We're investigating two cases that we think are related. The first is your smuggling case. We want to know who else is involved here in Gaborone or any other southern African country, as well as who your contacts are in China and Vietnam. The second case is the murder of—"

"I know nothing about any murders!"

"Listen and don't interrupt," Kubu growled.

"The second case is the murder of a Bushman known as Heiseb and a traditional healer whose name was Ramala—*Kgosi* Ramala, as he called himself."

"I tell you I know nothing about any murders!"

"That's what they all say," Kubu said to Samantha. "It's amazing how innocent everyone is until they're in court and the judge is going to sentence them." He turned back to Tomale. "You know that we have the death penalty here in Botswana, don't you?"

"I didn't kill anybody!" Tomale was screaming now.

Again he and Samantha laid out what charges they could already bring against her and what information they wanted on both the smuggling and the murder cases.

"I promise I don't know anything about any murders." Her voice was now low and breaking.

"Who is helping you with the smuggling? If you don't help us now, you'll spend the night in jail and we'll continue in the morning. This is your last chance to answer today; otherwise, I'm going home to my family."

Tomale slumped.

"There are two others in Gaborone that I know: Clarence Khumalo and Boy Sedombo. They bring me parcels sometimes. If I want to contact them, I leave a message at a number. If you give me my phone, I can tell you what it is."

Kubu nodded at Samantha, who left to find it.

He turned back to Tomale and grilled her for the next fifteen minutes, learning only how she was paid—in cash, given to her by Sedombo by hand.

When Samantha returned with Tomale's smartphone, it took

her only a few moments to find the number and give it to the detectives.

"Thank you," Kubu said. "We'll see you in the morning. A constable will come and take you to your cell in a few minutes."

Tomale jumped up. "You said I could go if I told you what you wanted," she screamed.

Kubu shook his head. "No. I said I'd go home to my family if you didn't. Have a good night."

As Kubu and Samantha walked back to their offices, Kubu said, "Put a trace on the number she gave us. Do that right away and say it is urgent. I want the information first thing in the morning. Then we'll bring in the two men she mentioned. We probably should take a SWAT team—they could be dangerous. Hopefully that will lead us to Dr. Hairong or Mr. Ho or whatever he calls himself. Then we'll be close to catching the people who committed those murders."

CHAPTER 47

When she got back to her office, Samantha learned that Lani Muru, the man Legotlo said had witnessed the abduction of Ramala, had been found and was being brought to the CID. Torn between the imminent arrest of the smugglers and following up on Muru, Samantha went to ask Kubu what to do.

"Muru could be important," Kubu told her. "Tomale's given us nothing that links the smuggling and the murders. Probably Khumalo and Sedombo will break, but it'll help if we have an eyewitness, and Muru might have seen one of them when Ramala was taken. You follow up on Muru. I need to arrange surveillance on Khumalo and Sedombo's homes. Then we can both focus on the smugglers when they're brought in."

So Samantha went back to her office and dug out the file she'd been building on Muru. Actually, there wasn't much: a few complaints of loitering, and a couple who had accused him of being a pickpocket, but nothing provable. She stuffed some scrap paper into the back of the file to make it look thicker, added a couple of pictures of the elusive Ho aka Hairong, and waited to be called.

Muru wasn't an impressive individual. He sat slouched in his chair. His clothes looked as though he slept in them—which he probably did—and he smelled as though he hadn't had a shower for weeks—which he probably hadn't. He looked at her insolently.

"Why've you brought me here? I've done nothing."

Samantha sat opposite him and opened the file. "Oh, you've done plenty. It's all in here." She tapped the file. "But what I want right now is some information. Maybe all this can go away." She tapped the file again.

"I don't know anything, either," Muru responded.

"Yes, you do. What did you see at Riverwalk on the fifteenth of last month?"

Muru frowned. "How am I supposed to remember that? That was three weeks ago." He shrugged. "Who says I was even at Riverwalk?"

"That's what you told Legotlo."

"That rat," Muru sneered. "That's what he does—rat on people. On his friends. I don't care what he told you. I didn't see anything. I wasn't even there."

"So where were you?"

"How do I know? Like I said, it was weeks ago."

"So how do you know you weren't there?" She indicated the file again. "It says in here you're always loitering around there, trying to find an unguarded pocket."

"That's lies. The shops don't like me being there because I sell tourists stuff cheaper than they do."

"Look, we know what happened to Ramala. We just want you to confirm it. Tell me what you saw."

Muru looked at her as though he didn't believe what he was hearing. "You crazy or something? These people are bad, really bad. They'll have you for breakfast." He snorted. "You're going to protect me? They send a girl to protect me."

"I'm not a *girl*!" Samantha could feel herself losing her temper, and let it happen. "Look, you pathetic excuse for a man, you cooperate, or we'll hit you with this." She waved the thick file at him. "You'll do time. You won't like *that*."

"Don't make me laugh. None of that stuff will stick. I'll be out of here in half an hour, once I get a lawyer. And I want one. You've got to get me one."

"Maybe you're right," Samantha said thoughtfully. "Why bother with you? Maybe we'll just let you go. We'll tell the press you were just helping us with your account of seeing the men who grabbed *Kgosi* Ramala."

That had the desired effect. "You can't do that!" he said, jumping to his feet. "I'll be mincemeat. They'll kill me. You can't do that."

Samantha said nothing, but she didn't break eye contact, and it was Muru who looked down first. "All right, if I help you, you'll keep me out of it, and that file gets lost?"

"I'll see what I can do."

Muru sat down. "Well, I was at Riverwalk. I remember now."

Samantha nodded.

"I spotted Ramala. He was walking round the front of the shopping center, coming towards the Mugg and Bean. I thought he'd remember me, maybe want to buy something, or lend me a few pula, or at least give me a cigarette." He paused. "You got any cigarettes?"

Samantha shook her head. "You knew him?"

Muru nodded. "Sometimes he helped me with stuff. Before he became so famous and rich."

"What time was this?"

"Early afternoon."

"And then?"

"Then I saw this big Chinese guy get up from a table and wave him over. After that I backed off. You don't get involved with those guys. Ramala joined the men at the table. Three of them. All Chinese. Thugs. It seemed fine at first, but then they start arguing. The big Chinese guy gets up and goes over to Ramala and says something into his ear. After that, there's no more arguing, and they all leave. The big guy holding Ramala's arm."

"They must've threatened him."

"Something like that," Muru said. "Their car was parked right at the front of the lot. Ramala and the guy walking with him get in the back, one of the others gets in the driver's seat, and the third walks away. Then they drive off."

Samantha dug in her file and produced the pictures of Ho.

"Was this one of the men?"

Muru looked at them carefully. "I'm not sure," he said. "It could be. These Chinese people all look the same. Is this a big guy?"

Samantha realized that she didn't know. "What happened to the third Chinese man?"

Muru shrugged. "He walked off round the back. Maybe he went to drive Ramala's car. I don't know."

"Can you describe the car the Chinese were in?"

"Come on. It was three weeks ago."

Samantha sighed. She'd gone to a lot of trouble to get Muru talking, but so far he'd added nothing to the story Legotlo had already told them. There had to be something more. She stared across the table at Muru until he looked away.

"Okay, look, I do remember something about their car," he said at last. "Actually, it was a double cab. I don't know what make, but it was silver, or maybe metallic blue—anyway a light color. Maybe gray, but not white."

Samantha felt a stirring of hope. There couldn't be too many cars like that around.

"Did you get the registration number?"

Muru shook his head. "But when it went out, I saw it had a sticker in the window. Like a Chinese flag. Yellow stars on a red background."

"Listen, Muru, you better not be holding anything back or you *will* need someone to protect you. I can talk to the newspapers anytime."

He shook his head. "That's it. Look, you going to get these guys? If you don't, I'm going to end up as dead as Ramala."

"We'll get them once we know where they are," Samantha said.

Muru looked at her incredulously again. "People say they run the casinos, everything! What's the problem?"

Samantha shook her head. "You better hope I find them."

CHAPTER 48

It wasn't difficult for the police to find out where the two men that Tomale had named lived. Clarence Khumalo rented an apartment in Old Naledi and Boy Sedombo owned a house in Extension 48, not far from the A1 highway.

Starting on Tuesday morning, each place was staked out by a plainclothes policeman armed with photos lifted from the men's driver's license records. They were to report back to Kubu and Samantha as soon as they'd made a positive identification. If the men left again, they were to be followed discreetly. Kubu didn't want them to become suspicious.

While this was happening, Kubu, Samantha, and Mabaku formulated a plan to take the men into custody with the least amount of risk.

"Remember, they may be dangerous," Mabaku warned. "We don't want any more bodies lying around."

They decided that the best plan was to ready two SWAT teams, one for each home. If the men returned home for the night, each SWAT team would attempt to arrest its man, hopefully while he was still asleep, in the early hours of Wednesday morning. Once in custody, the men would be taken to the holding cells at CID headquarters. Both places would then be searched for anything that would help with the poaching and murder cases.

"What if there are other people in the house?" Samantha asked as they reviewed the plans.

"Bring them all in," Kubu replied. "We can let them go later if we have to. I don't want anyone slipping through our net."

Mabaku nodded in agreement. "Let's hope we catch the right bastards," he said. "This whole mess has been going on too long."

KUBU'S PHONE RANG at seven o'clock on Wednesday morning. The head of the SWAT teams reported that they'd brought in three men—their targets, Clarence Khumalo and Boy Sedombo, as well as a third man, who was in the apartment with Khumalo.

"This third man. Is he Chinese?" Kubu asked.

"No. He's black. But I get the sense that he's a foreigner."

"Keep an eye on them," Kubu said. "I'll be there just after eight. Please let Detective Khama know as well. I'll contact the director."

KUBU DECIDED TO interview Sedombo first because he was the younger of the two men and unlikely to be the leader. Kubu wanted as much information as possible before tackling Khumalo.

The first hour was unproductive. Sedombo denied having anything to do with Tomale.

"I've never heard of her," he said repeatedly.

He also denied he was involved in any smuggling.

"I work as an auto mechanic. You can ask my boss."

Kubu took the details and left the room to ask Samantha to follow up. In return, she handed Kubu a printout.

"These are his bank statements for the last year. Some interesting deposits there." She handed Kubu a second stack of paper. "And these are Khumalo's statements. Some nice matches between the two. Seems cash is king."

Kubu spent a few minutes looking at what Samantha had given him. She'd taken the time to annotate them, so finding the withdrawals and associated deposits was easy. However, there were a number of sizable cash deposits into Khumalo's account that had no source.

"There's something else you should see," Samantha said. "Come with me."

She led Kubu to the evidence room, where, after completing the formalities, she retrieved a large evidence bag containing a briefcase. "They found it at Khumalo's apartment, under the bed the other man was sleeping in."

She slipped on some latex gloves and took the briefcase out of the bag.

"I picked the locks. They weren't very good."

She opened the top. Kubu gasped. The briefcase was full of American dollars, mainly hundreds and fifties.

"There's a fortune in there," he said.

"Nearly a hundred and twenty thousand dollars."

There were also two passports, both with the same picture. One was a Nigerian passport sporting the name Bernard Oni, and the other was a South African one with the name Bernard Qolo. Kubu flipped through them quickly.

"Neither has a Botswana entry stamp," Kubu said. "The man's in the country illegally, and at least one of these passports is a fake. Good!"

"RRA SEDOMBO," KUBU said, after returning to the interview room. "Please could you explain these five cash deposits for ten thousand pula." He read off the dates from the printout.

Sedombo hemmed and hawed and eventually came up with a story that he'd done some special work on a rich man's car.

"Five times?" Kubu asked.

Sedombo nodded. "It needed a lot of work."

"What is the name of the man who hired you?"

"I can't remember."

"Where did he live, then?"

Sedombo shrugged.

"Okay, where did you do the work? And what sort of car was it?"

"It was at the garage where I work. On Sundays."

"And the type of car?"

"A BMW seven series."

"And the color?"

"Black," Sedombo stammered.

"Do you know a Clarence Khumalo?"

Sedombo looked panic-stricken. "No. I mean yes. I mean, I've heard of him."

"Was it Khumalo who gave you these big amounts of cash?"

"No. It was the owner of the car."

Kubu pushed Khumalo's bank statements in front of Sedombo. "Look here," he said. "Every time your 'car owner' paid you, Khumalo withdrew the identical amount of cash from his bank account. I'm going to speak to him in a few minutes. I'm sure he'll confirm that he paid you these amounts. Then you'll be caught in a lie. And I'm sure that you know lying to the police is a major offense." He paused. "Have you seen the inside of our jails? They're not very nice."

Kubu stood up to leave.

"It was Khumalo," Sedombo whispered. "Please don't tell him I told you. He'll kill me."

"Kill you?" Kubu asked. "Have you seen him kill people?"

"No, never. But he'll beat me up if he knows I told you."

Kubu spent the next ten minutes extracting more information about Khumalo and what Sedombo did to deserve the payments. Eventually he confessed that he worked with people in South Africa to move rhino horns out of the country.

"What do you do for them?"

"I pick stuff up in Groot Marico, bring it into Botswana, and pack it for shipping."

"Where does it go to?"

"I don't know. Khumalo handles that."

ARMED WITH THE information from Sedombo, it didn't take Kubu long to get Khumalo to confess to also being involved in smuggling rhino horn from South Africa. His job was to coordinate and manage the operation in Botswana. He also confirmed that Sedombo was just a messenger.

Then Kubu turned to asking about the man who was sleeping in Khumalo's apartment. Immediately, Khumalo shook his head. "I'm not saying anything. Just a friend of a friend who needed a place to sleep."

"Do you know his name?"

"No. But it's Sam, I think."

"Who's your friend?"

"Just someone I know from a bar. Don't know his name, either. We call him Mick."

"So, let me understand this. You know someone from a bar, but you don't know his name. He asks you to let a friend of his stay with you, but you don't know his name, either. Is that right?"

Khumalo nodded.

"Well, let me tell you something," Kubu said, leaning forward. "These big cash deposits into your account, including one from two days ago—I think your friend gives them to you for managing his business here in Gabs. And I'm going to get his bank accounts and tie his withdrawals to your deposits. I'm sure the judge will be very interested in that."

He stared at the forlorn Khumalo.

"Who is he? What's his name?"

Khumalo just shook his head.

"And what about *Kgosi* Ramala?" Kubu asked. "Why did you kill him?"

"Kill Ramala? I've never killed anyone. And I'd be mad to kill a witch doctor."

"You know *Kgosi* Ramala?"

"Of course. Everyone knows of him. But I've never spoken to him."

"And Christopher Collins?"

Khumalo looked blank. "Who?"

Kubu was sure that Khumalo didn't know who Collins was.

"One last question for now," Kubu continued. "What are you doing with a hundred thousand dollars in your apartment?"

Khumalo looked as though he could fall off his chair. "A hundred thousand dollars? I don't have any dollars. It must be Bernard's."

"So it's not Sam now. And what is Bernard's last name?"

Khumalo didn't say anything.

"If you can't explain how that money got to be in your apartment," Kubu said, "I'll have to assume it's been stolen. And that you stole it."

"Good afternoon, Mr. Oni, or is it Qolo? Or perhaps neither." Kubu had just completed the formalities for recording the interview. He sat down.

"You're in a lot of trouble. Illegally in the country; trafficking a controlled substance, namely rhino horn; possession of undisclosed foreign currency; and murder."

"Murder? I've never killed anyone."

"In addition to rhino horn, we believe that you've also been exporting indigenous Botswana plants to China in contravention of biopiracy laws. We also think you killed a *Kgosi* Ramala and possibly a Christopher Collins in order to acquire plants that have the potential to prolong life. That could be much more valuable than rhino horn."

"Bullshit! I've never touched any plants, and I've never heard of those two people. You're bullshitting me."

"Let me lay things out for you, Mr. Oni. When you've heard what I have to say, I'm sure you'll find cooperating the best course of action."

. . .

"DIRECTOR, I THINK I was wrong." Kubu said. "I was certain the murders and the smuggling were linked, but now I'm not so sure."

"You mean this is all a coincidence?"

"Yes, I think so. I know you don't believe in them, Director, and neither do I. But I'm convinced this is an exception. There *is* a rhino horn gang—those are the four we have in custody, as well as the ones they've got in China. And there *are* people interested in plants promising immortality, but it's a different group. The Chinese involved in that are here in Botswana—Ho, the men who abducted Ramala, and maybe Chan at the embassy, and a few others."

"I still think they're linked," Mabaku responded. "Go and spend another day putting pressure on them all. Tell them we'll see them die in prison if they don't talk."

"Director, we can charge Tomale, Sedombo, and Khumalo right now, but I'm not sure about the fourth man. Let Samantha and me follow up a few leads before we go after him again. Anyway, I'll keep them all in custody. It'll soften them up to stew for another day in our fine accommodation."

Mabaku stared at Kubu. "Okay. One more day before we throw the book at the men downstairs."

"And the woman," Samantha said.

CHAPTER 49

First thing the next morning, Samantha went to Kubu's office and they planned what to do.

"I looked at the motor vehicle database last night," she said, "but you can only search it on owner's name or ID number and car registration number. You can't search by vehicle type or color or vehicle make. It's going to take forever if we have to go through it vehicle by vehicle. Edison never came up with Festus Moeng's vehicle using that approach."

Kubu reached for his phone and punched in an internal number. "Helenka? Good morning. I wonder if you can help us with a computer problem." He paused for a few moments, thanked her, and hung up.

"She'll be here in a minute. If anyone can work this out, she can."

An hour later Helenka came to Samantha's office with a memory stick.

"You know Excel?" she asked.

Samantha nodded.

"Okay." Helenka handed her the stick and left without another word. A bit puzzled, Samantha inserted the stick and opened the file on it. It was a large spreadsheet with thousands of entries— probably all the light motor vehicles registered in Gaborone, Samantha decided. The headings included all the attributes captured in the registration documents: the identity or passport number of the owner, nationality, and address; vehicle make, color, registration number, and year of first registration.

Samantha smiled. "Thank you, Helenka," she said out loud.

It took her a couple of minutes to sort the spreadsheet by vehicle type. Then she started checking which were registered as single or double cabs before she realized that the owners may not have included this detail on their applications. There must be an easier way, she decided.

After a few moments' thought, she sorted the spreadsheet again, this time on nationality of owner. There were less than a hundred with the People's Republic of China as their nationality, and when she selected the model type and checked which could be double cabs, she was left with just over twenty possibilities. Of those, only six had the light colors that might fit Muru's description.

She printed out the names and addresses of the owners, as well as the vehicle registration numbers, and set off, sticking her head into Kubu's office on the way out to tell him what she was up to. Kubu listened to what she'd done, nodded, and wished her luck.

She realized she needed it. Maybe the vehicle used to abduct Ramala wasn't owned by a Chinese individual; maybe it was owned by a company. Maybe it wasn't registered in the Gaborone area. Maybe the vehicle was from South Africa. At least she was pretty sure it wasn't a stolen vehicle—she'd checked through the list of those while waiting for Helenka.

All these possibilities bounced around Samantha's head as she drove off to the first address.

· · ·

THE HOUSE WAS in an upper-middle-class neighborhood and protected by a wall and electric gates. She rang the intercom, waited half a minute, and then tried again. There was a click, and an accented voice said, in English, "Yes? What you want?"

"Hello, I'm from the traffic police. I need to do a routine check on your vehicle registration. It will only take a few minutes."

There was silence, but through the gate she saw the front door open and a man walk down the driveway. He stopped some distance away. "How I know you police?" he asked.

Samantha held up her identification, and the man walked closer so that he could read it. After a few moments he pressed a remote control and the gate slid open just enough to allow her in before he closed it again. "What you want?" he repeated.

"I'm Detective Khama. Are you"—she checked her list—"Mr. C. H. Dong?"

The man nodded.

"There've been some problems with vehicle registrations. Some numbers have been duplicated by the computer. I need to check your vehicle against my information."

"You want see vehicle? In garage. I bought. Cash. Nothing wrong with registration." He made no move toward the garage.

"I just need to check it. Then I'll leave."

The man seemed to be considering his options. She didn't have a search warrant, so if he refused, there was nothing she could do about it. But why would he do that if he's got nothing to hide? Samantha wondered.

"Okay. You come." He walked off toward the garage door, which opened with another press of the remote.

The vehicle parked there was an Isuzu KB double cab. The color was a light metallic blue. Samantha swallowed. This could be it. She walked around the vehicle, but there were no stickers on any of the windows. She asked the owner to lift the hood so that she could check the engine number. She had no idea where to look, but fortunately it was on a plate in an obvious position. Finally, she took a picture with her cell phone, in the hope that Muru might react to it.

"Hey! Why you take picture?" The man seemed suddenly agitated.

"Just for my records. Everything is in order. Your registration is fine."

He digested that, apparently uncertain how to react. A woman came out of the front door and called out something in Chinese, and he answered her sharply before turning back to Samantha. "You go now," he said, pointing to the gate.

"Yes. Thank you for your help."

Once the gate closed behind her, Samantha felt relief. Either she'd upset the man or he'd been hiding something. Either way, she was pleased to be out from behind the walls and the electric gate.

She put a question mark next to the vehicle on her list.

THE NEXT VEHICLE on her list was in a less affluent part of town, and she could walk up to the door and knock. To her surprise, it was opened by a black man. Samantha showed him her identification, gave him the speech about duplicate car registrations, and then said, "I'm looking for a Rra L. E. Sin. Is this the right address?"

"Yes, Rra Sin lives here, but he's not in at the moment. I'm Jonas. I just work here."

"Is the car here?"

"Yes. Rra Sin went out with another man."

"Can I see it?"

Jonas looked dubious. "I'm not sure Rra Sin would like that."

"I just want to check the license disk. It will take a minute and save me another trip here." She smiled at him. "It would be a big help."

Jonas shrugged. "You won't touch anything? Come through to the back; the side gate's locked."

They walked through the house to the kitchen and out the back door. The vehicle, parked under a carport, was a beige color, not metallic, and had several dents and scratches. The whole situation struck Samantha as wrong for Chinese smugglers, but she had to check. She walked up to the passenger side to check the registration and inhaled sharply when she saw the large red and gold sticker on the back window. She covered her surprise by asking, "Chinese flag?"

The man nodded. "Rra Sin is very proud of his country. Always telling people how great it is."

Samantha took a picture and checked the model and registration number. "What does Rra Sin do?"

Jonas shrugged.

"Any idea when he'll be back?"

Jonas shook his head. "You done?"

Samantha nodded, and he led her back through the house.

When Jonas opened the door, a man was walking up the path toward them. He was Asian, at least six foot, and well built. He glared at Samantha and Jonas.

"Where's Sin? Who's she?"

"Mr. Sin is out. She's—"

"I'm just leaving," Samantha interrupted. She nodded to the man, brushed past him, and headed for the street. She sensed he was staring at her as she walked to her car.

Although she'd recognized him at once, she had no intention of taking him on alone. He was the man who sometimes called himself Ho and sometimes called himself Hairong.

CHAPTER 50

Samantha took her time leaving, opening the driver's window and fiddling with the ignition keys. She wanted to be sure that Ho went into the house before she moved. Then she pulled off and headed down the street, but made a U-turn as soon as she was out of sight and drove slowly back until she could see the street in front of the house. Then she pulled over next to a group of shrubs and phoned Kubu.

"You're sure it's Ho?" She could hear that he was excited.

"Yes. I only saw him for a moment, but I was right next to him."

"And he doesn't know why you were there?"

Samantha hesitated. "I told the man who works there I wanted to check the car, and he showed it to me. Perhaps Ho will guess what I was after."

"I'll grab a couple of armed constables and come right away. Call me on my cell phone if there are any developments. And don't try to take him by yourself. It's too risky." He was gone before she could reply.

After several minutes, she heard a vehicle coming up quickly behind her. It passed, pulled up outside the house, and a man jumped out of the passenger side and hurried inside. The car raced off.

Samantha checked her watch, wondering how long Kubu would be. Although it felt like ages, it had only been ten minutes since she'd phoned. *If they make a run for it, I'll have to follow them and hope Kubu catches up,* she decided.

Suddenly she heard a car approaching, moving fast. It slowed, and then pulled up in front of Sin's house, blocking the driveway. Kubu's unmistakable bulk emerged from the front seat, and two uniformed men jumped out to join him. Hugely relieved, she drove up to join them.

KUBU SENT ONE of the constables round the back of the house and positioned the other at the side of the entrance. Then he hammered on the door. "Police! Open the door! Police!"

There was no reaction, so Kubu repeated the demand and banged on the door again. Eventually the door was opened by a man who was clearly Asian and, like Ho, heavily built. But it wasn't Ho.

Kubu held up his identification. "I need your ID," he said. "Keep your hands where I can see them."

The man said nothing, but he reached for his back pocket, turning so Kubu could see what he was doing, and pulled out a Chinese passport, which he passed over to Kubu.

"You are Sin Gowei?" Kubu asked, as he checked the passport. The man nodded. "And you're the owner of the double cab parked at the back?" Again the man nodded. "Is there anyone else in the house?" Another nod. "Call them all out here. With their identification." Kubu didn't offer to return the passport.

The man called out, and another Chinese man and a black man appeared. Kubu decided Samantha was right: this was definitely Ho or Hairong or whatever his real name was. His Chinese passport, however, showed him as Hairong Feng.

"What you want?" Hairong asked.

"You know very well what this is about," Kubu told him.

The other man was Joshua Mfundi, a Motswana. He looked very scared and had a bruise around his right eye. That's because of me, Samantha thought with regret. Because he was trying to be helpful.

"We're taking you all into custody," Kubu told them.

"Why?" Hairong asked.

"On suspicion of smuggling illicit materials, illegal removal of human remains, kidnapping, and murder. That'll do for a start."

Hairong looked at him impassively. "We arrested?"

"Not yet," Kubu replied. "Turn around and put your hands behind your backs. You have to be handcuffed for the trip to the CID."

"I had nothing to do with this!" Joshua burst out in Setswana. "I just work here for Rra Sin. Clean house. Cook rice. Why're you arresting me? I've done nothing!"

"Then you have nothing to worry about," Kubu replied in the same language. "Now turn around and put your hands behind your back. Don't make me tell you again."

Joshua may be the weak link, Kubu thought. Maybe this is going to be easy.

BUT IT WASN'T. By six o'clock the detectives had had enough and called it a day. After the three men had been taken away, Kubu and Samantha headed to Mabaku's office to fill him in.

"Well?" Mabaku asked as they came in. "What've you got?"

"Very little, dammit," Kubu replied, allowing his frustration to show. "After three hours of questioning."

Mabaku frowned, but waited for the story without comment.

"First there's this Joshua character. I think he knows nothing. He's scared to death, and I think he's what he says he is: a domestic worker for the man called Sin. He showed Samantha the car at the back of the house—it's a double cab and has the Chinese flag sticker in the window, just as the witness to the abduction described—and why would he let her in if he was involved? And our guess is that he took a punch to the face for doing so. He denies that, but we're sure that's what happened."

Samantha nodded.

"As for Sin," Kubu continued, "he's said very little. He wants a lawyer, and we'll get him one, but what he has said all backs up the other man, whose real name is Hairong. They've obviously aligned their stories. He agrees that he owns the double cab with the flag sticker but says lots of Chinese display their flag like that, and, of course, he denies having anything to do with Ramala." Kubu shrugged. "That brings us to Hairong Feng, which is the name on his passport. He's as cool as a Kalahari spring. The only thing he admits to is buying stuff from the herbal shop at Africa Mall and mailing it to China for testing. It was a commission from some herbal remedy operation in Qingdao, he says. He has an answer for everything."

"What about the coffin issue?" Mabaku prompted. "That was also shipped there."

"He denies it all, flat out. He was never in Kachikau; he knows nothing about the girl who supposedly died of malaria; and he's never heard of a person called Ho and never called himself that."

"But we have the video from the embassy! Does he deny that too?"

"No, but he claims he knows Chan at the embassy and visited him that day. He says that his job involves looking for import and export opportunities for China, and that Chan helps him with that. But that's where there *is* a flaw in his story. Either Chan lied and deliberately gave us the wrong video, or he'll contradict Hairong's story."

"What about the man at customs?" Samantha asked. "Didn't he also see Ho? And Muru may be able to identify him or the vehicle. One of them will break his story. And there's a possible connection to Ramala. According to Ramala's appointment book, he had a meeting with 'Hair On' the afternoon he was taken. 'Hair On' could be how he wrote Hairong."

"We need a search warrant," Kubu said. "We need to go through that double cab and link it to Ramala's grave—the first one—and build up a forensics case."

"I'll see what I can do," Mabaku said.

Kubu paused before he continued. "The amazing thing is that there seems to be no link with the rhino horn smuggling. Nothing has come up there with a local Chinese connection. So this Hairong seems to be doing his own thing on the herbal remedies. But I don't know what his connections are or where he's getting his information."

"What about the third man?" Mabaku asked. He often surprised Kubu by how much detail he remembered about a case. "There were supposed to be *three* men who abducted Ramala, weren't there?"

Samantha nodded. "We think that's probably the man who dropped off Sin at his house before we took them into custody. Sin gave us a name and address, but so far we haven't traced him. Maybe he's made a run for it."

"If he's panicked, that could work for us," Kubu added. "If we catch him, he may break. The other two are confident we can't prove anything."

"It seems that they're right," Mabaku said sourly. "And you can't hold them forever without charging them. You better get onto the embassy, the witness, and the customs guy first thing in the morning." He started to pull a file toward him—a sure sign that the meeting was over—but then he shoved it away in disgust. "The hell with it! Look, we've made a lot of progress in the last few days, and we'll nail these bastards, too. Great job tracing them through the double-cab truck, Samantha. Come on, let's go get a drink."

Kubu and Samantha looked at one another with amazement. Mabaku passing out compliments and buying celebratory drinks was unheard of.

Mabaku led the way out of his office with Kubu and Samantha following, speechless.

CHAPTER 51

The next morning did not start well. Samantha did manage to track down Muru and show him the pictures she'd taken of Sin's vehicle. However, when he saw the one from the driver's side, he said he didn't think the color was right, and when she showed him the passenger side with the flag sticker, he said it was what he'd seen. He refused point blank to attend a lineup, and when she showed him a collection of pictures of Chinese men, including Hairong and Sin, he failed to select either of them. Samantha wasn't sure that he would pick them out in any case; he obviously wanted as little to do with the matter as possible. Frustrated, she headed back to the CID.

At about the same time, Kubu was speaking to Tole at customs. Unlike Muru, Tole seemed to enjoy being involved with the case—perhaps it was a break for him from the monotony of paperwork. He looked at all the pictures carefully, but then shook his head.

"I wasn't really concentrating when Rra Ho was at the airport. I was talking to the people loading the plane. I just felt very sorry for him. It was so sad to lose a young daughter. But I didn't really look at him closely. He was Chinese..." He went through the pictures a second time. "How tall are these men, rra? Sometimes Chinese people are short, but I remember thinking he was quite big for a Chinese person."

Well, maybe that's worth something, Kubu thought. He thanked Tole and took his leave.

Instead of returning directly to the CID, Kubu took a detour to the Chinese embassy. He had some trouble getting past the security guard at the entrance, but his police ID and his demand to speak urgently to Mr. Chan got him in. At reception, he was asked to take a seat and wait. After twenty minutes, he was still waiting. Eventually a man wearing a dark blue suit approached and addressed him in flawless English.

"Good morning, Assistant Superintendent. My name is Zhang. I'm the assistant to the ambassador. Would you please come with me to my office?"

Kubu was puzzled by this development, but he followed Zhang, and nothing more was said until they'd settled at a conference table in the man's impressively large office.

"Would you like some green tea?" Zhang inquired. "Or coffee perhaps?"

Kubu accepted the coffee, and Zhang placed the order with his secretary.

"Assistant Superintendent, you're probably wondering why you're talking to me when you asked to see Mr. Chan. In fact, the matter is rather embarrassing for us here. Mr. Chan has been recalled to China."

"Recalled to China? Why?"

"That is why it's embarrassing. There are indications that, perhaps, Mr. Chan was not following embassy procedures correctly."

Kubu waited. That didn't sound like a reason either to recall Chan or to be embarrassed.

"It may be," Zhang continued, "that Mr. Chan had gone rather beyond his brief here and was involved in certain activities that are not appropriate for an embassy official."

"Are you saying he was engaged in some criminal activity?"

Zhang hesitated. "I wouldn't want to go as far as that. We're not sure of the details at this point. However, we think his activities were likely inappropriate and certainly not sanctioned by our government."

"Mr. Zhang, right now I'm investigating two murders, as well as the illegal removal of human remains from Botswana, and—with the help of your law enforcement officials in Shanghai—the smuggling of rhino horn into your country. We believe Mr. Chan can help us with these cases. If he's no longer here, I'd like to speak to him by phone."

At this point the tea and coffee were served by the secretary, who also handed Zhang a folder. Zhang glanced at it before he replied.

"I'm afraid that won't be possible, Assistant Superintendent. Right now Mr. Chan is not taking calls." He gave a formal smile, but held up the folder when Kubu started to protest. "Perhaps we will be able to obtain the information you need. I have here a list of Mr. Chan's contacts in Gaborone. I think you will find some of the names interesting." He passed the document across to Kubu.

While he drank his coffee, Kubu scanned it. He spotted Hairong Feng's name, but there was no one called Ho or Sin on the list. He did pause when he saw Jonah Gampone's name. That was interesting, but then, of course, Gampone's business cover was exporting goods to China. None of the other names meant anything to him. Zhang was looking at him as if he expected the list to be enlightening.

"Would it be possible to see Mr. Chan's diary for a certain date?" Kubu asked him.

"If you have a specific query, I'll check."

He's trying to be helpful, but not too helpful, Kubu thought. I wonder just what Chan was up to. "I'd like to know who he saw on Thursday the twenty-ninth of October."

Zhang nodded, left the office, and was away for quite some

time. When he returned, he passed Kubu a typed list of Chan's appointments for the day. A Hairong was on it, but not a Ho.

"Deputy Ambassador," Kubu said, "when I interviewed Mr. Chan before, he told me that he'd met a Mr. Ho on that day and helped him with paperwork to return the body of his dead daughter to China. He also said he hadn't asked Ho for identification because the man was so distraught. Subsequently he sent me video footage, from the security gate, of the man he said was Ho. The pictures turned out to be a Mr. Hairong Feng, who is on this list. There is no one by the name of Ho."

There was a long pause. "It seems that Chan lied to you, Assistant Superintendent."

"Yes, and that lie makes him at least an accessory to the crimes I'm investigating. It's critical that I interview him."

Again Zhang took his time. "I regret that I must point out that Mr. Chan is covered by diplomatic immunity and so can't be extradited from China. On the other hand, we will certainly follow up this matter with him as we pursue our inquiries into his conduct. We will share that information with you when we have it."

"Sir, that's not good enough. It now seems to me that Chan was behind these murders—and everything else—using Hairong to do his dirty work, smuggling, and stealing medicinal plant knowledge from the local people. You can't be serious that he can hide behind diplomatic immunity!"

"I'm afraid that is exactly what I am saying, Assistant Superintendent. But rest assured that if you're right, Chan will be dealt with very severely."

Kubu controlled his temper. He wasn't going to make any progress by haranguing Zhang. The matter would have to be taken up with the ambassador himself, by the commissioner, or even the minister. However, Kubu was pretty sure that even they would learn only as much as the Chinese government wanted them to know, and not a word more.

The worst part was that the evidence he had managed to obtain from Zhang supported Hairong's story. Kubu couldn't stand the thought that they might have to let him go.

As soon as he was back at the CID, Kubu collected Samantha, and they both went to see Mabaku.

"It's Chan," Kubu announced. "He must have been behind the whole business of trying to identify the longevity plant. He knows Hairong, who was obviously hired to do the dirty work—he and his friends. I'll bet they attacked Heiseb and killed him by accident, and then they had to get rid of Collins too.

"But Chan wanted Heiseb's organs tested, so they stole the body from Ian's morgue, and Chan used his position at the embassy to fake the documents needed to ship the body to China. Probably they went after Ramala because they thought he might already have the plant. And I'll bet that the embassy sent Chan back to China when the arrests were made on the rhino horn smuggling—he's probably involved in that as well! The whole thing is the Chinese again! You have to get the commissioner to pressure the ambassador to extradite Chan." Kubu was fuming.

Mabaku thought about it. "Calm down, Kubu. Let's talk it through." He paused. "Why would they have moved Ramala's body from the original grave?"

There was silence for a few moments before Kubu responded. "Gampone always said that killing Ramala at his house was a warning to him. Perhaps when the rhino horn smugglers in China were satisfied about him, they decided to take off the pressure."

Mabaku and Samantha looked dubious.

"And how did Chan find out about Heiseb in the first place?" Mabaku persisted.

"Perhaps from that herbal medicine shop?" Samantha suggested.

Mabaku shook his head. "That could be the connection to Ramala, but Heiseb was never involved with anyone here. Except Collins. Could there be a link there?"

Kubu turned that over in his mind. "Thabo," he said after a while. "The link could be Professor Thabo. I've never trusted him. I always felt he was hiding something. Maybe the Chinese were paying him for information. He knew about Collins's work, and even tried to find Heiseb himself. From what we've learned about this, the only other person who knew about Collins's work was Ross, and Ross had his own agenda. I can't see him working with the Chinese."

"Why don't you pay Professor Thabo another visit," Mabaku suggested. "In the meanwhile, I'll bring the commissioner up to date about what's going on."

Kubu found Thabo in his office at the university. "*Dumela*, Assistant Superintendent. I didn't expect to see you again," he said as he waved Kubu to a chair.

"Why is that, Professor?"

"Well, after your big breakthrough with the rhino horn smugglers, I thought you'd tied up the cases."

Kubu nodded. "Yes, we've arrested the smugglers, and we're pretty sure we know now how that links to the murders, but we need to build a watertight case. We're getting close, but the missing piece is how these people were getting information about Collins and Heiseb. We think you can help us with that." Kubu stopped and waited.

"I've told you everything I know."

"Professor, I'd like you to think about this very carefully. We're very close to the culprits now. Your evidence will clinch it for us and see them brought to justice. But, without it, we may not be able to make the case stick. They'll be free. And they'll know that you are the one person who can send them to jail for a very long time, or to the gallows." Kubu paused. "And they've already killed at least two people, probably three."

"Are you threatening me?"

"Not at all. I'm asking you to consider your personal safety.

These people are smugglers, biopirates, murderers. What would you do in their position?"

Thabo looked uncomfortable and started playing with a pen on his desk.

Kubu let the silence grow.

"I haven't done anything wrong," Thabo said at last. "I'm a consultant. I give people advice, the benefit of my expertise. That's how I make a decent living. Professors don't earn as much as they should."

"I understand, Professor. No one is accusing you of anything." At least not yet, Kubu added to himself. "I'm asking you to help us get to the bottom of this matter, to get these people put in jail before they strike again."

"Well, I actually did tell someone about Collins's work. He was interested in life-extending plants, and I told him about the Bushman who had a very long memory. I told him I thought that it was highly unlikely to be due to some herbal remedy, but he was keen to get as much information as possible, and was willing to pay well for it."

Kubu nodded. "That's why you set out to find who Collins's subject was. Why you made the trip to Ghanzi and New Xade."

"Yes," Thabo said. "But I had no idea that it might lead to Heiseb's death! I was just trying to help set up a deal. I'm sure you can confirm that from Collins himself when you find him."

Kubu shook his head. "We're almost certain that Collins is also dead."

"Why would they do it? Collins was the link to Heiseb. Heiseb was the link to the plant. Why kill them?"

"We'll find out, with your help. Now, exactly what did you tell Chan, Professor?"

Thabo looked surprised. "Who is Chan? I don't know any Chan. I was helping a man called Gampone, Jonah Gampone. He's a businessman."

Kubu didn't answer. His view of the case had suddenly morphed.

Gampone. The man who'd said he'd like to live forever, who'd paid Thabo for information on Collins and Heiseb, who'd consulted Ramala, and who had connections to Chan and his Chinese contacts. All along Gampone had been playing not a double game but a triple one.

CHAPTER 52

Kubu was totally distracted as he drove back to his office, nearly having an accident just outside the university by failing to yield to traffic in the circle, and then narrowly missing some pedestrians on a zebra crossing farther down the road.

If I weren't driving, he thought, I'd kick myself.

In retrospect, it was obvious that the kingpin had to be Gampone. He was well positioned to know about the trade in illegal goods, his business allowed him to move stuff around the world, and he had all of the right contacts.

"Damn!" Kubu said out loud.

As soon as he reached the CID he headed for Mabaku's office, but he met Samantha in the corridor, coming in the opposite direction.

"It's Gampone," he told her. "Where's the director?"

"He's with the commissioner about the Chan issue. What about Gampone?"

"Let's get some tea and go to my office."

Soon they sat down with their tea and a few cookies and Kubu filled Samantha in on his meeting with Thabo. He could see the puzzlement fading from her face as all the pieces fell into place for her also.

"So there was a connection after all," she said. "And it was Gampone. He was involved both in the rhino horn smuggling and the search for the magic plant, but there was no connection between the two operations. He kept them completely separate."

"Don't forget his business. That was also separate, and it's what gave him the contacts he needed for what he was really after. The problem is that it's going to be really hard to bring him down."

Samantha looked surprised. "But we have all the pieces now!"

Kubu nodded. "But what can we prove? Gampone was out of the country when Ramala was killed, and I'm sure he didn't go after Heiseb himself."

"How do you know?"

"Because Gampone would never have wanted Heiseb dead, nor Collins. They were his only connection to the plant. Ramala was a desperate plan B, and Hairong screwed that up by killing him at Gampone's house."

"What about Chan, then? Where does he fit in?"

Kubu shrugged. "My guess is that he's in trouble over the rhino horn smuggling. Why were they moving it through Gaborone anyway? He was Gampone's contact with Hairong and so on, but I doubt we'll get anything useful out of that."

"So we get Hairong to confess."

Kubu shook his head. "I doubt that, too. A confession sends him to jail for life at best, but if he just denies everything, we can't prove much, and there's no link to Gampone."

"Well, what about Sin and the other one?"

"Maybe. But even then it just becomes their word against Gampone's."

"At least we can throw the book at Gampone for the rhino horn smuggling!"

"Perhaps so, but his lawyer will say he was helping us, and we can't deny that. He'll get off with a light sentence, if anything at all."

"Dammit! We're always hamstrung by having to follow all the rules while the criminals can do what they damn well like and get away with it! What *can* we do?"

But Kubu's mind was elsewhere. "I need to think this through. Call me when Mabaku comes back." He leaned back and put his feet on the desk.

Samantha took the hint and left him to it.

It's the plant, Kubu thought. It's at the center of everything. Where is it? What does it do? Does it even exist? If we could follow it, somehow it would lead to Gampone.

He closed his eyes and relaxed. Soon he was snoring lightly, and a kaleidoscope of different thoughts and images flashed through his mind. Every now and again, a frown creased his face and his eyes fluttered, then he slept again.

Suddenly he woke up.

Of course, he thought. There *is* a connection between the rhino horn smuggling and the search for the plant. They aren't independent at all. The rhino horn itself does nothing—it's not an aphrodisiac and certainly doesn't cure cancer. And the plant is just something rare growing in the Kalahari, probably with no fantastic properties at all. The connection isn't the items, it's us. It's our greed to have them.

He picked up his half-drunk tea, but it was cold. He checked his watch and saw that it was after five o'clock. Then his thoughts returned to greed.

Heiseb had the plant but wouldn't share it with his friends at New Xade. He wanted it just for himself. As for the rest, they preyed on the greed of others to feed their own. Collins was excited about his academic theories, until he realized the commercial potential of the plant. So he went to Ross, who spotted the huge profits it could make for him. And it may be as much that greed as concern for Collins that has Ross trudging about the Kalahari. And Ramala was the same. He was a run-of-the-mill witch doctor wanting more. Then he realized what would sell—a secret potion for long life. And Gampone is the greediest of all, willing to do anything to get what he wants.

And that gave Kubu an idea.

It was after eight o'clock by the time Kubu reached Gampone's house. It was dark, and Kubu wondered if Gampone was out. Could he have gotten wind of what was up? If so, Kubu's plan would collapse.

He pressed the bell, wondering whether his trip was going to be a waste of time. But after a few moments, Gampone opened the door.

"Assistant Superintendent? This is very late to call."

Kubu nodded. "We need to talk, and it's urgent. May I come in?"

Gampone hesitated, then nodded. "We can go to my study."

"There's no one else here?"

"No, I'm alone."

"Good." Kubu followed Gampone to his study and took a comfortable chair. There was a glass of red wine next to the chair Gampone chose.

"Ah," said Kubu. "You're having a nightcap. I'll join you."

"Of course." Gampone fetched a glass for Kubu.

"Now, how can I help you, Assistant Superintendent? I'm an early riser, and I've got a lot of catching up to do now. I thought the smuggling issue was resolved."

"I'm not here about that," Kubu said. "The smuggling was really always a sideshow, wasn't it?" He took a sip of the wine. Not bad, he thought.

"What do you mean?"

"That was never what you were really interested in, and neither was your business."

Gampone appeared puzzled.

Kubu sighed. "Let's not waste time. I know all about Collins and Heiseb and smuggling his body to China. I know all about Chan and Hairong and his thugs. And I know all about Ramala. That was a real mistake, killing him here, wasn't it?" He smiled. "You can't get good help these days."

Gampone's face was blank. "I've no idea what you're talking about."

"Of course you have. I have Hairong and his friends in jail. Chan is detained. Thabo has told me everything. It's all cut and dried."

"I'm not talking to you without my lawyer."

"Rra Gampone, I'm not here to arrest you. I want to see if we can help each other. Do you have the plant?"

"What plant?"

Kubu sighed. "Rra, please. Did you find Heiseb's plant? The one he used to heal wounds, cure diseases, extend life. Do you have it?"

Gampone took a large sip of wine. "You said you know everything. Why are you asking me these questions?"

"My daughter is very ill. I thought you might be able to help me." He shrugged. "Maybe then I could help you too."

Gampone took his time replying. "What if I do have something? Maybe I can help you. But what do I get out of it?"

"I'll leave here with it. Hairong hasn't confessed yet, and I can make sure it takes a while before he does. You have money. You can make a new start somewhere else."

Gampone said nothing for some time. "Let's have another glass of wine," he said at last. He refilled the glasses. "What's the matter with her? Your daughter."

"Complications from HIV."

Gampone considered that, taking a sip of wine. He's judging me, Kubu thought. So be it.

"I do study plants, Rra Bengu. I have some remedies—"

Kubu interrupted. "I'm not interested in your remedies. Do you have Heiseb's plant or not?"

"It's not that simple."

Kubu put his glass down on the side table and stood up. "It seems we don't have anything to discuss, Rra Gampone. Please don't try to leave. I'll have men watching you."

"Please sit down, Assistant Superintendent. I said it wasn't simple. I didn't say it was impossible."

Kubu hesitated, then resumed his seat and took another sip of wine. "I'm listening."

"I have a sample of Heiseb's potion. It should be enough to help your daughter now, but she'll need more. And we need it too, Rra Bengu, you and I, to live the sort of lives we deserve. The world needs it, and the world will pay for it. Whatever we ask."

"What are you saying?" Kubu knew very well, but he wanted to reel in his fish slowly lest the line break.

Gampone's eyes glittered. "Your thinking is so small, *Assistant* Superintendent. What are you paid? Barely enough to support your family decently, I'd guess. Now you want to give me a chance to get away in exchange for some potion—a once-off to help your daughter." Gampone smiled. "Yes, I can start a new life somewhere else. But we could *both* have a new life right here!"

Kubu shook his head. "Rra Gampone, I don't want anything to do with murderers and smugglers. I came to you because I'm desperate. Otherwise I'd be here with a warrant for your arrest."

Gampone shook his head. "I had no choice. I had no way of getting what I needed except by using Chan's thugs. But they're idiots! If you and I were working together, we'd need none of that. You have contacts, the authority of the police. Together we could identify and farm the plant, live very long lives—maybe forever!—and be fabulously wealthy!"

Kubu shook his head. "It's nonsense. We'd be caught. There are laws about biopiracy."

"Not if you're on the inside."

There was a long pause. At last Kubu said, "I know the head of a pharmaceutical company in the US. I know he's interested. We could use him to sell it."

Gampone nodded and smiled again—the smile of someone who knows he's won.

"I do have contacts," Kubu continued pensively. "I have a very loyal constable at New Xade, and others who'll do what I want. But no one gets hurt in the process, is that agreed?"

Gampone nodded quickly. "Of course not. That was never what I wanted."

"Then why on earth did you kill Heiseb?"

"You think I'm an idiot? Of course I didn't kill him. I told Hairong to kidnap him, make him point out the plant, and then keep him on ice. They roughed him up and killed him by mistake."

"And Collins?"

"They followed him to get to Heiseb, and he was there when they grabbed the Bushman. He saw Hairong take Heiseb into the desert and come back with plants. Then Heiseb tried to get away, and Collins managed to get out of the vehicle and ran to help him. But it was too late; Hairong had broken his neck. They couldn't let Collins go after that. But they made him tell them everything he knew. I have all that information."

"So what happened to him?"

Gampone shrugged. "They buried his body somewhere away from the road and abandoned his vehicle."

Kubu digested that. "And Ramala?"

"He claimed to have the secret! He also had connections with the Bushmen—or at least his father did—but the stuff he sold was rubbish. He was a charlatan."

"So you killed him too."

"I was overseas! I thought Hairong could manage it; I certainly gave him enough money. But the idiot brought Ramala here! When he told me, I made them move the body, but it was too late. You already knew he'd been here. How did you find out?"

"I've known it all for some time. But it's more complicated than

I thought. We can't let Hairong talk. I could arrange an accident in jail. I've no sympathy for him after what he's done." He paused. "Now, do you actually know where the plant grows? You said Hairong made Heiseb get some."

"That was a weed. Hairong knows nothing and was duped. But I'm very close. I have all the Shakawe contacts from Ramala. At least Hairong knows how to make people talk. And Collins also did a lot of talking. He showed Hairong everywhere he'd been and told him everything he knew. If I'd been there myself . . ." He shrugged. "But I have enough. Together we'll find the plant, all right."

"Where do the other Chinese fit in? Not Hairong and his thugs. The ones in Qingdao."

Gampone looked surprised. "You do know everything, it seems. There's a lab there that does work for me. The analytics and so on. We don't have the technology to do it here, and anyway it would be too risky. It would get out."

"And all this was financed by the rhino horn, wasn't it? It wasn't from selling cheap carvings to China."

Gampone said nothing, but didn't deny it.

"Fifty-fifty," Kubu said after a pause.

Gampone hesitated, but Kubu could tell it was just for effect. His greed will always win, he thought. He should be happy just to get away with what he's done, but he'll risk everything for what he wants.

Gampone nodded.

"Okay, show me everything you've got."

It wasn't much, but it was enough. Some pressed plant samples and notes from Collins, a couple of small containers from Heiseb— one with some dried leaves, and one with a little ointment—which Gampone offered to Kubu, who pocketed it without a word.

They shook hands and Kubu went out to his car. Once inside, he took his cell phone from his pocket and said, "I'm in my car, Samantha. Did you get all of that?"

"Every word."

"Okay, tell the police cars to move in. We know this is the only road up to the house. He can't go anywhere."

As he waited for the cars, he wondered if he would have been tempted by that ointment if the news from Nono's doctor had been bad. I'm not immune, he thought. I'm glad I wasn't faced with that.

When the first car arrived, he headed back to the house and knocked on the door. Rra Gampone was probably having a celebratory third glass of wine. He was in for a big disappointment.

CHAPTER 53

"You could've been killed, just like the others," Mabaku said. "Why didn't you call me before you went out there?"

"Director, you were with the commissioner and I didn't want to disturb you. And I wasn't there to arrest Gampone, just to talk to him. I didn't think it was dangerous at all, and Samantha was listening in, with backup nearby."

"Well, his lawyer is definitely going to scream entrapment. You should've just arrested him and brought him in for questioning."

"On what grounds, Director? We had no proof that he'd done anything, and Hairong and Sin weren't talking. We would've had to let them all go."

"So what are you going to charge them with now?"

"Well, we've made some progress with hard evidence. Our handwriting guy says that the writing on the manifest that was used to send the coffin to China is Hairong's. Then, Zanele's people have found some hairs in Sin's double cab that are Ramala's, and the tracks outside Gampone's garage match Sin's tires. And when we searched Hairong's home, we found the smartphone that was used to send the second email to Mrs. Collins. Also, immigration caught the third man who abducted Ramala, as he was trying to leave the country—his visa was fake and we'd alerted them to check all Chinese men trying to leave the country. His name is Li Yong. We think he's just Hairong's sidekick and does what he's told. It turns out that the fingerprints on the phone we found in Ramala's car were his."

"Useful, but probably not enough to convict. And what about Gampone? Do you have anything hard on him?"

"There's always a weak link, Director," Kubu replied, "and in this case it's our Rra Li. I spoke to the prosecutor about him. He is willing to ask for a reduced sentence if Li cooperates—a life sentence with the possibility of parole, instead of the death penalty. We confronted Li with two things: Zanele just confirmed that his hairs and prints were among those found in Collins's four-by-four, as well as prints on the phone in Ramala's car. He jumped at the chance and confessed to being present at the murder of Collins and Ramala. He says that Hairong and Sin pushed the limits on the torture, and both Collins and Ramala died because of that. But he insists that Heiseb's death was accidental."

"Is he willing to testify in court?"

Kubu nodded. "We also asked him who was paying Hairong, but he didn't know. Of course, Gampone confessed to that when I was at his house, so we have that link established."

"And what did he say about the rhino horn smuggling?"

"Nothing. As I suspected, the only link between that and the plants is Gampone. The two groups didn't know about each other."

Mabaku stood up and walked over to the window. The baboons from Kgale Hill were in the parking lot again. "They'd better not crap on my car," Mabaku muttered, "or I'll shoot the lot of them."

He turned back to Kubu. "So what can we charge Gampone with?"

"Kidnapping; accessory to murder, unless Hairong testifies that Gampone told him to kill Collins and Ramala, in which case, murder; and manslaughter, for Heiseb's death; as well as a number of lesser charges, including a variety of charges around smuggling; and theft. Also, last night we grabbed the things Gampone had shown me—the pressed flowers, and notes that Collins had made. We also found Ramala's stone box—empty, of course. We've definitely got Gampone, but unfortunately it'll be difficult to get the death penalty since he wasn't present at any of the murders."

"And the rhino horn gang?"

"We'll get all of them lengthy sentences. For once, the Chinese are cooperating. Unfortunately, when we checked with CITES, they knew of the powder that Gampone had and had approved of him using it to land the big fish in China and Vietnam, so we can't link him to the smuggling."

"And what's happened to the Americans?"

"I spoke to them on the phone this morning. They found nothing, as I expected. They're leaving the country today. It's very sad for Mrs. Collins. Must be difficult not to have closure. I was hoping that one of the Chinese thugs would tell us where Collins's body is, but Hairong and Sin aren't talking, and Li can't describe the place. I don't think we'll ever find it."

"And Ross?"

"He's probably torn. He was a good friend of Collins, but he would have loved to find the plant."

Mabaku shook his head. "All this over rhino horn that does nothing and a plant that doesn't exist. It'll be interesting to see what the judge makes of it! Anyway, you and Samantha did a really good job on this one, Kubu. Take the rest of the day off; you deserve it."

"It's Saturday, Director."

Mabaku smiled. "So it is."

With that he sat down and opened a file.

ON HIS WAY home after the meeting, Kubu stopped at Game City to buy a bottle of South African sparkling wine and a tub of chocolate ice cream. After all, he thought, it's time to celebrate. This evening the family is going to be together for the first time in what seemed like ages.

Joy and Tumi were on their way back from Mochudi with Amantle, who was going to stay for the weekend. And he was going to the hospital to take Nono home. The doctor had phoned the day before to say she'd improved enough to be at home.

And, of course, he'd successfully solved two cases—with Samantha's help, he had to admit. He'd considered inviting her for dinner but had decided against it because he wanted the evening to be for family only.

KUBU WAS SITTING on the veranda when Ilia jumped up and raced for the gate, yapping enthusiastically. Obviously she's heard Joy returning, Kubu thought.

He stood up to open the gate, but before he'd even left the veranda, Tumi rushed up the stairs.

"Where's Nono?" she asked.

"In her bed," Kubu replied.

Tumi rushed inside and seconds later he heard her squeal with delight.

"I'm so happy you're home," he heard her say. "You're not allowed to get sick again." Kubu smiled. Oh to be young again.

He then greeted his mother, and the two of them sat down to chat while Joy headed off to the kitchen. And it wasn't long before she carried a tray onto the veranda, with all the trappings for the kind of afternoon tea that Kubu liked. There was a plate of mixed cookies and, to his surprise and delight, a homemade carrot cake.

When Joy called, Tumi ran out and shouted, "Mommy, Mommy, we don't want tea. We want ice cream. You promised. You promised. I'll take it to Nono."

Joy hesitated only a moment before nodding. "Go and get it, Tumi. And two bowls, and two spoons. And don't forget the chocolate sauce. It's on the counter."

Minutes later, Tumi disappeared with their two bowls, and Kubu was sure they were shoveling ice cream into their mouths as fast as they could swallow it. It wasn't long before Tumi ran out and asked for more.

"I see you didn't eat much," Joy said. "Most of it's on your face." She smiled. "You can have a little more now—half a scoop only, otherwise you'll spoil your dinner. I have a big treat for you."

KUBU SERVED THE sparkling wine before dinner, then opened his best bottle of South African cabernet sauvignon for the meal that Joy was preparing. In reality, it was an inexpensive wine, but given his delight at Nono's return, it tasted like a fine Bordeaux.

The treat was a roasted leg of lamb that Joy had liberally spiced with many cloves of garlic, smothered with olive oil, dusted with rosemary, and served medium rare. As sides, she served roasted potatoes and fresh beans, lightly fried with butter and almonds.

The dessert was, of course, chocolate ice cream covered with chocolate sauce. Amantle and Joy passed on the ice cream, and Tumi and Nono could only manage small helpings. However, Kubu couldn't resist, and he enjoyed two big servings.

"That was a delicious dinner, my daughter," Amantle said as Kubu stood up to clear the plates. "Thank you for having me stay with you. I am tired this evening and will go to bed now."

She turned and went into the kids' room, which she always used when visiting.

Tonight, Kubu thought, is the perfect time to put what happened between us to rest. We're both mellow, and Nono's home and on the mend.

"Joy, my darling, I'll do the dishes in the morning. It's such a beautiful evening. Let's go and sit on the veranda. I have something to say."

CHAPTER 54

For Kubu, the intense few weeks ended the way they had begun—
with a quiet morning at the CID and a call from Ian MacGregor.

"How are you doing, Kubu?"

"Not bad, Ian. And you?"

"I'm fine. If you're not busy, why don't you come over? I've
something to show you."

Kubu checked his watch. "Sure. I'll be there in half an hour."

When Kubu arrived at Ian's office, he found him sucking on
his pipe, unlit as usual. Ian gestured to a chair. "How are Tumi
and Nono?"

"Fine. Tumi's full of beans as usual; it's hard to keep up with her.
And Nono's almost back to her old self. The doctors are pleased with
her progress since she left the hospital. The cocktail of ARVs she's
taking now seems to be doing the trick. But . . ."

Ian nodded. "It's a worry. Probably always will be. You need to
take it one day at a time, my friend."

"I suppose so."

"And Joy? How are the two of you getting on?"

"We're doing well, Ian. After Nono came home, we had a good talk. There are still a few rough edges, but they're not sharp enough to cut anymore. I think we were just so stressed that we didn't really know what we were doing." He hesitated. "I never really thanked you properly, Ian. Without you, this might all have ended in disaster. Did you know Joy would reject the *muti* if she was actually faced with her daughter using it?"

Ian laughed. "If I were that good, I'd have my own TV program and lots of money! Relationships are hard, Kubu. Even the really good ones, like yours with Joy."

"Well, anyway, I owe you a drink. In fact, several."

Ian smiled. "I look forward to taking you up on that. I know a place that has a pretty decent single malt." He paused. "Anyway, as I mentioned, I want to show you something. I got back the report on the teeth."

For a moment Kubu was puzzled, until he remembered the teeth Ian had extracted from Heiseb and sent for analysis. "From the Danish laboratory?"

Ian nodded. "They found it very difficult. But take a look at the conclusions." He passed a document to Kubu, who was relieved to see it was in English. He turned to the last page.

By using the two independent techniques described in detail above and taking the overlap of those two estimates, we have been able to obtain an estimate for the age of the specimens you sent to us. Again we emphasize the experimental nature of the techniques, should these be necessary for presentation in a court of law. A 95 percent confidence interval for the age would be no older than 180 years and no younger than 130 years.

We hope this helps you with your work and research.

Kubu read it twice. "They're saying he was at least one hundred thirty years old? Maybe more?"

Ian nodded. "Their mean estimate was one hundred fifty-five, but there's a twenty-five-year error of measurement with their tests."

"So those stories he told were true. He *had* been hunted by the Germans; he *had* been shot with a black-powder bullet."

"It looks like it. I know this will sound strange to you—especially coming from a rational Scot—but this is what I expected. When you've cut up as many bodies as I have and looked at as many organs, it's pretty obvious when something is highly unusual."

"So the plant will be real, as well. There's something growing in the Kalahari that can at least double a human life span."

"That's not so clear, laddie. Maybe Heiseb was just a genetic freak. Did we ever trace his body? I'm still angry about that break-in."

"That's a dead end. The herbal medicine operation in Qingdao denies any knowledge of it, and I'm sure the body disappeared pretty quickly once the police came to call."

"Too bad," Ian commented, but he didn't sound particularly upset.

Kubu hesitated for a few moments and then said, "Gampone had a little of the ointment Collins told his wife about. I took it as part of the scam I pulled to get Gampone to confess on tape."

"Ah, the Kubu who never bends his principles," Ian said, with a twinkle in his eye. "And what happened to this ointment?"

"I still have it. You're the only person I've told about it."

Suddenly, Ian's smile faded. "Kubu, I've been thinking about this ever since that report came through from Copenhagen. Suppose there *is* a longevity plant out in the desert. Suppose we confirm it with my reports, the Danish analysis, and your ointment. Think about what would happen."

Kubu had already pondered the consequences. Just the rumor of the plant had led to greedy people being attracted like flies to a carcass, resulting in three murders. The news that the plant actually existed would start a stampede to the Kalahari, bringing with it waves of bribery, corruption, and violence. It would be the end for the Bushmen. And countries had collapsed under outsider greed for resources much less valuable than this.

"Do we really need to live longer lives?" Kubu asked eventually. "Are we short of people on the planet?"

Ian said nothing.

"What will you do with this?" He passed the report back to his friend.

"I'll write, thanking them for their trouble, and file it. If anyone asks about it, I'll say it's full of a lot of scientific jargon but the results are inconclusive."

"Mabaku never believed in it anyway," Kubu mused.

There was silence for a few moments, and then Ian asked, "And what will you do with that ointment?"

That was a difficult one for Kubu, and he took his time over it. Suppose Nono . . . But he refused to think about that.

"I'll give it to you," he replied. "For your file."

"You are a brave man, my friend," Ian said. "But it is better for all that no one knows about it."

AUTHORS' NOTE

Throughout sub-Saharan Africa, witch doctors hold influential positions in society. Most people believe in them and their powers to some extent. Even Western-trained scientists may carry a residue of belief.

Most witch doctors are traditional healers. That is, they use a combination of potions and suggestion to help people. For the most part, these potions, called *muti* in southern Africa, are made from a variety of herbs and plants. Occasionally, they add some part of an animal's body, such as the heart of a lion. A few may even use human body parts.

Biopiracy is the exploitation of a country's endemic plants and the protection of traditional knowledge of their properties. Many countries now have outlawed biopiracy.

Hoodia, mentioned in this book, became a test case when the South African Council for Scientific and Industrial Research wished to exploit its appetite-suppressing properties in partnership with an international pharmaceutical company. The CSIR's interest was sparked by the Bushman tradition of chewing the plant to suppress feelings of hunger. After protests that traditional knowledge was being stolen, a royalty arrangement was eventually worked out with the Bushmen. Ultimately, the proposed drug was never developed, and the Bushmen received no royalties.

The Kalahari is a huge area, and it's known to host a variety of unusual plants and creatures. They are well worth protecting, if for no other reason than that they may turn out to have remarkable medicinal properties.

ACKNOWLEDGMENTS

With each new book, we have more people to thank for their generous help and support, because we keep leaning on those who have helped us before while finding new ones to impose upon.

We were very fortunate to have a variety of readers of drafts of this book giving us input and suggestions and catching errors. Our sincere thanks to: Steve Alessi, Linda Bowles, Pat Cretchley, Pam Diamond, Pat and Nelson Markley, Steve Robinson, and the Minneapolis writing group—Gary Bush, Sujata Massey, and Heidi Skarie. With all their comments, it's hard to believe that the book still has mistakes. But it probably does, and we take responsibility for any that remain.

Many people in Botswana have generously given us their time to make the book as authentic as possible. It's amazing to us that so many people in Botswana are willing to take the time to be bombarded by odd questions from two authors about *muti*, police procedures, and the like. We particularly want to thank Andy Taylor, headmaster of the wonderful Maru-a-Pula School in Gaborone, who has been extraordinarily patient with all our questions and requests, and invaluable for introducing us to people in the know. We received helpful information from Alice Mogwe, director of the human rights organization, Ditshwanelo; and Unity Dow, former high-court judge of Botswana, for which we thank them.

We would like to thank our editor, Marcia Markland, for her input and her support of Detective Kubu. We also thank Todd Manza for his careful copy editing.

Finally, we thank our partners, Pat Cretchley and Mette Nielsen, for their support, patience, and unfailing good humor.

GLOSSARY

Aardvark	Large ant eater which makes deep burrows. *Orycteropus afer.*
Bakkie	Slang for pickup truck.
Batswana	Plural adjective or noun: "The people of Botswana are known as Batswana." See MOTSWANA.
Dagga	Marijuana. *Cannabis sativa.*
Dumela	Setswana for hello or good day.
Hoodia	Cactus-like plant, eaten for energy and as a hunger suppressant. *Hoodia gordonii.*
Kubu	Setswana for hippopotamus.
Mma	Respectful term in Setswana used when addressing a woman. For example, "Dumela, Mma Bengu" means "Hello, Mrs. Bengu."
Motswana	Singular adjective or noun. "That man from Botswana is a Motswana." See BATSWANA.
Muti	Medicine from a traditional healer. Sometimes contains body parts.

Pap	Smooth maize meal porridge, often eaten with the fingers and dipped into a meat or vegetable stew.
Pula	Currency of Botswana. Pula means rain in Setswana. One hundred thebes equals one pula. One US dollar equals roughly ten pula. See THEBE.
Rra	Respectful term in Setswana used when addressing a man. For example, "Dumela, Rra Bengu" means "Hello, Mr. Bengu."
Setswana	Language of the Batswana peoples.
Steelworks	Drink made from kola tonic, lime juice, ginger beer, soda water, and bitters.
Thebe	Smallest denomination of Botswana currency. Thebe means shield in Setswana. See PULA.